Red Tape

David Michelson

The events and characters in this book are fictitious. Certain real locations and public figures are mentioned, but all other characters and events described in the book are totally imaginary.

Copyright 2010 by David Michelson. All rights reserved.

Visit the Web site at www.redtapethenovel.com

Printed in the United States of America.

Library of Congress Catalog: TXu 1-677-749.

ISBN 978-0-615-43031-7

Dedicated to the Tibetans.
May they be granted complete freedom in Tibet.

CHAPTER 1

Tibet, Present Day

This is suicide. But maybe that's what it's going to take. He had hoped to be inconspicuous in a black sweatshirt, black jeans, and a black cap. But with a pale white face and standing a few inches over six feet, Mason Hamilton protruded out from the crowd. At least his height would be an advantage today—his mission depended upon it.

Hidden behind a merchant stall, Mason watched intently as a hundred thousand Tibetans crammed themselves into the Barkhor, the central Lhasa Square. He had witnessed many protests during his years with Amnesty International—none, however, with the fervor that this one elicited. In any culture, when something core to a community was threatened, people passionately united. Today was that day for the Tibetans.

An elderly monk wearing a dusty maroon and yellow robe stepped onto a large crate in front of the Jokhang. The venerable monk was from the Drepung Monastery, one of the precious few not yet destroyed by the Chinese.

Using a microphone, the monk began to speak. Tongling Tsong, Mason's guide, leaned over to interpret.

"The Jokhang is ours! We will not let them take it down to build a factory! We fight, not with violence, but with no cooperation! We will not move!"

The crowd began to shout in unison, "Save Jokhang! Save Jokhang!"

The Jokhang was the holiest Tibetan temple. Its sacredness for Tibetans was akin to the Vatican for Catholics or the Western Wall for Jews. Day and night, the temple was filled with pilgrims who trekked great distances over rugged terrain, all to pay homage to Lord Buddha in this precious sanctuary. Seeing it torn down would be like watching one's mother being stabbed with a knife. There was nothing they wouldn't do to prevent this, even sacrifice their lives. And it might come to that. Today a meeting was being held in Lhasa between China's Minister of Commerce and a representative of Ingrols, a large U.S. retailer, to finalize demolition plans. The Jokhang was to be replaced with a massive Ingrols discount goods factory.

As the monk continued to exhort the crowd, Chinese militia arrived on the scene. Commanding the front of the temple, the militia shoved away Tibetans performing *koras*—the holy ritual where Tibetans circumambulated the Jokhang, spinning its prayer wheels while citing *"om mane padme hum,"* a blessed prayer for all beings that invoked wisdom, compassion, and realization of one's true nature.

A commotion at the front corner of the Jokhang revealed a group of Chinese soldiers hauling out two Tibetans who were resisting being pushed back from the temple. The crowd raised their fists and yelled at the militia's arrests. The revered monk responded by stepping down from the platform to do his own *kora* around the temple. As he did, one of the Chinese soldiers pushed him away.

"Stay back!" the soldier yelled.

In disobedience, the monk pulled out a picture of the Dalai Lama from his robe. He held it high, exalting his dedication to His Holiness. It was against the law in Tibet to possess the Dalai Lama's picture, let alone display it in public. Such allegiance to the Tibetan spiritual and political leader had led to over one million Tibetans being killed since China's invasion in 1949. Separatism, in the eyes of the Communist Party of China, was as much of an offense as terrorism was deemed in the West.

The Chinese soldier pointed his gun at the monk and yelled, "Give me picture!"

Damn, here we go, Mason thought. The air was too tight. Something had to snap.

Mason unclenched his fists, took a deep breath and tried to exhale his rising anger. The compassion he admired in Tibetan monks didn't come easily for him.

Ducking down, he unrolled his sleeve revealing a peace dove tattoo embedded on his forearm during his early years with Amnesty International. He reached into his pocket and pulled out a metal device enclosed in a small hand towel. He then scanned the area for Chinese militia. Drawing their attention would certainly get him arrested…if not killed.

Keeping the device hidden, Mason moved slightly away from the stall to get a direct view of the Chinese soldier in front of the Jokhang. He brought the eyepiece to his eye and zoomed in for a clear shot. Focusing on his target, he held the device steady, took another deep breath, and pressed the button. A red light illuminated—the digital camcorder was in operation.

As Mason began recording, the Chinese soldier reached for the picture in the monk's hand. The monk pulled back. The soldier stepped forward and grabbed the monk's arm. The monk pulled back even further in defiance.

"One more time. Give me picture or I shoot!" the soldier commanded.

The monk held the picture even higher and yelled, "Long live the Dalai Lama!"

The soldier grabbed his gun and shot straight into the monk's chest. The blast sent the monk reeling to the ground, blood gushing from his robes. The soldier leaned over and tore the picture from the monk's hand.

A Tibetan nun, standing next to the monk, bent down to her dying leader. The soldier shot her in the back of the head.

Armed only with waving pictures of the Dalai Lama, a group of a hundred *Khampa*—the statuesque Tibetan nomads from the *Khampa* region with their broad shoulders, red-braided hair and turquoise earrings—rallied together and charged the temple. The Chinese militia moved closer and aimed their weapons at the approaching Tibetans. An order was given and the militia opened fire, gunning down the *Khampa*.

The militia continued to fire their guns in frenzy throughout the Barkhor. The screaming crowd scattered wildly. A father scooped up his young daughter and ran frantically with her in his arms. A bullet went straight through his heart. The girl fell head first onto the pavement and died instantly. A five-year-old boy stood screaming over his dead mother—a gunshot sent him tumbling on top of her. The militia made no discrimination. Monks, nuns, men, women, and children were all gunned down in a sea of blood.

You bastards! Mason screamed to himself while trying to keep his hand from shaking as he maintained the camcorder's focus on the horror before him. He desperately wanted to leap in and assist the wounded. But he knew another Tiananmen was in the making. His best assistance could be to capture the bloodbath as his camcorder might be the only verifiable source for the world.

Mason jumped when he heard Tongling scream.

"Look! It's Liung Xilai!"

Tongling pointed at the Chinese Minister of Commerce standing atop a hotel overlooking the Barkhor.

Using the zoom, Mason focused on the man in the dark gray suit standing with his arms crossed, observing the scene. Next to him stood a Caucasian man presumably Kurt Redman, the American representative from Ingrols. With all the chaos, no one would have even known the men ultimately responsible for the massacre were passively watching it take place.

While Mason recorded, a second Caucasian man dressed in a dark blue suit, much older than the other two men, came out from behind them. Mason zoomed in on the man until the lens was fully extended. Though the man's face was barely in focus, he seemed familiar. A moment later, the realization hit Mason, causing him to joggle the camera—*What is the Vice President doing here?*

Jack Tenner, Vice President of the U.S., quickly shook hands with Liung Xilai and then was whisked away by several men Mason assumed were Secret Service. Mason hit *Pause* and pushed through the panicked crowd to get a closer shot. He wanted no mistake about the presence of the silent watchers.

Mason refocused the camcorder on the hotel, but by then the men had disappeared. He glanced in every direction but couldn't spot them through the crowd.

"There!" Tongling yelled, having followed him. His guide was pointing to the hotel's front door.

Liung and Redman reappeared guarded by five Chinese soldiers. The soldiers led the two men through the frenzy using their rifles as sticks to beat Tibetans in the way.

Mason kept filming. He searched for the Vice President, but Tenner was nowhere in sight.

As the soldiers were clearing a path for the leaders, a young Tibetan in his late teens ran up and broke through the circle of soldiers. Seeing the intense determination in the boy's movements, Mason focused the camcorder on the teenager as he jostled his way in front of Redman.

The teen reached into his jacket pocket.

Mason zoomed in.

Redman anxiously grabbed a rifle out of the hands of one of the Chinese soldiers. He pointed the gun at the teen and pulled the trigger. The bullet ripped through the boy's chest sending him hard to the pavement. As he fell, the boy's hand came out from his pocket and the object floated to the ground next to his head. It was a picture of the Dalai Lama.

Another blast of anger rushed through Mason's veins and reddened his pale complexion. He took a few steps forward to get a close-up shot of Redman's face with rifle in hand.

One of the Chinese soldiers spotted Mason videotaping. The soldier rushed towards him, screaming and pointing furiously.

Mason stopped recording and jammed the camcorder back into his pocket.

"Let's get out of here!" Mason yelled as he grabbed Tongling's arm. They bolted in the opposite direction, up Mentsikhang Lam, the main road at the west end of the Barkhor.

With the crowd still fleeing in panic, Mason and Tongling shoved through the frenetic scene. One woman ran hysterically in front of Mason. He tried to sidestep her but accidentally smacked into her shoulder, sending the woman to the ground. Mason turned and saw that the soldier was gaining on them. He quickly heaved the woman upright and then continued to run with Tongling by his side.

As they passed the Pentoc Guesthouse, they ducked into a cobbled alley and headed into Western Lhasa—the urbanized Chinese section of town where Tibetan homes had been replaced with upscale Chinese establishments and a mile strip of brothels, gambling dens, and discos.

Mason and Tongling zigzagged their way through several alleys until they found themselves near the tall Golden Yaks Statue, a monument signifying the liberation of Tibet. *Liberation my ass*, Mason swore to himself.

When they reached the Produce Market, merchants were frantically packing their goods trying to escape the craze. Mason saw a clothed table with no one working the stall.

He looked back. His assailant was not in sight.

He ran towards the table and pulled up the cloth. He and Tongling ducked underneath.

As Mason pulled the cloth back down, he noticed a few small items had fallen from his coat pocket on the ground several feet from the stall. Among them was a piece of paper containing a key piece of personal data, but he couldn't risk coming out from under cover to get it.

The soldier entered the Produce Market. His eyes darted back and forth. Scanning the area, the soldier looked down and saw the items Mason had dropped—a pair of sunglasses, lip balm, and the piece of paper. He picked them up and read the contents of the paper. It contained both Chinese and English characters. The soldier smiled and stuffed it into his uniform.

He then looked at the empty produce stall and aimed his gun directly at the hanging cloth covering the table. Bullets shelled the cloth, obliterating everything underneath.

CHAPTER 2

I'm crossing the Golden Gate right now. You should see the Bay...it's sparkling like a diamond," said Julia Hamilton, her green eyes narrowing from the glare of the San Francisco Bay.

"Did anyone ever tell you never to make a client jealous?" Janice's voice responded through a speaker in Julia's Honda Accord.

"If you weren't such a good friend I wouldn't have. Why, you don't have an ocean view from the hotel?"

"Very funny. The only ocean I can see from this Kansas City airport hotel room is in this travel book of Hilton destinations. So, what are you wearing tonight?"

"A black dress and pumps."

"You'll be the prettiest journalist there. I'll bet the Governor gives you more for your article...*when* you speak with him."

Julia didn't like the pressure from her friend, but she was a freelancer, and Janice was her boss on this project.

"I'll do my best. There'll be tons of environmental lobbyists at the Governor's dinner tonight. Cigarette litter may not be a priority on his mind."

"You got some heat to give him?"

"How about the fact that several trillion cigarette butts are littered worldwide every year, and that they are the most littered item in America...especially on our California beaches. And they aren't as biodegradable as everyone thinks. The plastic filters can take years to decompose. When the rain sweeps them into our water sources, the toxic chemicals build up."

"Good. And get a good quote from him...no matter what his opinion is. Need I remind you as Editor-In-Chief of the IJ, I need to make sure we sell this newspaper? Use that tenacity and great body of yours."

Julia paid the toll at the end of the bridge. "I'll get one...even if I have to flirt with one of his aides." At 32, five-foot six, with shoulder length dark brown hair, radiant eyes, and a captivating smile, Julia never had a problem turning heads.

"You're not going solo again, are you?" Janice asked.

Julia was tempted to hit the disconnect button. Her friend hardly let a call go by without driving that dagger.

"When do you need the article?" Julia replied.

"Sorry. One of these days I'll stop. It's only 'cause I love you."

"I know, but can you find a softer way of showing it?"

"Sorry. My husband says the same thing. I'll try. Hey, speaking of tough love, aren't you seeing your father soon?"

"In two weeks."

"It's been a while, hasn't it?"

"A few years. My perfunctory visit. So when do you need the article?" Julia repeated.

"By the 10th at the latest."

"Okay. Call me when you get back."

Julia hung up the phone and continued into the city. She thought about the upcoming visit with her father. In the last fifteen years, there were only a handful of them. Each time they were together, they argued about the lie that had altered their relationship. Janice once said that her father's lie had instilled a drive in her to reveal the truth—a gift that made her a great journalist. Julia would have tossed that gift in a heartbeat if it meant a chance to have met her mother.

As she drove past a Tibetan restaurant on Lombard, Julia thought about a recent message from her father saying he was leaving for India to attend some Tibetan Buddhist retreat. He'd be back before her visit. For a second, she wondered what he was doing over there right now...not that she really cared.

CHAPTER 3

"What's his name?" he demanded.

"Mason Hamilton," the voice answered through the speakerphone. "He dropped a bank receipt with his passport number—"

"Who is he?" the man interrupted.

"A human rights activist from Denver."

The man leaned forward in his black leather chair and took a puff of his cigar.

"You're *absolutely* sure he made the tape?"

"I'd bet my life on it."

"You are!"

The person on the other end cringed at the menace in the man's voice.

"Well get me the tape. Then take him out like those yak herders!" The man smacked the button on the speakerphone. The person on the other line didn't get a chance to reply. That didn't matter—there was no refuting the man anyway. For it was known what the man was capable of if one did. That's why he was known as the Predator.

CHAPTER 4

*M*ason picked up the phone and dialed the Congressman's office. Senator Green was his best connection to Washington.

Just a week ago, he and Tongling hid in large crates behind the stall as the Chinese soldier's shots rang out. Just a week ago, they survived the road connecting Lhasa and Nepal named *Friendship Highway*, a misnomer, as anyone caught escaping was ruthlessly murdered. Just a week ago, a thousand Tibetans were slaughtered…

"Senator Green's office," a woman's voice came on the line.

"Uh, yes," Mason uttered, trying to regain his focus. "I'm a long time friend of Richard. Is he in today?"

"I believe he's in a meeting. May I ask who's calling please?"

"Mason Hamilton."

"Let me double check, Mr. Hamilton. Please hold."

It had been a few years since Mason had last spoken with Green. He had called to congratulate Green on being elected Senator of Colorado. The two had become friendly earlier in their careers. Green had been one of Denver's rising prosecuting attorneys. Mason, now fifty-six, had worked for the Denver Post after his stint with Amnesty International. At the Post he wrote several glowing articles praising the way Green successfully prosecuted a case. The articles elevated Green's fame and catapulted his career. Green was very grateful and offered to be of help if he ever could; Mason was now hoping to call-in on Green's offer.

A familiar voice came on the line.

"Mason!" Green stated happily, glad to reconnect with his old friend. "I'm in a meeting and then headed to Washington. But I thought I'd say a quick hello and see what's up."

"Thanks. I'll get right to it then. I really need your help, Richard. I'd rather not discuss the matter over the phone. Is there any chance we could meet briefly before your flight? I wouldn't bother you unless I thought it was urgent."

After making arrangements to meet at Centennial Airport in an hour, Mason hung up and stretched his neck back to release some of his tension. He knew this was the beginning of going public with the tape. There was no turning back now—not that he wanted to anyway.

He looked out the window of his Evergreen home, just outside Denver. Dark gray clouds were steadily moving in over the mile high city. He grabbed his heavy hemp jacket as the local news had mentioned a cold front moving in which could bring an early snowfall. And with the nagging cough he picked up in India—where he had learned about the protest—he didn't want the cough to get worse.

Mason set the alarm to the house and then climbed into his cherished Prius. Despite his legroom being compromised, Mason was one of the initial enthusiasts to buy the hybrid and get 50mpg. He detested the fact that the U.S. was the world's largest emitter of greenhouse gases accounting for twenty percent of all emissions. *Go Eco* had been his motto for years. His secluded, sustainable, and natural home was built with the latest design in green building materials, passive solar heating, wind powered electricity, water conservation, and other renewable products.

As Mason emerged from the private road his house was built on and turned onto a main street, he didn't notice the black sedan parked near the corner. Having tapped Mason's phone line, the sedan's driver had listened into Mason's conversation with Green. The car pulled out and followed the Prius.

At Centennial airport, Mason parked in the public lot next to the Tac-Air Executive Terminal, one of three terminals at Centennial that served the ultra rich. As he opened his car door, a jet took off carrying the owner of the Dallas Cowboys—not that Mason would have known who that was even if he were told.

Mason entered the terminal lobby and checked around for Green. On the far side of a short hallway were glass doors leading out to the tarmac. An aircraft was parked with its stairs opened.

Having arrived early, and with no sight of Green, Mason stood in a waiting area that served complimentary tea, coffee and Oreos—a popular snack for pilots who flew Tac-Air. He downed a couple of the cookies while catching a bit of CNN. Another car bomb had detonated in the Middle East. Mason wondered whether he should have set off a bomb of his own by contacting CNN with his tape. *Not yet*, he thought. He needed to see this strategy through first.

After ten minutes, a black limousine pulled up in the circular drive outside the terminal. Mason watched as the driver got out and opened the back door. A fit, handsome gray-haired man in his mid-fifties wearing a navy blue suit climbed out carrying a small travel bag. If the Congressman ever ended his career in politics, his Richard Gere-like good looks would enable him to do the opposite of Reagan and Swarzenegger—go from politics to Hollywood.

As Green entered the lobby, Mason walked over to greet him. He extended his hand graciously. "Good to see you, Richard. Thanks for meeting on such short notice."

Green smiled, "Good to see you too, Mason—been awhile." He then turned and waved his hand to his driver indicating that the man was free to take off.

Green turned back toward Mason.

"How's Judy and the kids?" Mason asked.

Red Tape

"Judy's managing the interns and having fun with that. The twins are in their final year in college…almost off my payroll. How's Julia?"

"We're talking a bit more these days," Mason replied with some remorse in his voice.

"Glad to hear that. Always liked her."

"Maybe one day I won't be on her black list."

Green gave a compassionate smile and then quickly added, "Well I know you've got something important to discuss. We can sit here in the lobby and talk for a few minutes."

Mason informed Green of Ingrols' and China's deal to demolish the Jokhang and build the enormous Ingrols factory complex. He described how he recorded the massacre, Liung's passive observation, the murder of the Tibetan teen by Redman, and the astonishing presence of the Vice President.

"What? Tenner was there?" Green exclaimed. "I thought he was in Japan."

Mason escalated his tone. "No, he was on a hotel rooftop in Lhasa shaking hands with the Minister of Commerce while Tibetans were getting slaughtered."

"Are you sure it was him?"

"The glasses, the big nose, double chin…no mistake."

"I haven't seen any media coverage about all this," Green said completely bewildered.

"Hasn't been much. No journalists were allowed. I'm sure I'm the only one who recorded it all. I'll bet no one even knew the Vice President was there."

"And there was no violence on the part of the Tibetans provoking the shooting?"

"Their only weapon was a picture of the Dalai Lama."

Green shook his head.

Mason pulled out a couple of small articles to show Green.

"On top of that, I found two small articles in the People's Daily and the Wall Street Journal reporting that Ingrols and China finalized an agreement to open the factory. Those bastards had the gall to sign the deal *the day after* the massacre!"

Green took a look at the articles. As he did he asked, "Have you shown the tape or talked about this with anyone else?"

"Not yet."

"Why haven't you gone to the media?"

"I might. But I want to try to get support from D.C. first. I don't want to just bury Tenner, Redman, and Ingrols. I want the tape to be used in negotiations with China."

Green looked up at Mason, his eyebrows raised. "What kind of negotiations?"

Mason met Green's eyes squarely. "I was hoping you could connect me with someone in Washington who can do something about China."

"What do you mean?"

"China claims to have invaded Tibet to *liberate* the region. Yet this liberation is nothing less than genocide and cultural cleansing! They've murdered over a million Tibetans, destroyed 6,000 monasteries and are wiping out their culture. Tibetans are nonviolent, compassionate people just wanting to keep their way of life and spiritual pursuits. And here in the U.S., our government waves our flag, spouts declarations of human rights and freedom, and yet we don't put any real pressure on China to relieve their oppression of Tibet...'cause of one thing. Money. We spend over $300 billion dollars on products *made in China*. Most American flags are made over there for Christ's sake! We're live-in prostitutes and Ingrols is just one of the whores. The Vice President, too!"

"So what exactly do you hope to accomplish?"

Mason remembered the meditation he had learned in India and took a deep breath to calm his temper. He tried to deliver his message with a more composed tone.

"A meeting between the Dalai Lama and President Hu Jintao. The Dalai Lama's been under exile from Tibet for over forty-five years. He's been asking for decades for a dialogue with China to discuss some form of true autonomy for Tibet. He doesn't want complete independence. This tape could be just what's needed to make that happen."

Green looked down at the floor for a moment and then back up at Mason.

"That's a tall order. Trade and political relations with China are complicated. And needless to say, this is a delicate matter with the Vice President involved."

Green looked away again to ponder the situation. Then he glanced at his watch. He needed to end the conversation.

"I tell you what," Green finally added. "Let me discuss this with Ambassador Ruttlefield. He's the U.S. Trade Representative and part of the Executive Office of the President. He's ultimately responsible for trade relations with China and should have some clue as to the Vice President's involvement. He's probably the best person on the Hill that could help you because he's got the leverage within the administration. I served on the Ways and Means Committee with him, along with a few other subcommittees. I know him pretty well so I should be able to get you a meeting. But I can't promise he'll do anything. He's a long-time vet and his veins hover just above the freezing mark. He's also a tough negotiator. I'd say more, but I've got to run. I'll leave him a message tonight and won't mention it to anyone else."

Green stood up.

"Thanks," Mason said as he stood to shake the Congressman's hand. "I'll wait for your call."

"Watch your back," Green admonished, as he began heading toward his jet. "I imagine you're on the black list of more people than just your daughter."

Mason stood for a moment digesting the Congressman's words. *Probably so,* he thought, *but other than Julia, they're all on mine.*

CHAPTER 5

"He just finished the meeting," the driver said, trailing Mason out of the airport.

"Did he give Green the tape?" the Predator asked.

"No."

"Well, stay on his ass. And I want to know everything—how often he goes to the bathroom, the amount of gas put into his car, the number of fries left on his plate. Got it?"

"Yes, sir."

The Predator hung up and took a puff of his cigar. He knew time was of the essence. He looked at his watch and calculated the time difference. He picked up the phone again and dialed a secured number.

"It's me. What's the count?" the Predator demanded.

"Four right now and one probable," answered the other voice.

"We need eight!" the Predator insisted.

"We'll get the others. Don't worry."

"I'll stop worrying when we get the count." The Predator took another puff of his cigar.

"We will, but we need to keep the street quiet 'til then."

"Just get the count. I'll cut vocal chords if I have to."

CHAPTER 6

*M*ason scurried through Level Two of the Terminal West parking garage at Denver International Airport. Long lines were common at the one security entrance for all three concourses—he didn't want to miss his flight.

The meeting with Ambassador Ruttlefield got scheduled much quicker than imagined. Green had come through *big time*. Mason had received a call from Ruttlefield's assistant earlier in the day saying that the Ambassador would be in D.C. for two more days before heading overseas for a series of US-EU trade relations meetings. Unexpectedly, Ruttlefield wanted to meet Mason at his office at 7:30 a.m. the following morning, assuming Mason could catch a flight today. Fortunately, there was space on the last United flight out. Mason could also make it back to Denver in time for Julia's visit.

As Mason disappeared into the parking lot elevator, the driver of the black sedan pulled into a spot near the Prius. Within sixty seconds, the driver crept over to the car, quickly planted the electronic device underneath, and returned unseen to the sedan. He pulled out his cell and called his boss.

"Red-Eye Activated."

CHAPTER 7

*T*he final passengers boarded the plane. Mason buckled his seat belt. Seated on the aisle, he hoped the middle seat wouldn't be taken so he'd have extra legroom. The heavyset woman by the window had already leaned her head against a pillow. *Good,* Mason thought. *I don't feel like talking.* He turned on the overhead light and pulled out his New York Times.

"Excuse me," a man said standing in the aisle next to Mason.

Mason looked up to see a Chinese guy in his late twenties wearing a white t-shirt and jeans.

"That's my seat," the guy said pointing to the middle one.

Just my luck, Mason thought.

He stood, trying not to frown, and allowed the guy to pass. Mason then re-took his seat and immediately picked up his paper again.

Reading the *World* section, Mason came upon an article titled, *Vice President Sends More Jobs To Japan*. Vice President Tenner had spent several days in Japan the prior week outlining a plan to outsource more IT jobs to Japan for the defense, technology and energy conservation sectors.

Mason almost choked as he read this. The timing of Tenner's visit to Japan was during the Tibetan massacre. But Mason was sure that it was Tenner on his tape. *Could I have been mistaken?*

"Great, isn't it?" said the guy looking at Mason's newspaper.

Mason turned toward him. "What's that?"

The guy pointed to the article in the Times. "Asia's technology keeps transforming the world."

Mason turned his eyes back toward the paper. "Yeah, but in what direction."

"What do you mean?"

Mason glanced over briefly. "Let's just say I'm not a big fan of investing in Asia...no offense." Mason thought he might be Chinese, but wasn't sure.

"Why not?" the guy continued. "Smaller, better, cheaper, faster. That's what it's all about. See?" The guy reached into his pocket and pulled out a state-of-the-art Iphone. "This is so cool. It's got a cell phone, Ipod, and wireless connection all in one. Made in Taiwan."

Mason shook his head. He decided not to continue the conversation but the guy goaded him.

"Investment in China is making a great impact over there."

"Talk to the Tibetans and then let's talk *impact*," Mason said, turning the page.

"Well, I don't know much about Tibet, but I grew up in a poor village where we couldn't even afford a bike. Because of the big bucks from the West, my dad was able to get a factory job in Shanghai that helped us get not just a bike, but also cleaner water and more fans to battle the hotter months. He made enough so I could come over here and get an education. I majored in IT and made seventy G's my first year after graduation and was able to send money back to support my family. Now I'm working for a start-up in Silicon Valley and could make ten times that this year!"

Mason tried to focus on reading another article.

"What did your dad do?" the guy asked.

"Commercial banking."

"Good for him...and for you. See, it wasn't so bad having that silver spoon in your mouth, now was it?"

Mason turned toward him and gave a stern look. Just then a flight attendant shut the door to the plane. The guy from Shanghai looked over his shoulder and saw an empty row a few rows back.

"Hey, there's some extra room back there. I'm going to take it...long flight."

"Sounds good," Mason affirmed, relieved to have his space back and the trip in solitude.

After taking his new seat, the guy slouched down out of sight and sent a quick text on his Iphone. He then stretched his legs across the adjacent seats.

Mason tried to keep reading but couldn't. The kid had gotten under his skin, but not just in an irritating way. Mason knew, in a tiny corner of his mind, that the kid had a point that with all the money pouring into China, some people had better living conditions. But Mason knew about horrific conditions that many of them slaved under. And no progress was justifiable if it meant tearing down a temple to build a factory and slaughtering a thousand Tibetans in the process.

Mason closed his eyes. His father hadn't come up in conversation in a long time. Mason could hear his voice as if he were now in the seat next to him.

"Go to business school and make something of your life, god dammit," his father yelled at him, standing in the kitchen the night after Mason's graduation.

"I'm done with school!" Mason fired back.

"You need an MBA to make serious bucks. Look what it did for me."

"Yeah, look what it did for you! I think we've had ten meals together in ten years!"

His father raised his hand to slap him but stopped. "Hey, I worked hard to give you a freer and comfortable lifestyle!"

"There are people out there denied the right to freedom at all!"

"Focus on yourself first."

"I am."

"You call going off to Cambodia taking care of yourself?"

"My choice."

"Well I'll pay for business school, but not that choice."

"I don't want your money." Mason stormed out of the kitchen.

"You will someday," his father called out.

Mason slammed the front door of the house and never stepped foot in it again.

Turning off the overhead light, Mason shifted his legs to a more comfortable position. The words *you will someday* echoed in his mind. *Someday* had come several years ago when Mason's father died from a heart attack. An inheritance check came, and Mason's life turned on a dime...actually a hundred million dimes. His father had left him *ten million dollars*.

A dirty trick, Mason had first thought. *The old man probably wanted me to see what it was like to swim in it. Funny way to prove you're right.*

But the amount did shake up his familiar, minimalist lifestyle. He immediately gave half to charities and then quit his job at the Post to be an activist consultant. He built an eco-friendly home and drove a new Prius rather than his previous beat up Corolla. Though he still lived modestly, guilt set in about others having so little. He considered giving more away but wanted to make life easier for Julia some day.

Julia's face flashed in his mind. He was looking forward to seeing her in a few days. Perhaps once and for all they could resolve the conflict between them. It was too much like the relationship with his father. This weekend he'd swallow his pride and win back her heart.

CHAPTER 8

At 7:20 a.m. the next morning, Mason stood outside the Dupont Circle hotel weary-eyed. The flight from DIA to Dulles had landed well after midnight. Despite the long flight and late hour arrival, Mason had difficulty falling asleep. The anticipation of his meeting with the United States Trade Representative kept his mind buzzing. His strategy was proceeding even quicker than he had hoped.

With a chill in the air, Mason zipped his jacket up to his throat. His cough was still hanging around like a pestering mosquito.

He climbed into a taxi carrying a hemp briefcase with the tape and headed to 600 17th Street—the USTR building. When the taxi arrived, Mason got out and looked directly across the street at the Executive Offices of the President. He tried to catch a glimpse of the White House but the Executive Offices blocked the view.

He remembered learning that the presidential palace was constructed of an excessively porous stone. The permeability would dampen the interior if it were not for a thick coat of white lead that was applied about once every ten years at enormous expense. *No accident*, Mason often mused, that the building went through this cover up.

The Office of the USTR was responsible for developing, coordinating, and negotiating bilateral and multilateral international trade agreements, while ironing out any wrinkles that developed in trade relations. The USTR reported directly to the President and was the principal advisor on trade policy and affairs. One of the office's main duties was to expand market access for American goods and services. With the rapid expansion of the global economy in the last few decades, the USTR had quietly become one of the largest heavyweights at the top of the hill. Senators who meddled in the trade relation strategy of Ambassador Ruttlefield, the current USTR, quickly learned to respect his position or careers could tumble back down the hill.

As Mason approached the building, he noticed the *Winder Building* sign just to the right of the entrance. Named after Brigadier General William H. Winder, the building was built in the mid-19th century and was used during the Civil War as the headquarters for the U.S. Army. Mason remembered Green saying that Ruttlefield was a Veteran and a tough negotiator. *Oh great, the building probably gives the guy extra testosterone.*

Mason pushed the doorbell next to the sign.

"Yes?" a voice answered through an intercom.

Mason cleared his throat. "Good morning, I'm Mason Hamilton. I have a meeting with Ambassador Ruttlefield."

A security guard opened the door.

"Come in, Mr. Hamilton," a woman spoke from behind the guard.

Standing in the vestibule was a sharply dressed woman in an olive colored suit with shoulder length blonde hair. Though in her late twenties, she looked as if she could still be in college.

"Good morning, Mr. Hamilton. I'm Jessica—Ambassador Ruttlefield's assistant." She flashed the big smile that was routine for staffers throughout the capital.

"Nice to meet you." Mason shook her extended hand.

"You pulled this off pretty quickly."

"Yeah, maybe there really is something to the saying that providence moves when you commit to something."

Jessica laughed. "Well, if you can do that with the lottery, let me know."

Mason grinned.

"Ambassador Ruttlefield's office is on the third floor. We need to pass through security first."

Jessica led the way to the metal detectors. After they passed through, she led him up a flight of stairs and navigated through a maze of cubicles until they reached a waiting area with two black leather chairs situated beside a large mahogany door. On the door was a bronze plate engraved *Ambassador Burton Ruttlefield.*

"Mr. Hamilton, please have a seat. I'll let Ambassador Ruttlefield know you're here." Mason sat down as she disappeared behind the door.

As he waited, Mason took note of a few pictures hanging on the wall outside Ruttlefield's office. There was one of Ruttlefield standing with the President in front of the White House. Next to this was an older black and white. Mason stood up to get a closer look. It was a picture of two Army men. On the left was a young Ruttlefield, perhaps in his late teens, early twenties. Mason saw it was Ruttlefield by the resemblance from the older photo with the President. The young soldier next to Ruttlefield, who had his arm around Ruttlefield's shoulders, looked familiar. It then hit Mason—it was a young picture of Vice President Tenner.

The door opened up. Mason spun around. "Ambassador Ruttlefield will see you now, Mr. Hamilton," Jessica said politely.

"Thanks," Mason said, a bit thrown off by the picture and entered the dimly lit room.

The office contained several bookcases filled with international business trade texts. On the far side of the office, Ruttlefield sat behind an uncluttered mahogany desk in a black leather swivel chair. Directly behind the man was a six-foot pole holding a large U.S flag. *Probably made in China,* Mason thought.

Ruttlefield didn't stand to greet him, but Mason gauged them of equal height, with Ruttlefield having an additional fifteen years on him. The man had large, thick eyebrows and a stern face over a still-fit physique that spoke of hours of pumping iron in the gym. The sheen from his dark blue suit and the slick, combed white hair made Mason think that the polished veneer of a politician always seemed to hide something.

"Come in, Mr. Hamilton. Take a seat," Ruttlefield said pointing to the chairs in front of his desk. Ruttlefield remained seated behind his desk, keeping the barrier between them. No smile. No welcoming handshake.

Mason took the chair closest to the door. Keeping his jacket on, he placed his briefcase on the floor, without relaxing his grip on the handle.

"So I understand, Mr. Hamilton, that you have a tape of the event in Tibet?" Ruttlefield leaned back in his chair.

"I would hardly call it an *event*. And call me Mason."

"What would you call it…Mason?" Ruttlefield didn't make a similar offer.

"It was a *massacre*. A thousand Tibetans were killed in cold blood."

Ruttlefield remained silent as he continued to stare at Mason.

"And I've got on tape China's Minister of Commerce doing nothing about it as well as Vice President Tenner shaking his hands while the *massacre* is happening. On top of that, I captured the head of China operations for Ingrols murdering a Tibetan teen! And the next day, Ingrols and China signed the deal to—"

"What do you want from this meeting, Mason?" Ruttlefield cut him off.

Mason gripped his briefcase a bit tighter. He had hoped for a better welcome given the man's relationship with Green, though the Congressman did warn him of Ruttlefield's standoffish character.

"I want to discuss how this atrocity was yet another example of China's tyranny of the Tibetans. I could have gone to the media with the tape. They would have a field day with China, the Vice President, Ingrols, and Redman. But I've come to you instead."

"Why?" Ruttlefield titled his head.

"China's record in human rights violations is abominable. They've murdered over a million Tibetans and have practically destroyed their culture. I want this tape to show that violence and prevent the temple from being demolished and to force the Chinese government into meeting with the Dalai Lama to discuss an autonomous Tibet."

Ruttlefield tipped his chair back, gazed at the ceiling, and then locked eyes with Mason.

"First of all, I heard about what happened in Tibet. Tragic. But the Vice President was in Japan. You must have someone else on this tape. Secondly, from what I understand, Redman was acting completely in self-defense. Thirdly, the political history of Tibet is complicated. Matters of human rights and international territory lines do not fall under my jurisdiction. And finally, Ingrols has the right to do any deal it wants. Anytime. Anywhere. I can't stop that."

"Acting in self-defense?" Mason's voice rose. "The kid was threatening with a *picture* of the Dalai Lama!"

"Apparently Redman didn't know this," Ruttlefield retorted.

"Says who?" Mason challenged.

"I spoke with Minister Liung Xilai yesterday. He says the crowd was protesting aggressively."

Mason gripped the briefcase even tighter. "These are non-violent Buddhists for crying out loud! They had no weapons—only pictures of the Dalai Lama! Can you imagine being told that you can't put up someone's picture in your house?"

"This is China's concern, not ours."

"What about the genocide that's taken place over there for decades? Even today, Tibetans are beaten and executed for not embracing the ideology of the Chinese Communist Party. And yet our administration makes parenthetical comments about human rights and then turns its head, keeping our eyes fixed on our bank statements!"

"First of all, Mason, genocide is a loaded word. Second of all, our political and trade relationship with China is very complex."

"Complex? It's very simple. It's about three words....money, money and more money. We don't have any trouble fighting hard on their undervalued currency, their stealing of our intellectual property, or them restricting access to their markets for our products."

Ruttlefield shook his head.

"Are you familiar with the Panchen Lama?" Mason asked.

"No."

"He's considered the second holiest Tibetan after the Dalai Lama. In 1995, China abducted that six year-old boy to prevent the development of any Tibetan allegiance to the Lama. No one knows where he is...or even if he's still alive. He's the world's youngest political prisoner and yet no one demands proof of his whereabouts."

"That's outside my arena," Ruttlefield steepled his fingers under his chin.

"How about the fact that this massacre took place because Ingrols is trying to tear down the holiest Tibetan temple in order to build a factory complex for trade purposes...and then kills Tibetans in the process. Is this within your area? Or how about the fact that the average American spends a thousand dollars a year on products made in China thereby supporting the policies and practices of the Chinese government. Is this within your area?" Mason was at the edge of his seat, nearly touching Ruttlefield's desk.

"People are more concerned about their wallets than the Great Wall."

Mason ignored Ruttlefield's curt and non-cooperative responses.

"And it's fine that Vice President Tenner is supporting all this?"

"Like I said, Vice President Tenner was in Japan."

"He *was*," Mason argued. "But then he took a secretive trip to Tibet for the Ingrols meeting. I know it's him on the tape."

"Do you have the tape?" Ruttlefield demanded.

Mason hesitated. He felt torn. He had initially planned on playing the tape to gain a more fervent commitment from Ruttlefield to approach China. Mason figured that unless Saddam Hussein or Hitler were viewing the tape, any one else watching it would be deeply moved by the slaughtering of the innocent Tibetans. However, the man's defensiveness and history with the Vice President made Mason leery of going further. But he couldn't hold back now. Perhaps if Ruttlefield saw the tape firsthand, he'd be more apt to take action.

"Yes," Mason acknowledged apprehensively.

"Let's watch it," Ruttlefield pointed to a flat screen in the bookcase next to his desk.

Mason was hopeful that the larger screen of the TV would have greater impact than the tiny display on the camcorder. He reached down and unlocked the briefcase. Inside was a small black bag containing the digital camcorder and cables.

The length of the recording was exactly one hundred and eight seconds, which was auspicious for Mason when he first played it. 108 was a magical number in many spiritual traditions. Most malas or rosaries contained one hundred and eight beads for the one hundred and eight mantras that monks frequently cited. The number 108 was used in Islam to refer to God. Even scientifically, the distance between the earth and the sun was 108 times the sun's diameter. The distance between the earth and the moon was 108 times the moon's diameter, and the diameter of the sun equaled 108 times the earth's diameter.

After Mason attached the cables, he pressed *play* and the picture came through clearly. As they viewed the tape, Mason glanced over several times to gauge Ruttlefield's reaction. The Ambassador's reaction was the same—emotionless. Whether it was the elderly monk being shot, Tibetans being slaughtered, children screaming, the Vice President shaking hands with Liung, or Redman murdering the Tibetan teen, Ruttlefield didn't wince. He maintained a rigid and blank stare.

The tape ended. Neither said a word. Mason unplugged the cords and sat back down. The silence was interrupted only by the sound of a wall clock ticking.

Ruttlefield swiveled his chair and looked out a large window at the Executive Offices of The President across the street. Mason wondered what was going through the man's mind. After a long silence, Ruttlefield turned back to Mason.

"Quite a tape. Have you shown it or discussed this with anyone other than Congressman Green?"

"Not yet."

"Let's keep it that way. There are people I can contact who can lend their cooperation. However, I need you to leave me the tape."

"And who might they be?" Mason pressed.

"I can't say right now. I'll show it to those who'll be…" Ruttlefield paused, "interested in seeing it and in position to do something with it."

Mason shook his head. "If you can't tell me who you'll talk to, I can't leave the tape."

"That would be a mistake, Mason," Ruttlefield admonished. "First of all, it's in your best interest to give me the tape so that suitable action can be taken from here in Washington. And secondly, if you don't, I can get a court order to legally sequester the tape."

"Sequester the tape?" Mason repeated in disbelief.

"You have material that, if utilized with malicious intent, may interfere with, and potentially damage, U.S. interests in international trade relations. I have the legal right to prevent such occurrences and could easily get a court order to impound the tape."

"This isn't the kind of support I was hoping to get."

"This is Washington and you have to know how to play by the rules. Just give me the tape. I'll see it's given its due attention."

Ruttlefield extended his hand.

Mason put the camcorder back in his briefcase.

"Well, I think I'll find another game," Mason said as he locked the briefcase and started walking toward the door.

"Congressman Green told me that the Chinese know you have the tape. I must tell you that your life could be in danger. For all I know, it already is...*Mason.*"

Mason opened the door. He then turned around and said calmly, "There's an old Tibetan saying. *Tomorrow or the next life—which will come first, we never know.* For your own sake, I think you better watch your own karma...*Burton!*"

Mason slammed the door shut behind him.

Jessica was sitting at her desk and looked up in surprise.

"Is everything okay, Mr. Hamilton?" she asked in concern.

"I can find my own way out," Mason replied as he briskly walked past her desk.

"I'm afraid I'll have to escort you out, Mr. Hamilton. Security reasons. I'm sure you understand."

"Let's go then," Mason said curtly. He wanted out of the building immediately.

Neither of them said a word until they reached the side entrance.

As they approached the door, Jessica said, "Mr. Hamilton, I don't know what happened in there, but let me know if I can be of further assistance." She smiled and extended her hand.

Mason shook her hand and wondered if Jessica was just being customarily polite or truly sincere. But it didn't matter right now. He had to start plan B.

CHAPTER 9

*D*espite the cool temperature, Mason decided to walk off the anger. Besides, his next destination was only about a ten-minute walk up 17th Ave.

Following Mason, a man in a black suit turned the corner from the USTR building. He kept a decent distance back but maintained visual range.

When Mason reached H Street, a loud horn made Mason look around. A man in a black suit was crossing the street despite the *"Don't Walk"* sign.

At Farragut Square, Mason crossed the street to see the statue in the middle of the square. It was that of the Civil War Admiral David Farragut who had coined the phrase *full speed ahead* during the 1864 Battle of Mobile Bay, Alabama. Mason circled the statue and then, out of the corner of his eye, noticed the man in the black suit taking a seat on a bench on the southwest corner of the square. The man had no coat, no book, no newspaper—he merely sat with his hands in his pockets gazing about the empty square.

Mason switched gears. He headed to a Starbucks on the other side of K Street. Just to the left of the brew-house capital, hurrying commuters emerged from the Farragut North Metro station. Mason crossed the street and tried to get lost among the bustling crowd before slipping into Starbucks.

Five minutes later, Mason exited with a decaf latte in hand. He spotted the man in the black suit standing across the street looking in his direction. Their eyes met and Mason knew for certain he was being followed.

Mason glanced right. The entrance to the station was still packed. He maneuvered through the crowd and then looked back to see the man coming after him. Farragut's phrase *full speed ahead* crossed his mind. He tossed the latte into a trashcan and bolted up Connecticut Avenue, holding his briefcase tightly.

Mason passed Café Panini. He considered whether to go inside. Glancing back, he could see that the man in the black suit was still in view. *Too small a place*, he thought.

He darted ahead toward the luxurious Renaissance Mayflower hotel. When he reached the circular drive, he hurried through the rotating front door into the lobby. He stopped a bellman pushing a cart.

"Where are the restrooms?" Mason demanded.

"Through the promenade," pointed the bellman.

Mason dashed through the promenade on the white marble floor, trying to stay clear of yellow *"Caution Wet Floor"* signs. When he reached a sign indicating the restrooms were down a flight of stairs, he turned but didn't spot his follower.

He raced down the steps and entered the men's room where he locked himself into a stall. Trying to catch his breath again, he tried to suppress the nagging cough but couldn't. The sound reverberated throughout the restroom.

He listened for the door but no one entered.

With perspiration dripping, he grabbed some toilet paper and wiped his forehead.

Who was this guy? Could Ruttlefield have sent a watchdog that fast? Who else would have known he was in D.C. at the Ambassador's office?

He remembered Ruttlefield's comment about his life being in danger. Perhaps the Veteran was right. Given what he captured on tape, he was a walking time bomb. It was surely plausible that there'd be those who'd stop at nothing to ensure that the bomb was *defused*.

After waiting in the stall for fifteen minutes, Mason decided he'd probably lost his tracker. Heading back to the main corridor, he saw the man in the black suit sitting on a couch in the promenade about thirty feet away talking on his cell.

The man saw Mason and immediately jumped up from the couch.

Mason turned to run in the opposite direction but slipped on the wet marble and fell to the floor. The briefcase flew out of his hands. The case hit the floor and the lid flipped open.

Before Mason could grab the camcorder, the man ran passed him, scooped up the case, and charged down the hall toward an exit. Within a matter of seconds, the man was out of sight.

Mason lifted himself up and watched the man disappear. With a pain in his hip, he walked with a slight limp back to the lobby to find a payphone.

Near the registration desk was a bank of phones. He picked up one and placed the call. As the phone rang at the office, he glanced worriedly about the lobby. After three rings, the voicemail of the International Campaign for Tibet—where he had been heading—finally picked up. A recording explained that the office was closed until the following Monday in observance of a Tibetan holiday. Today was Wednesday. *Dammit,* he said, slamming the phone back on the hook.

He stood contemplating his next steps. He had originally planned to return to Denver on Friday to be back for Julia's visit. But a realization flashed through his mind. There was something he needed to do—and as soon as possible. It couldn't wait until Friday. And though it seemed imprudent, he knew it was the best decision.

He left a quick message for Julia and then grabbed a taxi to check out of his hotel. Within a couple of hours he was back on a plane to Denver.

CHAPTER 10

"What do you mean you don't have the tape?" the Predator barked into the speakerphone.

"When I grabbed the case off the floor, I saw the tape inside the camcorder. I figured that was it," the man in the black suit said. He was now circling the area around the Renaissance Hotel in his car looking for Mason.

"You didn't check it?" the Predator exclaimed.

"I did when I reached my car. That's when I found the blank. I'm not sure how he—" the man in the black suit stopped in mid-sentence realizing what happened. "Shit! He must have switched tapes in the men's room."

"Where is he now?"

"Don't know...but don't worry. I'll find him and get it. He must be staying in a hotel nearby."

"Find the bastard!" The Predator slammed his fist down on his desk and hung up.

CHAPTER 11

Who's after me? Mason wondered, staring out the window of the plane. The people who knew about the tape were Green, Ruttlefield, and, by now, probably Redman and Liung, and perhaps even Vice President Tenner. Green was an unlikely source given their long-term relationship, but he'd call the Congressman when he got home to feel him out.

Ruttlefield had said he had been in contact with Liung prior to the meeting. He knew the stakes if the tape went public. But could he have sent a tail so quickly? If U.S. nuclear land missiles can be launched on two minutes notice, organizing someone to follow him within two minutes couldn't be too hard given the Ambassador's position.

Another likely culprit was Liung. Mason figured the Chinese soldier who chased him in Tibet would certainly have notified his commanders after discovering his passport number. This meant his U.S. address could be easily traced. Perhaps the Chinese leader had some connection in the U.S. Or, perhaps he was in league with Redman. Redman had plenty at stake and could have arranged to have him followed from Denver.

No matter who was masterminding this, Mason knew it wouldn't be long before he'd be tracked again. He needed to complete Plan B.

Back at the airport in Denver, Mason made his way through the parking lot. Once inside his car, he put the key in the ignition. As he started to turn the key, he realized he wasn't sure where he had put the parking ticket. He pulled out his wallet and sorted through bills and receipts. There it was. He buckled his seatbelt and turned the ignition key. The engine's starter began to engage but didn't start. *Strange,* he thought—the car hadn't been giving him any problems. *The engine's probably cold.*

He tried again. This time the engine kicked in. He backed the car out and headed off.

As he did, other eyes were glued to a website. The GPS-Web Vehicle Tracking System showed exactly where Mason was driving. It didn't take long for the person to figure out Mason was headed home. He was back on Mason's trail.

CHAPTER 12

Julia opened the door to her one bedroom apartment. She slid the shoulder strap off of her brown, soft leather briefcase and put it on her desk in the living room. The clock read *9:00pm*—her usual quitting time.

She stepped out of her shoes, comforting aching feet after a long day of running to meetings throughout the North Bay. Living among the redwoods in Mill Valley had both its upsides and downs for Julia. The beauty of great hiking and running trails, as well as the conscious environmental community of the area, reminded her of the Colorado lifestyle she grew up in. But with freeway traffic in the Bay Area that would make anyone insane, she worked late hours to minimize driving time.

Julia headed into the kitchen and poured herself a glass of Pinot. She then sat at her desk and listened to her voicemail while flipping through the regular delivery of bills and ads.

The first message was from Janice thanking her for the great cigarette litter article and for completing it ahead of schedule along with the quote from the Governor, even though the best quote she could get was *I'm against litter of any kind.*

The next message was from a girlfriend confirming the meeting spot for their hike up Mt. Tam tomorrow. *Good.* Julia wanted the exercise before flying out the following morning to see her father.

The last one was from him.

"Hi. It's your father. I've got something important to talk to you about when I see you. Please don't cancel this time. I've got your flight details. I'll meet you," her father coughed a few times before continuing. "Sorry about that. I picked up a cough in India. I'll meet you on the other side of security. Can't wait to see you."

Julia erased the message. *He sounds a bit exasperated, but he didn't say to call back. Must not be that important. Maybe he's decided to move to India.* That would be fine with her.

She took her wine, sat on her couch and thought about her upcoming trip. It was to be a quick one—in Saturday morning, back Sunday evening. Just how she liked it. Two days, max. One day more and they'd be butting heads about what happened—they always did.

It was her thirteenth birthday. Her father had left her with a nanny and was on yet another journey for Amnesty International. It was his fifty-ninth trip in seven years; that was the number of pencil marks she made on the wall next to her bed every time he left.

When Julia came home from school, she saw a FedEx envelope outside the front door. She thought it might be a gift, and curious, she opened it.

Inside was a notification letter that a Tara Frazier had just died—the mother of Julia Hamilton. Julia stood there stunned. Her father had always said that her mother died of cancer soon after she was born. He never talked about her. Whenever Julia brought her up in conversation, he quickly changed the subject. There were no pictures of her around the house; he had claimed they were too painful.

When her father returned home from his trip, as soon as he walked in the door, she confronted him.

"What is this Daddy?" she yelled.

Mason put down his bags.

"What's going on?" he took the letter and read the contents. "Where'd you get this?" he demanded.

"Was Tara Frazier my mother?" she demanded.

Mason shook his head in disbelief.

"Was she my mother?" Julia cried again.

"Yes," he admitted.

"But you told me she died right after I was born. This says she died two weeks ago!"

"Julia, let me—"

"You lied to me about my mother!" Julia began sobbing and ran up the stairs toward her room.

"Wait! Let me explain." Mason paused. "I thought it would be best not to tell you!"

"Best for who?" She yelled back and locked herself in her room.

It was over an hour before Mason could give her his explanation. During his first job in Cambodia, Mason had a fling with an American woman who had been traveling on vacation. After the woman returned to the States, she discovered she was pregnant. It was Mason's child, and she tried contacting him by sending letters to the U.S. Post Office Box he had given her. Mason didn't find the letters until he completed his assignment and returned home—six months after Julia was born.

In desperation, he tried to contact the woman only to discover she had received a five-year jail sentence for drug possession and larceny. Mason was livid. The woman hadn't tried to track him down through Amnesty International though she knew he worked for them. She had the child and then fell to drug addiction. Social Services took the baby. Though Mason was by no means ready to be a father, he sought the legal help of a friend and gained full custody of Julia.

Mason explained to Julia that he had looked out for her best interest; he was afraid that if she knew about her mother, that it would scar her life. Julia ended up scarred anyway.

Julia took another sip of wine to ease the familiar anger that the memory always elicited. She hated her father not only for lying but also for having denied her any chance to meet her mother. She would have done anything for that. It didn't matter that the woman had been imprisoned for several more sentences during those years. Perhaps Julia would have been a positive spark in her mother's life, inspiring her to take a new direction. But that would never happen. After a few unsuccessful suicide attempts, her mother had finally succeeded—she hanged herself in jail using her bed sheets.

CHAPTER 13

As a branch of UNESCO, the World Heritage Committee (WHC) oversees the identification, protection, and preservation of significant cultural and natural heritage sites around the world. Since 1972, over 800 international properties in 182 State Parties had been accepted under the strict guidelines of UNESCO. For a property to be inscribed or removed from *the list*, the participating State Parties on the WHC had to abide by its operating decision-making rules. With twenty-one members comprising the committee, and two-thirds of a quorum needed to affirm a decision, the Jokhang Temple was eight votes from being taken off from the list.

The Predator put out his cigar and tossed the butt into the bin under his desk. He proceeded to dial the secured number.

"What's the count now?" he asked.

"Five yes's, and three no's at this point. The other four are undecided," the person responded.

"Who's in?"

"Lithuania—who chairs the committee. We've also got Kuwait, Benin, and Canada. Then of course, there's the U.S."

"Who's against?"

"New Zealand, India and the Netherlands."

"The three of them help run this committee, dammit! Can't Xinsheng do something about that?"

"I doubt it. They're all loyalists to the list."

"Who's on the fence?"

"Chile, Cuba, Morroco, and Korea. But Xinsheng is certain he'll get three of the four. He says he's got enough to hold the meeting. Don't worry."

"I'm tired of people telling me not to worry. I've gotten to where I am because I worry! How much longer?"

"A couple of weeks. But the construction company is set. The temple can be torn down right away once the committee OK's it."

"Well, light a fire under Xinsheng's ass."

The Predator disconnected the line. As long as Hamilton's tape didn't go public, the deal would soon be done.

CHAPTER 14

*M*ason watched from his car as the few customers who had been standing outside the front door entered the bank. It was 9:00am. He had been waiting for the last five minutes with the doors locked. It was too risky to stand in the open with the tape. Perhaps it was two sleepless nights that contributed to his paranoia; more likely it was being chased twice in two weeks that made him feel like a mouse trying to escape the wrath of a persistent cat.

Mason got out of his car and scanned the lot. Nothing unusual. He swiftly headed inside the bank where he was welcomed by one of the staff.

"Good morning. How may I help you today?" said a smiling bank representative.

"I need a safe deposit box," Mason requested.

"Right this way."

The representative led Mason past the new accounts platform toward the rear of the bank. As they reached a staircase leading to a lower level, a man seated in the new accounts waiting area peered above the magazine he was reading. He watched as they disappeared under the *Safe Deposit* sign just above the staircase. The man had been one of the customers waiting outside the bank before it opened.

He tilted the cap he was wearing down to cover more of his face. Placing the unread magazine down on a table, he then strolled out of the bank.

The tracking device was working like a charm.

CHAPTER 15

*I*t just ended, honey," said Green to his wife on his cell as he walked out the front door of the Denver West Marriott. He had attended a fundraiser for the American Heart Association. The Thursday night event had been sponsored by the Clinton Foundation, which had joined the AHA's bandwagon to fight the mounting concern of childhood obesity. Over 12 million children in the U.S. were overweight and exhibited high blood pressure, elevated cholesterol, and type-2 diabetes. Green had been a supporter of the AHA ever since a female colleague died at fifty-five from a heart attack, thereby contributing to the statistic that cardiovascular disease was the number one killer of both men *and* women.

"When do you think you'll get home?" his wife asked.

Green paused and glanced at his Rolex. "Well, it's about ten fifteen so I should be home by eleven-ish. I need to take the Loop because 70 is closed. Guess there was an accident with this crazy snow."

"I'll wait up. Drive safe."

"Will do."

"Love you."

"Love you, too," Green echoed and closed the phone lid.

As he departed the parking lot in his newly leased Jag, he didn't notice the black sedan follow him out.

Green checked his office voicemail. There were two messages. The first was from his assistant mentioning that she had prepared the copies of the bill being distributed at Monday's Transportation and Energy Committee meeting. She then reminded him she was flying to Jamaica first thing in the morning for her long overdue vacation—where she could *not* be reached by phone *or* email. Green smiled. He knew how hard she worked. She deserved the time off.

The second message was from Mason Hamilton. Mason was back from D.C. and needed to talk but would save the details for when they spoke. *I'll call him in the morning,* Green thought.

Driving carefully in the snow, Green steered his way through the winding hills of the Lariat Loop toward his custom built home on Lookout Mountain. He noticed a car in his rearview mirror following a bit close. He was surprised because the road curved frequently over the steep terrain. Even at mid-day the road was treacherous.

With the headlights practically sitting in his back seat, Green started to get pissed off. Coming to a short straightaway, Green slowed down to let the annoying driver go by. But instead of passing, the black sedan accelerated and smashed into the trunk of the Jag, snapping Green's head back.

Green tried to steer the car into the embankment away from the cliff-side but with the slippery condition and force of the sedan, the Jag veered back toward the cliff.

Ahead was a guardrail protecting another sharp curve in the road. Green slammed his foot on the brakes but with increased power from the sedan behind, his car flipped over the guardrail, tumbling end-over-end down a three hundred foot drop until it smashed into trees below. The impact jarred open the driver's door, and the seatbelt snapped, hurling Green's lifeless body of the car.

The driver of the black sedan turned around and headed back toward Denver. As he did, a smile crossed his face as he thought, *what you don't know, won't hurt you, but what you do, will kill you.*

CHAPTER 16

"Welcome, Mr. Hamilton," said the bank associate looking at him to confirm the picture on his ID.

"I'll need you to sign here to match your signature to the signature card," she said slipping him the form over the desk outside the Safe Deposit vault. "I'll also need your social security number and current address please."

After verifying the information matched, she explained that she would retrieve the bank's Master Key since no box could be opened without both a customer's and the bank's key for security purposes.

"Well, I've actually lost both of my keys," he stated. "I know this is going to sound crazy, but I opened my box yesterday. When I left the bank, I put the safe deposit keys on the passenger seat of my car. I stopped at Whole Foods Market on the way home and when I came out, my car had been stolen. Since then, I've been dealing with the police and other urgent matters. This is the first chance I've had to come in. I really need the contents from the box now."

"Mr. Hamilton, as you were probably told when you rented the box, we have a strict policy of not opening a customer's box without one of their keys. If a customer loses both keys, we must arrange for a locksmith to drill open the box. It costs one hundred and fifty dollars. You can then rent another one if you'd like. Fortunately, we contract with a locksmith around the corner. If you have the time, I can call him now."

"Yes—the sooner the better," he nodded.

Within 30 minutes, the safe deposit box had been opened and the contents were removed. Actually, the *content* was removed—all that was in the box was the tape.

Red Tape

49

After collecting the money, the associate asked, "Would you care to open another box?"

"Not today, but perhaps soon."

He left the bank with the tape in hand and drove to a nearby dead end road where he wouldn't be seen. He rotated the rearview mirror toward himself.

Reaching beneath his shirt collar, he found the edge. Slowly he pulled the latex rubber mask that had been covering his head. The disguise worked flawlessly—a bit itchy and hot—but effective. The clandestine photos taken of Hamilton had allowed for a perfect disguise to be crafted. In addition, the man had rehearsed Hamilton's signature and memorized his personal information.

He pulled out his cell and made the call.

"I've got the tape," he said to the Predator.

"Good. Make the delivery and continue the routine."

The Predator hung up, took a quick puff of his cigar, and then picked up the phone to make the call.

"We've got it," the Predator confirmed.

"That's a relief," the voice responded.

"Give me the status."

"We got Cuba. Their Urban Historic Centre of Cienfuegos was recently approved so they felt obliged. Just two to go."

"Don't let up."

The Predator hung up. He leaned back in his chair and reviewed a text message on his cell. The characters slowly moved across the tiny screen—*No wife. One daughter named Julia.*

CHAPTER 17

A red light flickered on his answering machine. Mason thought it might be a message from Green as he had yet to hear back from the Senator. When he hit playback, it was Julia's voice that came through.

Got your message. I'm still coming tomorrow. I'm out all day hiking so let's talk when I see you. Got to run. Bye.

Good...she's still coming, Mason thought. His plan was to pick her up at the airport tomorrow and head to a secluded hotel outside Denver. He'd explain all the details then, both of what had happened as well as his strategy for moving forward. He had held off saying anything thus far. He hadn't wanted to worry her. But he couldn't wait any longer. Despite their friction, she was the one person he could trust.

He sat in his large reading chair and thought about the upcoming meeting he had scheduled for later that evening. The old familiar pain was back...and the drug he'd get tonight from his supplier was the only relief he knew.

He wasn't proud of this shady side of himself. It went against everything he believed. Sometimes he justified it by thinking everyone had *some* form of addiction; this was his. Yet, his savvy intellect could see through this veil.

Over the years, he had become increasingly bitter and isolated. He never married, as work was his true love. But the one thing he dedicated his life to—fighting against social injustice—had produced little progress in his eyes. If anything, there were more merciless acts in the world today. The list went on...9/11, Iraq, Darfur, etc. In his younger days, he could block out the feelings of helplessness and unworthiness by tapping into his humanitarian passion. But that reserve tank was empty. And he was wiser...or at least older. He could no longer deny feeling like a failure.

He had stumbled across Tibetan Buddhism a few years back. He was drawn to the spiritual teachings that claimed to provide a way out of suffering. He sunk his teeth in deeply, as he did with everything. He took several trips to Dharamsala, India—the exiled government of the Tibetans and home of the Dalai Lama. There he not only bonded with the Tibetan community but also learned that his drive for justice, peace and harmony in the world was a way to feel more connected with humanity. The eastern view was that all of life was interconnected. Although people, the environment and all material form seemed to be independent, this was a superficial view of reality. There was a deeper unification to be seen and understood. If one could experience the true interdependent nature of existence, one could transcend the pain that came with feeling separate.

This wasn't Mason's experience, however. Though books and teachers testified to the reality that *"we're all connected"* and *"everything is one,"* Mason didn't feel it in his bones. At the end of the day, he still felt desperately alone. It was this despondency that kept calling him back to this drug—for the high he would receive tonight, though temporary, was his one saving grace.

A few hours passed when there it was. The ritualistic knock at the front door. Two taps, followed by one, followed by another two. *Right on time as usual,* he thought.

Mason made his way to the front door. When he opened it, his head jolted back a bit. She was by far the sexiest one yet. Wearing a low cut, spaghetti strapped black dress that tightly covered her hourglass figure, the Victoria Secret-like knockout had long blonde hair that fell down just below her shoulders to the tops of her well-proportioned breasts. Her slim, long tanned legs led down to elegant black stilettos, which added a couple of inches to her 5'6" height.

Scanning the dazzling features of her body, he quickly surmised she was probably a reward for him being such a good customer.

"Well, in or out?" she asked after letting him inspect the merchandise.

"Sorry. C'mon in," Mason said, quickly turning his eyes to the ground as he opened the door wider to let her in.

She strutted by him into the foyer carrying a black purse in one hand and a small cooler in the other. He hadn't noticed the cooler at first—his eyes fell on more important things.

"I was asked to bring you a fine selection," she said, as she caught his eyes glance at the cooler.

"That's a first," he said, as he locked the door behind her.

"We're upping our service for our best customers." She turned back and smiled at him.

He didn't return one.

"Actually," he murmured, "I could use a drink. I've had an intense couple of days."

"I bet I can help with that too," she said with a smirk. He felt her words penetrate his pelvis but continued to avoid her eyes.

Taking the cooler out of her hand, he walked her through the foyer toward the living room. He always preferred his house as the rendezvous point—a hotel could be too conspicuous. And the house was situated far enough away from his neighbors so no guests could be seen coming or going.

They walked past a set of Ashiko African drums and an ancient Balinese mask—recent collections that would remind him of his travels years with AI. In the center of the spacious living room was a sectional sofa fronted by a large wooden coffee table made in India. He placed the cooler on the table and opened it to find bottles of Heineken, Grey Goose, Baileys, and Dom Perignon—all on ice.

"Quite the assortment," he admired.

"The best always get the best. And given what you're paying, they told me to take good care of you—until midnight that is. That gives us two hours, however you want to use them...*and me, of course.*"

"Getting right to it, aren't you?" he said keeping his eyes fixed on the contents of the cooler.

She stepped up next to him and whispered into his ear.

"Well if you prefer, we can talk about the weather or who you think will win the Super Bowl this season. I like the Cowboys myself. That's because I've always liked *Cowboys*." She gently grazed his chest with the nail of her forefinger. He felt a rush pulsate through his veins like the hit a cocaine user gets on the first sniff.

"What's your name?" he asked.

"Star."

Mason knew Star wasn't her real name. But that didn't matter—he wasn't building a relationship anyway. It just added to the fantasy.

"Let's head to the bedroom...Star," he asserted.

"Sounds good to me. Which way?" She tilted her head sideways and flashed a sexy smile through the strands of blonde hair that fell across her face.

"Follow me."

He began walking in the direction of the bedroom.

"Don't forget the cooler," she reminded.

He turned, picked up the cooler, and headed toward two large doors on the right side of the living room.

In the middle of the bedroom, across from the four-poster bed, was a long matching dresser, on top of which were piles of magazines that Mason had read cover-to-cover. They included the latest issues of The Atlantic Monthly, National Geographic and Newsweek.

"What's your drink?" he asked as he pushed aside a few magazines and put the cooler down on the dresser.

"Whatever you're having. I want to be on the same playing field."

"Heineken works for me."

"Perfect. I've got a bottle opener in the cooler."

After they each took a few swigs of beer, she took the bottle out of his hand and put both bottles back in the cooler. She stepped closer and slid the back of her hand across his chest.

"You see, I really do like cowboys," she said again with a seductive grin. "I like watchin' 'em get in the corral and rope them bulls. Inside this body has always been a cowgirl."

She reached into her purse and pulled out a couple of long pieces of rope and black gloves. "How about a little rodeo, cowboy?" She tilted her head to the side again and looked at him out of the corner of her eyes while pretending to make a large lasso with one of the pieces.

"And which one of us is to be the bull?" he asked.

"Like I said, I want us on the same playing field. So let's take turns. You choose first."

Mason stared at her intently, deliberating whether to go through with it all. It wasn't too late to stop. The last time he had done this, he swore he was done. *No more* he had promised himself. He needed to find a different way to alleviate the incessant deep-rooted pain when it arose. But right now, the uncontrollable urges of his body override his mind.

After a long pause he finally broke the silence.

"Okay, cowgirl. Let's see you ride."

She smirked. "Well then. Let's prep the bull."

She slipped on a pair of thin, black leather gloves. Kneeling down in front of him, she first untied and removed his black shoes.

She then slid her hands up his black corduroy pants until she reached the belt. As she unbuckled it, he closed his eyes and took a deep breath. She slowly unzipped his pants and removed each pant leg.

Then, starting at the bottom of his long sleeved blue shirt, one by one she slowly unfastened each button, kissing his waist and chest right where the button had been. After undoing the top one, she stood up, kissed his neck and then whispered softly in his ear, "Time to get in the corral."

She escorted him to the bed where he laid down on his back, still wearing his unbuttoned shirt, underwear, and socks. His eyes were glued to her every move as she stood aside the bed and wrapped one piece of rope around his left wrist making sure his sleeve protected his skin. She then wound the rope tightly around the nearby bedpost. He was aroused, knowing he couldn't get free too easily.

She slid her hand over his body as she walked to the other side of the bed and then tied his right wrist in the same fashion. Using a second piece of rope, she tied each ankle over the socks to the other two posts by the foot of the bed.

With her clothes still on, she climbed on top of him and positioned herself on his crotch. She started to ride him like a bull, moving her pelvis up and down on his. The friction got him hard beneath his underwear.

He closed his eyes and took several deep breaths to try to release his tension. The erotic sensation quieted his mind and pushed away the loneliness.

After a few minutes of foreplay, she slid off and brought the cooler next to the bed. As she climbed back on him, he opened his eyes and stared at the black, sexy dress, imagining the finely shaped curves underneath.

"I can see things are heating up for the bull," she said with another sexy smile.

She reached into the cooler and pulled out a small piece of ice.

She started sensuously massaging his bare chest with the ice, using her tongue to lick the wet trail. He closed his eyes again, leaned his head back and did all he could to just breathe. His pelvis started moving up and down against hers. The stimulation was almost more than he could take.

"More?" she asked.

"Uh-huh," he nodded, knowing he was past the point of no return.

She reached into the cooler and pulled out a larger piece. She moistened his lips with the ice and slowly licked the wetness with the tip of her tongue. With his eyes still closed, he tried to meet her tongue with his. She pulled hers back teasingly and instead, parted his lips with her fingers and gently placed the ice cube into his mouth. He started to suck on it like a baby taking to a pacifier.

Then, in a swift moment, she rammed the large piece of ice down into this throat. His eyes widened immediately. She leaned harder and jammed her forearm against his windpipe.

Mason shook his head and tried to throw her off with his pelvis but her pressure was too strong. He wildly jerked his arms and thrashed his legs but couldn't free them—she had tied the ropes tautly. For a slender woman, her body was in extremely strong condition, and using her weight to keep him down, she compressed the ice further into his throat, jamming the airways. His began convulsing. His eyes widened even further. She maintained a firm pressure as he flailed helplessly until his body gave way and went completely limp. She continued to press in case he was pretending. But he wasn't.

She slid off and put what remained of the ice back into the cooler. It was one of her favorite weapons.

After untying his arms and legs, she placed the ropes in her purse. The shirt and socks had done their job by protecting the skin from rope burns. She removed the garments—except his underwear—and threw them on the floor by the pants and shoes. She then covered his body with the comforter to make it look like he had died in his sleep.

After inspecting the scene to ensure nothing had been left or was out of place, she grabbed the cooler and walked out of the room, turning off the light. She had been careful not to touch anything in the house before putting on her gloves. No prints would be found. She checked to make sure the front door was locked to eliminate any sign of forced entry. Success in her position was predicated on attention to fine details.

Then, finding the door to the garage, she pressed a button that opened one of the doors. Once it was completely raised, she clicked the button again. She ran and ducked under the closing door, carefully stepping over the sensor so the safety mechanism wouldn't trigger and reopen the door.

Scanning the area to make sure no one was in sight, she then walked briskly to her car, started the engine, and pulled away.

Her boss would be proud of her execution.

CHAPTER 18

Where is he? Julia wondered, searching the Denver arrivals area after her 6:30 a.m. flight from San Francisco. She looked for her father among the twenty or so people waiting. An older gentleman extended a rose to a woman wearing a Victorian hat who had been on her flight. As they kissed, she felt a slight pang in her heart; it had been a few years since her lips had touched someone else's like that.

Julia was surprised not to see her father there—he was usually very punctual. *Perhaps he's in the restroom or just coming in from the parking lot.* She would have tried his cell phone, if he carried one.

After several minutes, she checked the baggage claim area though she was sure he had said he'd meet her on the other side of security. Not there, she stepped outside to scan the cars picking up other passengers. No sign of the Prius.

She returned to security again wondering if she missed him somehow, but no luck. Checking the information desk, there were no messages. *Hmmm. This is strange.*

She pulled out her cell and called the house. No answer.

Could he have gotten in an accident?

After waiting another half hour, she gave up and decided she'd take a cab to the house.

* * * * *

Almost an hour later, the taxi pulled up in front of the eco-designed home. Julia looked out the taxi window at the stone exterior of her father's house. Her gut tightened…just like it always did whenever she saw him.

She paid the driver and made her way along the slate walkway toward the house. Scanning the grounds for any signs of movement, she saw nothing stirring in the mid-day sun.

She rang the doorbell. No answer. She tried knocking a few times but again, no answer. Cupping her hands, she looked through a tall window to the side of the door. No signs of life. The alarm system wasn't activated. *That's weird,* she thought. He always put it on when he left the house.

She walked over to the garden next to the door. On her last visit, her father had mentioned an extra key hidden under a small rock. She reached under the rock—still damp from the melted snow—and found the key.

Upon entering the front door, she called out, "Hello?"

There was dead silence.

"Dad?" she called louder as she walked inside. Her voice echoed through the foyer.

After closing the door, she placed her bag down and walked past the drums into the living room. To her right were doors leading to his bedroom; one of them was slightly ajar.

Heading over to the bedroom, she stood outside the room and called out again, "Dad, it's Julia."

There was still no response.

She opened the door and looked inside. Mason was lying on the bed with his head turned to the side.

"Dad?" she said, loud enough to awaken him. "Dad! Dad!"

He didn't stir.

Julia's heart began to pound. She rushed over to the bed. *Oh my God.*

CHAPTER 19

With a blank stare, Julia slowly ran her fingertips around the rim of her coffee mug. No tears had come, just a blanket of shock.

It had been two hours since her 911 call. An ambulance had arrived quickly and transported her father to a mortuary. Cops had sealed off the house from concerned neighbors. Investigators had completed a couple of rounds of inquiry with Julia; she had been requested to wait for one more.

A burly man entered the kitchen wearing a brown suit. He whispered something to an officer standing by the doorway. The officer turned and pointed toward Julia seated at the wooden table.

"Julia Hamilton?" the man said, as he approached her.

Julia looked up solemnly at the man with short salt and pepper hair, a square chin and broad shoulders. "Yes?" she answered.

"My name is John Carlton. I'm with the FBI." Carlton extended his hand and shook hers. "I'm sorry."

"Thank you," Julia said, feeling Carlton's strong grip. *Why is the FBI here?* She wondered.

"I know you've already been through this but I'd like to ask you a few questions?"

"I'm pretty tired and don't know what else I can say."

"I'll keep it short. Got some questions others haven't asked."

"Okay." Julia sat a bit more upright.

Carlton sat in the chair across from her. As he did, the fifty-year-old agent couldn't help but notice Julia's beautiful green eyes, despite their weariness.

Julia spotted a lengthy scar on the Carlton's neck just above the shirt collar. She tried not to stare and focused on what he was saying.

"The FBI is now heading the investigation for reasons I'll explain in a second. But first I want to let you know that the preliminary results indicate your father's death was due to some kind of respiratory condition. We're waiting for a final report from the medical examiner. Did you know of any respiratory problems he might have had?"

Julia leaned back in the chair surprised by the diagnosis.

"No," she said. "But he was in India recently for a few weeks. He left me a message when he got back saying he picked up a cough over there."

"Did he have that condition prior to India?"

"No. My father was in amazing health. At fifty-six, he had the body of a thirty-five year old. I can't imagine his condition being bad enough to kill him."

"Well, India is certainly a place to pick up viral infections." Carlton leaned back and folded his arms. "Besides, we haven't found any clues of foul play. There were no prints anywhere...except for yours. No marks on his body. So at this point, a respiratory condition makes the most sense."

Julia didn't like the *except for yours* comment. *He can't possibly think it could have been me.*

Carlton switched directions. "Do you know of anyone who would be considered some kind of enemy to your father?"

"I did go over this with the detective earlier. My father was private...very private. But none that I know of." Julia thought about the conflict between the two of them but it certainly didn't fall under enemies.

"Let me explain why the FBI is in now charge. The night before last, Congressman Richard Green was found dead. His car went over an embankment on Lookout Mountain. In speaking with his staff, evidently your father left him a message yesterday. He also called Green earlier in the week. That's why we're involved. Do you know anything about your father's relationship with Congressman Green?"

"You're not suggesting my father had something to do with Congressman Green's death are you?" Julia was stunned. Despite her difficult relationship with her father, she knew he wasn't a murderer.

"No. Could be two separate incidents. The road conditions were bad, but we need to check every angle."

"You said my father called him yesterday, after the Congressman was found dead."

"Yes."

"That would mean he didn't know Green was dead," Julia retorted.

"That's possible," Carlton said, trying to be careful not to paint Hamilton too much of a suspect. *Of course Hamilton could have placed the call to make it look like he wasn't involved.* Carlton chose not to go there.

"Do you know anything about their relationship?" Carlton tried again.

"Not much. I remember my father saying that he helped the Congressman many years ago. But it's not like they were very close friends. My father hadn't mentioned him in a while."

"Do you have any guesses why he would have contacted Senator Green?"

"No," Julia said curtly, not liking the line of questioning.

Carlton sensed her discomfort and decided to back off. "Well, like I said, they're probably separate incidents. But we'll need to check your father's phone records and do a little investigating."

"That's fine."

Carlton was about to get up when he asked, "Is there anything else you can add?"

"The only other thing I told the detectives earlier is that my father left me a message two days ago saying that he had something important to tell me but wanted to tell me in person."

"Anything more because that could be helpful?"

"No, that was it." Julia rubbed her eyes.

Carlton could see she was tired. "Why don't we continue at another time? I know you've had quite a day."

"It certainly has been."

Carlton stood and shook her hand. "I'll be in touch."

Once alone outside the house, Carlton pulled out his cell and dialed the number. "It's me," he said. "She had nothing on the Green connection. And it turns out Hamilton picked up a cough in India. Seems like we've got our case. I'm not sure she's buying it though."

"Keep an eye on her," said the voice on the other line.

"Will do," he affirmed, knowing that wouldn't be hard to do.

CHAPTER 20

As requested in his will, there was no memorial service for Mason. After time spent studying in India, he had viewed the body as a temporary dwelling. He had learned that true essence didn't die with the death of the body, so he saw no need to memorialize it. Instead, his will instructed that in the event of his death, his body was to be cremated. And, as Julia learned in a brief phone call from her father's attorney, the remains were to be scattered at her discretion.

At first, Julia thought the cremation process wouldn't be too tough. She thought she had compartmentalized the relationship into a manageable box. But that box opened up when she put Mason's remains into one. A wrenching tension now flooded her gut and a pervasive heaviness weighed down her body. The emotions took her by surprise; and she wasn't sure exactly what she was feeling. Discovering the facts of a story was more her expertise than understanding deeper emotions about her father.

During the two weeks in which she arranged the cremation and his affairs, Julia stayed at a hotel about twenty minutes from her father's house near Bear Creek Lake Park. Sleeping at the house would have been too disturbing. In addition, being near the park would allow her to get some daily hiking in, as well as be closer to the city for handling matters related to Mason's death. She was allowed to use her father's car but had been asked not to remove items from the house just yet.

Julia had just finished breakfast in her hotel room when agent Carlton called.

"We've got the final report from the coroner."

"What's it say?" Julia asked sitting on the edge of the bed.

"Like we thought, it indicates that your father's death was a result of pneumonia. They found a viral infection that had spread throughout his lungs. Both his trachea and lungs had substantial inflammation. There was a trace of alcohol but nothing that would have caused any harm. The coroner estimates that he died some time between ten o'clock at night and one in the morning. Given that there's no other evidence, we're certain that the pneumonia was the cause."

Julia shook her head. "I know that's what the report says, but I still can't believe his condition was that bad. There must be other leads," she persisted.

"We have no other leads...and we've found no connection between your father's death and Congressman Green's. In fact, given there was no criminal act, and with all the cases going on in the Denver area—especially Congressman Green's—we can't spend any more time on this one."

"You're dropping the case?" she said raising her voice. She stood up and began pacing the floor by the nightstand.

"Julia, again there's no evidence of homicide. We've done all we can at this point. I'm sorry."

"Two weeks? You call that an investigation and doing all you can?"

"If someone steps forward with evidence, I'm certainly willing to explore it."

"This is crazy."

"Julia, it's natural not to accept what happened. I've been down this road many times. And—"

"I'll investigate this myself if I have to!"

"Julia—"

It was too late. She hung up the phone.

CHAPTER 21

*I*n 1969, Elizabeth Kubler-Ross wrote *On Death and Dying*, the renowned text that outlined the five stages a person goes through when suffering from terminal illness or dealing with a sudden loss: denial, anger, bargaining, depression, and acceptance. Julia had read the book in college.

Since her conversation with Carlton, she wondered if her reaction to the autopsy report and the stopping of the investigation was a case in point. Maybe she was refusing to accept the findings. Maybe her anger toward the Feds was a form of denial. Maybe the anger was some form of long-held suppressed rage toward her father. Was she displaying the classic signs of Kubler-Ross's first two stages? It was possible she had been told the truth. This was the FBI and a professional coroner. Who was she to question their assessment?

Yet with every cell in her body, she knew that her father had not died of pneumonia, even though she found it hard to imagine someone wanting to murder him. The fact that he had called her wanting to discuss an important matter indicated something was up. Perhaps he had uncovered highly sensitive information that someone didn't want to him to reveal. Someone may have gotten into his house and poisoned him with some untraceable substance. *Could happen,* she thought—she had watched CSI Miami a few times.

Despite their tumultuous history, she couldn't turn her back on the peculiarities surrounding his death. Her sense that there was more to the story propelled her to explore for herself what happened. Like her father, she had a knack for research and investigation; it's what made her a good journalist. She could still hear his voice from when she landed her first job for the San Francisco Chronicle. *"Be persistent but not a pest and the story will come to you."* She was certain the truth was out there; all she needed was her tenacity to find it.

Julia parked the Prius in front of her father's house. The yellow barricade tape that previously covered the entrance was gone. Entering the front door, she immediately felt the emptiness. The couple of times she had been inside since his death, there had been a cop present. Now walking through the house alone, the empty silence felt ominous.

She first checked the master bedroom where her father was found. Carlton had claimed that the Feds had investigated and hadn't discovered anything. *Perhaps they missed something.*

Under the bed were some dust balls, but nothing more. She checked between the organic mattress and the box spring—nothing there either.

Inside his walk-in closet, his shirts and pants were hanging neatly. Her hand grazed across the long sleeve shirts. *I've got to do something with his clothes.*

She glanced down and noticed something barely sticking out from between a pair of his shoes. She leaned over and picked it up. It was a boarding stub from his trip to India. She put it in her pocket to keep as a memento.

Next was the master bathroom. On the far side was a large vanity covered with recycled stone. Julia opened the reclaimed wood cabinets underneath and found various toiletry items. Nothing seemed out of the ordinary. Next to the sink was a large medicine cabinet. In it were first aid items and creams, but no medications that showed a recent illness—no antibiotics, no pharmacy bottles, no cough syrup.

Moving on to his office, Julia sat down at his rustic desk and filtered through a stack of papers. One article caught her eye. It was a recent newsletter from The International Campaign for Tibet. On the cover was a story of how Chinese border police opened fire on a group of Tibetans trying to flee to Nepal across the Nangpa Pass in the Himalayans. A 17-year-old nun was killed.

Julia shook her head as she gazed at the picture of the nun who had been murdered. She knew the incident would have deeply upset her father. Despite their troubles, she had always admired his passion for social justice. It had been both his desire for truth, as well as his failure to tell it to her, that had propelled her into journalism. And now his death was a story whose truth needed discovery.

She put down the newsletter and continued her search. On the right side of the desk were two drawers. Julia pulled open the bottom drawer and moved her hand through file folders containing paid bills and bank statements. *Could someone have had a financial motive to kill my father? He seemingly had plenty of money.* She tucked the thought away to explore later.

In the top drawer was an assortment of pens, paper clips and small office items. As she reached into the back of the drawer, she discovered a small piece of paper with a phone number. There was no name. The number was local.

Curious, she picked up the phone and dialed the number.

"Denver Dreams," a woman answered.

Julia didn't recognize the name. "Excuse me, what is Denver Dreams?"

"We are an entertainment club. May I ask what you're looking for?"

"What kind of entertainment club?" Julia asked in confusion.

"We have various services. What are you interested in?"

Julia was confused by the aloof responses. "Well actually I'm calling on behalf of Mason Hamilton."

"Oh yes. How may we be of assistance?"

All of a sudden, a horrible suspicion crossed Julia's mind. She immediately hung up and raced to the kitchen to pull out the yellow pages. Turning the pages to the *E's*, she thumbed down...Erosion Control...Escalators...*Escort Services*. She checked all the listings under Escort Services. There was none for Denver Dreams.

Another thought came and she went back to the office and booted up her father's computer.

Once on-line, she pulled up *ask.com*. Her father had told her that he used this search engine instead of Google ever since Google began colluding with China to censor websites pertaining to Tibet, Taiwan, and China's human rights violations. Google had justified its move saying that the search engine would bring greater freedom throughout China despite the censoring. Mason convinced her that the real freedom Google desired was the free lifestyle that exorbitant profits would provide its management and investors.

She did a search for *Denver Dreams*. When the listing appeared, Julia's heart skipped a beat. There it was—a website for one of Denver's escort services.

Julia shook her head in disbelief. As if her father's death wasn't enough, now she had to deal with dredging up iniquities about his past. *How could this be? This didn't seem like him.*

She glanced at the phone and thought about calling Carlton. He'd want to know what she discovered. But he had told her he was finished with the investigation. Her discovery would probably be like junk mail thrown in the trash.

Julia scrolled for the address to Denver Dreams on their website but none was listed. She searched the Web but couldn't find it. Directory assistance didn't have it either. Her last resort was calling a friend at the Chronicle who could track down addresses through a special database. Within minutes, she had the location.

* * * * *

"She's leaving the house," said the driver of the black sedan after having listened in on Julia's phone conversation. The wiretap was still in place.

"Stay on her ass," the Predator said, having trouble lighting a match for yet another cigar.

* * * * *

The directions Julia got from MapQuest took her into Denver's LoDo, the 25 square block of the renovated historic downtown district that now hosted a hundred pubs, sports bars, cafes, restaurants, discos and some thirty art galleries. Many of the warehouses had been converted into upscale lofts for convenient city living. Several high-rise business hotels were nearby, not to mention the illustrious Coors Field.

Julia pulled up to a large gray building just on the edge of the LoDo. On the front of the building was a bold sign, *Adult Video Library*. She was a bit nervous walking in the store; she'd never been in one.

An overweight guy was putting sex magazines in a rack. The man looked over as he heard Julia enter.

"I'm looking for Denver Dreams," Julia said, keeping one hand on the doorknob.

"Next door," he motioned with his head with a quizzical look on his face.

"Thanks," Julia said turning her face away quickly as she shut the door.

The adjacent building to the porn shrine showed no indication of what was on the inside. There was no sign or street number.

Julia wondered how an establishment like this existed in such a revitalized area. Then she realized, *Maybe that's why.*

She pressed the doorbell but couldn't tell if it rang. There was no answer. She pressed it again—still no answer.

Julia turned the doorknob and was surprised to find it unlocked. The door opened into a large waiting area with plush beige carpet and brown leather couches. Directly across from the entry was a long counter that looked like a reception desk at a hotel. A bell had sounded as she opened the door. A woman, slightly overweight wearing an awkwardly tight fitting black dress emerged through a doorway behind the counter.

"May I help you?" asked the woman.

"Yes, I called earlier…on behalf of Mason Hamilton," Julia said, wanting to withhold her identity.

"Oh yes. I wasn't sure what happened when the phone line was disconnected."

Julia had to think.

"I'm sorry about that. Someone had walked in the room and I didn't want her to know I was on the phone with you. I thought I'd come speak to you in person."

"How did you find us?" the woman inquired, staring at Julia with penetrating eyes.

Julia hesitated. She didn't want to explain her connection at The Chronicle.

"Mr. Hamilton told me," she blurted out.

"Mr. Hamilton never stepped foot in this place," the woman retorted.

Julia tried not to wince. Instead she avoided the woman's response.

"I'd like to know the date Mr. Hamilton used…your services."

"We can't give out that information. It's to protect our clients' privacy. And what is your relation to Mr. Hamilton?" asked the woman in a firm tone.

Julia decided the truth was the best approach now. Besides, she had a bit of negotiation power that might add leverage to her position.

"Well, actually he's my father. And he was found dead recently. I found your number in his office desk and that's why I called."

The woman's face tightened as she swallowed hard.

"The police have followed every lead," Julia said, even though there weren't any. "And they've found nothing...so far. They don't know about my father having your number. I just discovered it in his house. If you don't tell me when he used...your *services*, you'll leave me no choice but to contact them. I don't have to tell you the trouble they could make."

"Okay, you've made your point. Hold on."

The woman disappeared through the doorway. Within a minute, she returned with a notebook.

"Mr. Hamilton called us two weeks ago on Thursday night October 3rd. We sent out a new girl to his house the following evening. He always preferred it there."

Julia froze. It was hard hearing *he always preferred it there*. This meant it happened several times. But just as shocking was the date of his last visit—October 4th—the night he died!

"And who was the woman that...visited him?" Julia tried to stay composed.

"A new girl had come in late that day. After interviewing her, I hired her on the spot. I asked when she could start. She said immediately. I had Mr. Hamilton lined up that night so I thought I'd give him a nice surprise since she was very sexy and he was such a good customer."

Julia tried to stay focused. "Is she here now?"

"No, it was the strangest thing. She came in that night after the job and said she changed her mind. She took her cut and quit."

"What time was that?"

"About midnight."

"Do you have her name or any information about where she lived?"

"Listen. I don't want any trouble with the cops but I think I've helped you enough already."

"I appreciate that. But it would really help if you could give me any information about her at all."

The woman looked away for a moment. Julia couldn't tell if she was trying to recall information or avoiding the conversation. But after a long pause, she turned back to Julia.

"All I know was that she went by the name Star, but her real name was Jane. She said she had just moved to town and was staying at the Keen Apartments next to the Ramada Hotel by Speer and 26th. I checked over there to make sure she wasn't giving me the run-around. The manager confirmed it. That's all I know. Okay?" The woman closed her notebook and started to head toward the back.

"Thank you," Julia said as she quickly turned to head out the door.

Julia left the building and jumped in her car to find the Keen Apartments. She wasn't aware of the black sedan that was still on her tail.

CHAPTER 22

As Julia drove away from Denver Dreams, she remembered that Carlton had said he was going to check her father's phone records. Her father had called the escort service the day before he was murdered. Something as outlandish as Denver Dreams should have stood out like a neon light—this couldn't have been an oversight. *Were the Feds trying to protect his privacy? Did they not want to cheapen his memory by not telling me? Or, was there some reason they didn't bother to follow up on the lead?*

On her way to the Keen apartments, Julia stopped by a woman's clothing store in the LoDo. She immediately pulled over into a vacant parking spot. When she emerged from the store, wearing a blonde wig, sunglasses, red lipstick, blush, and purple shawl, her look had changed dramatically.

The Keen apartment building was located just across the river. The run down, two-story building still exhibited its original gray aluminum siding. Much like at a cheap motel, all the apartments faced outside with digits on the doors. Julia approached the unit that displayed a small rusted sign saying *manager*. She knocked on the door.

When it opened, an unshaven man in his fifties stood in the doorway, scraggly hair, a heavy-set build, and a half tucked in white t-shirt sagging over his baggy gray pants.

"I'm looking for my sista, sir," Julia said to the manager with a strong southern accent. "She's been missin' over two weeks, bless her heart. She's run out on her husband. Did ya'll rent an apartment in the last two weeks to someone named Star?"

"No—haven't rented to anyone named Star," the man grumbled at a pitch just above the TV that was blaring The Jerry Springer Show in the background.

"How 'bout Jane? She always wished momma had named her Jane."

"Well," the man scratched the top of his head. "Come to think of it, I did rent one of the furnished studios a couple of weeks ago to a woman named Jane. She paid the first month's rent in full. Ain't seen her around though."

"Which room is she in?"

"Against our policy to give out that info."

Julia decided it worked once—maybe she'd get lucky again. "Well, I'm bettin' she's already skipped town and isn't in the room any longer. The cops are tryin' to help us out. If y'all like, I could have 'em come down here. But it'd sure save you a lot of hassle if I could take a quick peek and see if her things are still there."

Julia saw the man's eyes check her out.

"Well...I can't let you in alone," he finally said. "I'll have to go with you." He reached behind the door and grabbed the master keys hanging on the wall.

They walked up a flight of stairs just outside the manager's door and then along the second story walkway. Jane's unit was situated around the corner of the building near the back end of the complex. Julia refrained from any small talk as they made their way.

When they reached the apartment, the manager knocked on the door. No answer. He knocked again louder; still no response. He inserted the key and opened the door.

The blast hit them both immediately, knocking them back a few steps. Julia's head snapped backwards. The stench was practically unbearable. Lying outstretched on the bed was a woman with her face covered in blood. Large bloodstains were splattered on the pillowcases and the wall above the woman's head. A .38 caliber revolver was in her hand.

"Holy shit!" the manager hollered. "I'll call the cops." The manager dashed down towards his apartment.

Julia held her breath as the putrid gas emitting from the dead body wafted toward her. She took a quick glance at the woman who had apparently blown a hole through her forehead. Whatever sex appeal the woman once had was replaced by a deathly repulsiveness of a stiff corpse.

On the verge of vomiting, Julia considered running to her car when she noticed a purse on a chair by the bed. Still holding her breath, she grabbed a hand towel on the dresser and used it to open the purse. *No prints*, she thought.

Julia pulled out the woman's wallet, careful not to touch it with her fingers. Inside she found two driver licenses; a Meredith Kennedy from Washington, D.C. and a Jane Nichols from Kansas City. Seeing the *Jane* ID, a flash of anger electrified Julia. She knew instinctively this was her father's killer.

She glanced over to the doorway to see if the manager was coming. She grabbed a pen and a piece of paper from her own purse. Quickly, she copied the info from both ID's and then put everything back just as she found it.

She stepped to the doorway and peeked down the walkway.

The manager was still not in sight.

In the opposite direction from which they had come was a different stairwell. Julia bolted to the staircase and down to the ground level.

Staying close to the building, she ran under the walkway so that she'd be out of sight in case the manager was above her.

As she got nearer to her car, she saw him coming out of his apartment. She slipped behind one of the columns that held up the walkway. She waited for him to climb the stairs and run along the concrete above her.

After he passed and turned the corner, she darted for the car. She jumped in and pulled out as quickly as she could. Speeding out of the lot, she whipped off the wig and glasses. *Phew.* No one else had seen her. What she didn't know was that around the corner a red light was blinking on a computer. Someone knew every step she had taken and every person she had witnessed—both alive and dead.

* * * * *

The Predator was driving in his car when his cell phone rang. He had made it absolutely clear to his watchdogs that he was only to be called at this number in an emergency.

"She found Star," a voice said through the speaker on his cell.

"Dammit!" the Predator cursed angrily.

"Do you want me to take her out?"

"Not yet. A dead father *and* daughter would be a feeding frenzy for the media. When it's time to do something, I'll let you know."

The Predator disconnected the call. He was pissed. He was just one vote away as Chile had just come on board. With the tape in his possession and the temple about to be destroyed, he was soon to be home free. Hamilton had been an inconvenience that had to be taken care of. Now his daughter was following in his footsteps. The Predator *did not* like to be inconvenienced.

CHAPTER 23

The drive back to the hotel was a blur. Thoughts bounced around Julia's mind like a pinball machine. First, the idea of her father having sex with prostitutes was a shocker. Yes, he was a loner and had very few relationships in his life. But he wasn't the type. He was too moralistic for this, despite the lie about her mother. Yet, the truth was staring her in the face...*and it was a bloody one at that.*

Second, Julia was certain that she had uncovered her father's murderer. It all added up. Carlton said her father died between ten o'clock and one in the morning. The woman at Denver Dreams said she saw Star at midnight. The woman must have killed her father and then returned to Denver Dreams to quit, and collect her cut. And this would explain why there was no burglar. Her father would have let Star in and then locked the front door. She could have easily exited through the garage and the front door would have remained locked.

But how did the woman kill him? Did she suffocate him with a pillow? He was too strong for that...unless, he was drunk. But the coroner's report showed no suffocation and just a minor amount of alcohol in his system—which meant he probably had a drink with her. Perhaps she slipped something into his drink? Clearly, Star/Jane/Meredith—whatever her name was—wasn't a prostitute at all. The murder had to have been pre-meditated; her father's death was made to appear from natural causes with not a single clue to the contrary.

But why would Star commit suicide afterwards? *Unless it wasn't a suicide at all,* Julia thought. Her death could have been made to look like a suicide. Perhaps she was killed so she wouldn't talk. If so, why? What did her father know or do for all this to be happening?

Julia realized she was probably dealing with pros. *How* it all happened really didn't matter. What mattered most was *why*.

As Julia opened the door to her hotel room, she halted. The light was on in the closet. She was sure she hadn't left it on when she had left.

She flipped the light switch by the door and the foyer became illuminated. Nothing moved.

To her right was the bathroom. She slowly reached her hand around the wall and turned on the bathroom light.

No one was inside. She noticed, however, that the curtain to the tub was drawn. She couldn't remember if she had left it like that.

Grabbing her hair iron by the sink, she approached the white curtain with an intense stare. Her heart was pounding.

Ready to strike with the iron, in one swift move she swept the shower curtain open. The tub was empty.

She turned back and slowly walked out of the bathroom with the hair iron still in hand. Approaching the closet door, her body was too tight to breathe. Again, ready to strike, she slowly opened it.

Empty.

She then flipped the switch to the main area of the room. The bed sheets had been pulled down and a piece of chocolate was resting on her pillow. A bathrobe had been laid upon the bed. *Turn down service,* she realized and sighed relief.

She turned on the T.V. for some background noise to calm her nerves. The local news was reporting on Congressman Green. She realized that she had been so preoccupied with her father's death that she hadn't given Green's any attention. The report explained the case was still under investigation but there had been no evidence of a homicide.

Julia recalled Carlton mentioning her father had phoned the Congressman's office twice. It is it possible the two of them talked about something that led to both of their deaths? Within two weeks, her father, Congressman Green, and her father's murderer were dead. Perhaps there was a connection. If so, this killer was making sure each death was traceless. *Could she be next?*

It was then she saw the red message light blinking on her hotel phone. She checked the message center and discovered it was from her father's attorney, Brad Benson. He wanted to meet to discuss her father's estate along with other *important* information.

"Why don't people leave details," Julia said out loud.

She picked up the phone and dialed Benson's number. Within a minute, they had arranged to meet at the Cherry Hills Country Club for breakfast the next morning to go over her father's estate.

After the call, Julia double-checked to make sure the door to her room was locked and the latch was engaged. She then took a long, hot, and much needed bath.

Thirty minutes later, a bit more calm and focused, she was back at the computer. An idea had occurred to her in the tub. She wanted to do another search.

This time she typed in the words, *Meredith Kennedy Washington D.C.*

CHAPTER 24

Brad Benson pulled his rusted Toyota 4Runner into the parking lot of the Cherry Hills Country Club. He snickered, as he often did, when passing the luxury line of shiny Mercedes, Lexus, Audis, and Jaguars. He called them *actor tractors* because that's what he saw them being used for—*hauling around big egos.*

It wasn't that Brad couldn't afford one. As a thirty-eight year old successful attorney, he grew up in the sphere of the ultra rich, and still played in that circle. He just chose to play on the edge of it. While colleagues wore elegant Brook Brothers ties to arbitrations, Brad wore his green downhill skier or his orange and blue Denver Broncos tie. And while most colleagues spent Saturdays at the office, Brad was off bungee jumping, zipping down black diamonds, or mountain biking in the Rockies.

Brad navigated his 4Runner into a space between a BMW and a Prius. It wasn't just the out-of-place hybrid that drew Brad's attention to the car. He recognized the car based on the *"Save Tibet"* bumper sticker on the backside of the Toyota. He quickly guessed that Mason's daughter was now driving her father's Prius.

Brad walked toward the clubhouse tossing his keys in the air and catching them backhanded while whistling Kool & The Gang's *Celebration*. He had won a case yesterday and was in a good mood, though he knew he would have to tone it down for this meeting.

Wearing an olive suit and Halloween-decorated tie, he entered through the front doors of the clubhouse and sauntered into the lobby. Sitting in a large leather chair in the entryway was a very attractive brunette wearing a loose gray sweater and black pants. He hoped it was Julia. Though he drew the line when it came to dating clients, he at least enjoyed coming close to it.

"Julia?" Brad asked as walked up exuding a confident smile.

"Yes. Brad?" Julia said, in surprise, as she stood to greet him. She had anticipated a stodgy estate lawyer, especially when he suggested *The Club*. She didn't expect a young, handsome GQ type who looked like Matthew McConaughey.

"That'd be me," Brad said extending his hand. "Sorry to meet under these circumstances."

"Thank you." Julia shook his hand firmly.

"Let's head into the dining room," Brad said pointing to the far end of the hallway. "We can get a bite to eat and discuss everything in there. Are you hungry?"

"Actually, I am," Julia said as they started walking down the hall. "I haven't eaten much since I've been in town."

"Good, my family has been members here for years and the breakfast buffet is to die for—" Brad stopped, realizing what he said. Julia stopped as well.

"Sorry, Julia," Brad apologized. "That wasn't very sensitive."

Julia smiled. "Well, that apology was. So no worries."

"Thanks for letting me take my foot out of my mouth so I can eat." Brad returned the smile.

After their plates were full, they sat at a table overlooking the pristine golf course. Brad turned to her. "All this must be hard on you, especially with it being so sudden."

She wasn't sure how to respond given the complexity of her relationship with her father, and her recent discoveries.

"There's been quite a range of emotions," she said as she cut into her fresh cantaloupe.

"Yeah...I can imagine," Brad said, taking a bite of a warm blueberry muffin.

"So how long did you know my father?"

"A few years. We met about five years ago before I started my own practice. I was working then for a firm that took some pro-bono work with Amnesty International here in Denver. I was given the assignment and worked with your father, who was a volunteer. I guess he liked the way I handled myself, because he asked me to do his estate shortly after the AI project, just as I was leaving the firm."

"Did you have much contact with him?"

"Not much. He seemed pretty private. The last time I spoke with him was about six months ago when he had me make a few changes to his estate. I must say, though, that he had a young spirit for a...middle-aged guy."

"You can say older, that's okay."

"Just trying to be sensitive given that's not always my forte." Brad took a sip of coffee. "Have the cops given you final cause of death? The last I heard was that it was some respiratory problem."

Julia took a sip of orange juice thinking about how to answer the question. Though she had a good first impression of Brad, she still didn't feel comfortable revealing what she had stumbled upon.

"Well, that's what's been concluded. The medical examiner reported that he died of pneumonia. There was no other evidence, so they've already dropped the case."

"You don't sound convinced."

"Frankly, I'm not. He was very youthful, like you said...and in great shape. He wouldn't have just died in his sleep with no warning."

"Yeah, does seem odd. But these guys are pros—they know what they're doing."

Julia thought Brad was right, but "pros" might be in a different way.

"Well, as I mentioned on the phone," Brad said, putting down his fork, "I want to go over your dad's will."

"Okay."

Brad pulled out a notebook. "First of all, he left his house and belongings to you with the exception of his car. He'd like to have the Prius donated to the Colorado Environmental Coalition. He wanted to support their efforts."

"Sounds like my father," Julia agreed.

"Whenever you're done with the car, I can make arrangements to have it donated."

"That's fine."

"As far as his financial assets, he designated eighty percent of his assets to go to you. The other twenty percent he wanted donated to several organizations including Amnesty International, The International Campaign for Tibet, and again the Colorado Environmental Coalition. His total assets, not including the house, were about three million, which means you'll inherit about two and a half once all the red tape is worked through. Some of that will be taxed, but I'll get us through a few loops and you'll net about two."

Julia's eyes almost popped when she heard the figure. She knew her father had received substantial money from her grandfather but had no idea how much.

"Wow. We never discussed money, so I didn't know what he had."

"Well, it'll be yours soon. The process should take a month or two, at most. Your dad set it up to give the minimum to Uncle Sam. He said that Sam was no uncle of his."

Julia grinned. "That sounded like him too."

"And one last thing," Brad added as he pulled out a package from his coat. "Your dad sent me a confidential package for you. He had attached a note saying if anything should happen to him, he wanted you to open the package alone."

"That's strange," Julia said taking the package.

"Even stranger is that the package was sent just a couple of weeks ago. It was post marked October 4th."

Julia's eyes widened. "That's the day he died!"

"I know. It arrived at my office the following Monday, the 7th. I thought I'd give it to you when I saw you."

Julia looked at the bubbled wrapped mailer with no return address. "Did his note mention what it is?"

"No."

"I wonder why he sent it to you and not directly to me?" Julia pondered.

"For some reason he didn't want you to open it until he died."

"I wonder if this has anything to do with his death?"

"Guess it depends on what it is."

"Is there anything else? I'd like to check this out. I need to go to my father's house to do a few things."

"No. I understand."

Julia stood up and put the envelope in her jacket.

"I'll walk you out," Brad said.

Brad marked down his member's number on the bill and then escorted Julia out the club to the driver's side of the Prius. He leaned back against the passenger door of his Toyota and pulled a business card out of his wallet.

"Well, I must say I'm curious as hell as to what's inside. Call me if you want to talk about it. Here's my card. It has my home, office, and cell numbers."

"Okay."

"In either case, there'll be some paperwork for you to sign in a few days. If I don't hear from you by then, I'll check in with you. Perhaps we can sign documents over lunch, just to make sure you're getting enough to eat." Brad flashed his smile. "I know a great place in LoDo."

She smiled back. "Thanks, Brad. I appreciate all your support."

Julia got in her car and drove off. As Brad watched her car leave the lot, Brad climbed in his truck and pulled out his cell.

"Hey, it's me. Just finished," Brad said, when the man picked up on the other line. "Are we set for Sunday?"

"Yep," the man answered.

"Good."

"It should be another massacre."

"Yeah," Brad said. "It'll be good to kill those bastards."

"They deserve it after all they've done to us in the past. I want to see those bums on their hands and knees, begging for mercy."

"I think our guys can make that happen. They're all pretty pissed off and ready for revenge. We've got a few new weapons, too."

"Yeah…give 'em a taste of their own medicine."

"We should get there early to stake our spot. How 'bout I pick you up at ten?" Brad suggested.

"Sounds good."

"See you then," Brad said, starting to hang up. "Oh, and one more thing. Wear your Broncos shirt, Dad. It's shirt day. We want to drown out those Chiefs fans."

"You got it."

"Later." Brad ended the call. He pulled out of his spot and left the club.

Thirty seconds later, the black sedan backed out of a space that had been two rows away.

CHAPTER 25

She slowly opened the package. A wave of apprehension made her fingers tremble as she sat on the sectional sofa in her father's living room. Inside were three items: an envelope, a digital tape with a VHS tape adapter, and a twined bracelet.

She pulled out the enclosed letter from the envelope. It was from her father, dated Thursday, October 3rd 10:00pm.

> *Dearest Julia,*
> *If you are reading this, then most likely I have been killed before meeting you at the airport on Saturday. In case this happens, I wanted you to have a copy of this tape that I made in D.C. I've also written a description of what happened since my escaping Tibet. I hesitate doing this, because I don't want to put you in danger. But what happened is too important to keep silent.*

Julia's heart sank as she then read the details of the last two weeks of his life. He described it all: the Ingrols' deal to tear down the holy Jokhang, the massacre in Lhasa, the presence of the Vice President, his subsequent contact with Congressman Green, his meeting with Ambassador Ruttlefield, and the chase where he switched tapes. The original digital tape was stored in a safe deposit box at the bank. The keys were in a blue coffee mug in the upper, middle kitchen cabinet.

He pleaded for her to continue his mission. He wanted her to use the tape to affect China's policy toward Tibet, though she should be wary of the danger. He suggested contacting Green, the International Campaign for Tibet, or the media, but warned against Ruttlefield. The blue and white twined *Save Tibet* bracelet was handmade by Tibetans; he hoped she'd wear it for good luck.

Julia was stunned by the shocking incidents, but it was the end of the letter that moved her the most.

> *Julia, I know how deeply I hurt you by holding back the truth about your mother. You've had every right to use it as a shield to keep me at bay. For years I thought I was doing the best thing...both for you and me. I know we continued to get into arguments about that. I guess it was never easy for me to admit I was wrong. Well, I see now that I was and have such strong regrets about what I did. I wish we could have completely torn down this wall between us. I hope someday you'll be able to forgive me and not continue to carry the anger in your heart.*
>
> *You have no idea how proud I've been of you. I probably should have told you that more often. I love you so much more than words can convey. I wish I were there to hug you good-bye.*
>
> *Love you forever,*
> *Dad*

Julia put down the letter on the coffee table and sat back into the sofa. Her throat tightened and her heart sank. Tears formed in her eyes as she looked out a window. She could feel the passion her father had for the Tibetans and imagined the duress he must have experienced with all that had happened. But more importantly, she could feel his remorse for their estrangement, as well as his deep love. She had never heard him apologize like this.

Damn you, Dad! She banged her fist down on the couch. *Why wait until now?*

Her eyes continued to well until the tears could no longer be held back. Then, for the first time since her father's death, like storm clouds finally bursting, Julia broke down and cried.

CHAPTER 26

This is beyond horrible, Julia thought, as she brought her hand to her face as the ghastly scene on the tape unfolded before her eyes. Innocent Tibetan men, woman and children were brutally slaughtered.

The lens zoomed in on Liung watching the massacre and then the Vice President shaking hands with him. As Redman fired the bullet into the Tibetan teen's chest, Julia had to look away and stop the tape. *I can't take anymore.*

Julia sat there with her head in her hands, shedding more tears. She understood why her father must have been fuming about the Ingrols deal and the massacre. He would have stopped at nothing to hold the perpetrators accountable; and it was clearer now why someone kept him from doing so.

She went to the kitchen and found the blue mug containing the keys to the safe deposit box. Thought he didn't mention it in his letter, perhaps there were other important items he stored in the box as well.

Arriving at the bank, Julia approached a representative who had just finished speaking with another customer.

"Excuse me," Julia said.

"Yes?" the representative turned toward Julia with a smile.

"I'd like to open my father's safe deposit box. He died recently and has left me the contents."

"I'm so sorry to hear that. Let's go downstairs."

After checking Julia's ID outside the vaulted area, the woman remembered the name Hamilton.

"Actually Ms. Hamilton, your father no longer has a box. He chose *not* to open another one."

"What?" Julia asked in confusion.

"Yes, we had to get a locksmith to open the box he had rented."

"What do you mean?"

"Mr. Hamilton said he had lost his keys—which was strange. He had just opened the box the day before. He said his car was stolen after he left the bank and the safe deposit keys were in the car. Our policy is that if a customer loses both keys, we need an independent locksmith to drill open the box."

Julia grimaced. His car hadn't been stolen…nor were the keys lost. Why would her father make up a story about it? Unless *he* hadn't made it up. *Someone else got to the box!*

"Do you know which day it was?" Julia pressed

"Yes. October 4th. I remember because it was my birthday. It was right before my manager threw me a party here at the branch."

"Can I ask what identification you require?" Julia asked.

"A photo ID. We also match the signature to the signature card. In addition, we confirm the person's social security number and address." The bank associate was getting apprehensive. "What did you mean when you said you wanted to open his box. Do you have the keys?"

Julia hesitated and then said, "No. It must be a different set. Sorry for the misunderstanding. Thank you. You've been very helpful." Julia turned and hastily walked away. She had heard enough. She knew the people she was dealing with had the power to undetectably eliminate *people*, never mind a tape.

Julia got back into the car and sat for a moment as the pieces of the puzzle were coming together. Her father had written the letter on the 3rd after putting the tape in the safe deposit box. Brad had said the package was post marked on the 4th. This meant her father mailed the letter and copy of the tape the next day. Clearly someone disguised as her father came into the bank that day with a fake ID, forged his signature, and presented his personal data. The person made up an excuse to get the box opened. Whoever it was somehow knew her father had put the original tape in the box the day before. Also, the impersonator would have been a male. *Perhaps he was the one that killed Meredith Kennedy?*

Julia picked up the cell. She knew she needed help. The situation was too much to handle by herself. She didn't trust Agent Carlton. Green was dead. And she certainly couldn't approach Ruttlefield.

There was only one person she could call.

CHAPTER 27

*H*e didn't know what to say. And he wasn't used to being speechless. Brad swallowed the last bite of his chicken sandwich and leaned back in the booth in which he and Julia were seated.

Julia had called him from the bank saying she needed to see him as soon as possible. He had finished a deposition downtown and suggested they meet at the LoDo Bar & Grill. Julia had filled him in on all the details of what happened since stumbling upon Denver Dreams.

"Are you sure it was the Vice President on the tape?" Brad questioned.

"No doubt about it."

"Well I know I've been one to buck the system, but you should call the cops, even though you're not sure about this agent, Carlton."

Julia leaned forward tensely. "Brad, I can't do that yet. Something's going on here. The Feds must have known my father called Denver Dreams. They saw his phone records. They knew he called Green. And the way they dropped the case so quickly, I think they're involved somehow."

"You think the Feds are covering this up?" Brad challenged.

"My father mentioned he had a tough time with this guy Ruttlefield. For all I know, he's buddy buddy with the Feds."

"You think the United States Trade Representative is part of a conspiracy as well? I don't know, that's a real stretch."

"Why not? The Vice President's involved."

"You think *he's* covering it all up?" Brad questioned, as he took a sip of his water.

"Whoever's master-minding this not only killed my father but murdered this woman Meredith and Congressman Green, all with no traces. Perhaps the Chinese have some connection here and had my father killed. They know he made the tape. Maybe it's Redman. He certainly wouldn't want to be exposed."

"Let's say any of this is true. Your life could be in danger too, Julia. I think you need to get some protection. I say call the cops."

Julia shook her head. "I've thought about that. Whoever it is wouldn't kill me."

"How can you be so sure?"

"The person has the original tape and doesn't know I have a copy. Besides, if I were killed, it'd be way too suspicious. Right now there's no evidence of my father's murder. But if a father *and* his daughter were to die inexplicably so soon apart, that would make the front page of The Denver Post and might even get Larry King interviewing everyone from Denver Dreams to the President."

"What about hiring a private detective?"

"I might. But right now I don't trust anyone. I trust you because you were my father's attorney. And as much as I had issues with him, he always had good instincts about people. That's why I'm asking you. I need your help, Brad. I can't do this all alone," Julia pleaded.

Brad crossed his arms and continued to sit back in the booth. He looked up at one of the twenty-five HD TV screens mounted throughout the restaurant. A star player from the Broncos was being interviewed about the upcoming playoffs. Normally, Brad's eyes would be glued to the T.V., but he remained focused inwards. He was contemplating what she had told him. After a moment, he turned his head back to Julia.

"I don't know, Julia. This is way over our heads." Even as Brad said this, he was torn. He knew this job was for those with badges. Yet there seemed to be some validity in everything she said. Also, he hadn't stopped thinking about her since breakfast. There was something about her that immediately got under his skin.

"Why not go public with the tape now?" Brad asked, trying one more angle.

"We can always come forward with the tape. If we just do a bit of research first, we might learn something that will make it accepted more quickly and have more impact."

Brad fell silent again and looked down at his plate. It was hard to refuse her, looking into her pleading eyes.

"Please, Brad. I really need a friend right now. I have no one else I can turn to."

"What did you have in mind?"

"Some research this afternoon. There isn't much time to keep the Tibetan temple from being destroyed and these people, whoever they are, from taking more action. I was hoping you could check out Ingrols—who they are, what they're doing in China, and anything you could find out about this guy Redman. I want to check into this *whore* who killed my father. Between your legal research ability and my journalist background, maybe we'll find a pearl—or a whole necklace."

Brad leaned forward resting his arms on the table. "Well, I've got some paperwork that could wait 'til tomorrow. I guess some searches on the Net and a few calls wouldn't kill me..." Brad stopped and winced. "Not the best choice again, was it?"

Julia reached across the table and gently put her hand around his forearm. "Thanks, Brad. I really appreciate it."

Brad felt the touch run through his whole body. It had been a while since he felt such a rush and his breath hitched in his chest.

"You know," Brad coughed and switched topics, "with Halloween approaching, this is spooky. Did you know this restaurant and the club next door, Mattie's House of Mirrors, used to be a brothel? Supposedly it's haunted. From time-to-time paranormal investigators set up specialized videotape machines here. They claim to have captured shadows and voices whispering."

"You're kidding, aren't you?"

"No. I'm serious."

A chill went up Julia's spine giving her goose bumps. "That's too weird."

The waiter brought the check.

"Good timing," Julia said to the waiter, as she grabbed it. "My treat this time, Brad. I insist."

"Okay. But to set the record straight, if you weren't my client, I wouldn't let that happen." Brad smiled.

Julia returned the smile. She then looked at Brad's Halloween tie, decorated with skeletons. She remembered an expression her first boss told her about the world of journalism. *Be careful where you dig 'cause you might find bones.* She had already proven this true in finding Meredith. She looked back up at Brad's eyes. She decided to keep this saying to herself.

CHAPTER 28

"Who is he?" the Predator demanded, jumping up out of his black leather office chair to pace around his desk.

"Brad Benson. He was Hamilton's lawyer," a voice replied through the speakerphone.

"Has she told him anything?"

"Don't know. She's been using her cell. But she went downtown to meet him again."

The Predator paced another circle behind his office desk. He was livid—too many loose ends and yet now someone else was in the picture.

Finally breaking the silence, the driver of the black sedan asked, "Do you want me to take him out?"

The Predator put his hands on the desk and leaned over the speakerphone. "I'll tell you exactly what I want you to do." He dictated a series of instructions.

A light then flashed on the Predator's phone. "Got to go," he said. "Call me when it's done."

The Predator clicked onto the other call.

"What's the count?" he commanded.

"We got the last vote," said the voice on the other line. "Korea is in. We're all set. The meeting's been scheduled in two weeks—that was the soonest date that would accommodate everyone's schedule. It'll be in Beijing...home court advantage."

"Let's make the fat lady sing," the Predator said.

"Do you have the payment ready?"

"That doesn't happen until the decision is final!"

"Yes, but—"

"No buts. Get my votes, then you get your dough."

That was all the person on the other line wanted to hear.

CHAPTER 29

She looked at her watch—it was a minute to seven. Julia climbed up the stairs to Brad's townhouse, which was located in a new development inside the Denver Tech Center. They had agreed to meet at his place thinking it would make for a more private setting and allow them to do more Web surfing if they needed it.

Pulling out a mirror from her purse, Julia brushed her hair with her hand and applied gloss to moisten her lips, which had dried from the cool autumn air.

As she pressed the doorbell to Brad's three-bedroom corner unit, Julia was surprised to be looking forward to seeing him once again. It was the third time today. And it wasn't just his support that was appealing.

When the door opened, Brad's head was cocked to the right with a cordless phone between his right shoulder and ear. He had a glass of red wine in his hand.

"You can do it buddy," Brad said into the phone. He waved for Julia to come in.

Julia walked into the foyer and Brad closed the door behind her. He pointed his forefinger in the air to suggest he'd be off in a moment.

"Yeah...I know. Uh-huh. That's normal. But remember pal, fear comes from thought. No thought, no fear."

Julia glanced at Brad as they stood in the foyer. He was wearing jeans and an un-tucked black cotton t-shirt. She got a better look at his strong physique once he shed the suit.

"Just take a deep breath and picture your mind like an empty sky. And when it's completely clear, then let go and fall. Okay? Got to run. Call me when you're celebrating. Later."

Brad hung up the phone.

"Sorry about that. Buddy of mine's about to go bungee jumping for the first time—scared to death. Can I take your coat?" he asked as he put the wine and phone down on a console.

"Sure, thanks."

As Julia removed her coat, Brad noticed the black blouse she was wearing fit tighter than the loose sweater she had worn earlier. With jeans and black boots, Julia's slim athletic body was appealing. *Don't forget she's a client*—he'd have to keep telling himself this.

"Can I get you something to drink?" Brad asked after hanging up her coat. "Wine? Beer? Water?"

"Actually, a glass of wine sounds good."

"Pinot okay?" Brad asked, picking up his glass.

"My favorite."

The hardwood floors led them into a living room with cathedral ceilings and recessed lighting. The natural stained pine trim throughout the townhouse gave a rustic feel in contrast to its contemporary style. In the living room sat a gray sectional sofa that wrapped around a large coffee table. It faced the back wall, which was fronted by a huge colorful fish tank next to a fireplace burning with a crackling fire.

"The pizza should be here in about ten minutes or so," Brad said. "I'll get you some wine. Make yourself at home."

Brad headed into the kitchen. When he returned with a second glass of wine, Julia was standing by a collage of pictures on the wall above the fireplace. Several displayed Brad and college buddies wearing Colorado University sweats with beers in hand.

"I miss those days sometimes," Brad said, noticing Julia gazing at the photos. "Nothing like freedom without responsibility." He handed Julia her glass of wine.

"Thanks," she said.

Brad looked at the pictures. "I've got too many clients these days to be as foot loose and fancy free any more."

"Bungee jumping sure sounds a bit foot loose to me," Julia replied with a smirk.

"A guy's got to keep some of his youth. All work and no play makes regrets one day."

"I know that one," Julia said taking a sip of the wine.

"A workhorse, eh?"

"The news never sleeps…so neither do I."

Julia pointed to a picture of Brad and a beautiful blonde.

"College sweetheart?" she asked.

"Yep," Brad said as he took a sip of his wine. "Ex-wife, too."

"What happened?"

"Well, Amanda and I first dated during college. We broke up after graduation 'cause she wanted the marriage trail and I still wanted to burn some on the slopes. So we went our separate ways—for a while. I became a ski bum in Aspen. Then after a few years, when I thought I had gotten it out of my system, I applied to CU law school. My folks were lawyers, and I liked the perks that came with the gig. When I got accepted, Amanda and I got back together. We tied the knot when I passed the bar. But after two years of my continued weekends on the slopes, CU football games and golf courses, she untied it. She wanted to make babies, and I was still being one. Guess I had a little too much trouble transitioning out of all that freedom."

"Good for you to own up to that. Most guys usually point the finger the other way."

Brad launched into his Jimmy Buffet imitation. *"Some people say that there's a woman to blame, but I know, it's my own damn fault."* Brad grinned as he took another sip of wine.

"Guess we shouldn't have you drink too much of that?" Julia said with a smile.

"I do a mean karaoke I must say."

Brad bent down and stirred a piece of wood to boost the flames of the fire. Then he turned back to Julia.

"So, ever been married yourself, other than to your work?" he said with a smile.

"No."

"Not even engaged? I would think a beautiful woman like you would have been flocked with offers.

"One proposal but turned it down." Julia's eyes fell away.

"How come?"

Julia hesitated. She looked up at the pictures again. "Let's just say men haven't always been trustworthy and loyal."

Brad sensed her discomfort on the topic and decided to back off. As he did, a device was planted on the sliding glass door behind the dining table. With a range of a hundred feet, the electronic gadget could pick up any audible sound in the room. The person hiding outside in the bushes was now monitoring every word they said.

Julia turned to Brad. "So what did you find out this afternoon?"

"All right, well, let's sit on the couch and I'll fill you in."

After they sat down, Brad began. "Back in the '70s and '80s, Ingrols was reaping in the big bucks. But with the rise of stores like Walmart and Target, Ingrols has been spiraling downhill fast. A friend of mine who's a CEO in the retail business told me they're on the brink of bankruptcy. When I told him about the planned factory in Lhasa, he mentioned that the word on the street is that Ingrols is formulating an entirely new brand name to better market their products. They're betting the farm that this will recover their image, which the company desperately needs. By building their own factory, Ingrols will cut out many of their suppliers and produce their own goods, saving them a ton of dough. If the strategy works, it'll mean billions of dollars to the company and its investors. If not, the stock will be worth only enough to buy penny candy."

"Why in Tibet?"

"From what I was told it'll be cheaper for Ingrols. Laborers in the region will work for even less wages than in Taiwan or Shanghai. Also, China probably agreed to subsidize some of the construction cost if Ingrols agreed to build in Tibet. China wants to bring greater prosperity there—of course it's another way for them to squeeze out the Tibetan presence."

"I'm guessing if the tape got out, it would blow up Ingrols' strategy…not to mention bury this guy Redman and the V.P. Did you find out anything about Redman?"

Brad took another sip of his wine. "I read an article that said he's climbed the Ingrols' ladder during the past twenty years and has been in charge of their Chinese operations for five years. This deal would be by far the biggest feather in his cap. I'm sure his career's riding on it."

"And if the world learned he murdered people in the process, he'd have a tough time getting a job at McDonalds."

"Not only that, he's responsible for Ingrols' compliance with international labor laws. I found two lawsuits being brought against Ingrols. Workers employed by Ingrols' suppliers have been forced repeatedly to work overtime—often fifteen-hour shifts—and don't get paid for it. Management locks them in the factory to meet Ingrols' deadlines. I also found a suit filed by the family of a worker who had been severely beaten by a supervisor for complaining about the lack of clean air and being denied permission to go to the restroom more than once a day. That worker's no longer with the company and his whereabouts are unknown."

"That's horrible!" Julia exclaimed.

"Yeah. These suits are rare because workers are threatened they'll be fired and have their work permits confiscated if they complain, especially when labor inspectors examine working conditions."

"And Ingrols can be held liable for all this?"

"They're contractually obligated to enforce certain codes of conduct with their suppliers."

Julia shook her head. "I can't believe they get away with this."

"People are easily blinded when they've got dollar signs in their eyes. You'd also think that Chinese workers wouldn't want to work for only twelve cents an hour given these conditions. But there are over 1.3 billion people in China and most of them live in remote rural communities and work in rice fields. The youngsters move to the cities to get factory jobs where they keep just enough of what they make to live on and send the rest back to support their families. Compared to us they get paid peanuts, but it's a helluva lot more than making nothing but rice."

Julia shook her head.

"And many in Washington," Brad continued, "believe that our investment in China is bringing them into the global economy, increasing their dependence on our wallets, and paving the road to democracy."

"So our government doesn't twist their arm because we're too busy making money while building up their muscles," Julia angrily.

"We've made that mistake all over the world trying to forward our own interests."

"What do you make of the Vice President's involvement?"

"Hard to say. Perhaps there's even more to this deal than we know. Maybe he's negotiated with China something for the U.S. if they don't object to tearing down the temple."

"And what he wouldn't do to keep the tape from getting out. He'd take a nose dive if he did…and that wouldn't be pretty given the size of his."

Brad chuckled and took a sip of wine.

"You don't think he could have had your father killed, do you?"

"I wouldn't put anything past Washington at this point. As far as the timing, my father said Green called Ruttlefield the morning of October 1st. Ruttlefield would have known the potential blow to the Vice President and called him. They could have investigated my father before his meeting in D.C. on the 2nd and had his phone tapped while he was gone. The escort service said my father called on the 3rd. Perhaps Meredith Kennedy worked for the government. She could have flown to Denver the morning of the 4th, just in time to kill my father."

Brad stared at her in amazement. "Perhaps you missed your calling, Ms. CSI. You should have been a detective or a trial lawyer."

"Well, I'm guessing we're just scratching the surface."

"Did you find out anything about this Kennedy?" Brad asked.

"No. I was hoping to get more leads but didn't."

"So where do we go from here?"

"I've been thinking about that. On my father's desk was the newsletter from the International Campaign for Tibet. He mentioned it in his letter, and you mentioned it at breakfast."

"Right."

"I checked them out. They're headquartered in D.C. and have some political clout. Needless to say they'd be supportive and trustworthy. I'm thinking we call them on Monday and get them the tape.

In the meantime, we can see what we can come up with on Meredith Kennedy."

"Makes sense."

Outside the townhouse, a car pulled up to the front. A teenage boy got out with a pizza in hand. As he did, the driver of the black sedan approached the boy.

"Excuse me," the man said. "I'm a neighbor and want to play a joke on my friend. I'd like to pay for his pizza, and if you wouldn't mind letting me borrow your hat for a moment, I'd like to deliver the pizza myself. I owe him one."

"I'm not supposed to—"

"Here's an extra twenty bucks. C'mon, it's not that big a deal."

"Well...okay," the boy conceded as the man slipped him two tens.

"If you wouldn't mind waiting in the car, I'll return the hat when I'm done."

The boy got back in his car while the man put on the hat and took the pizza to the front door. As he disappeared under the shadowed awning, the man opened the box and poured Saxitoxin over the pizza. The colorless, tasteless and odorless substance was one of the most deadly poisons. It couldn't be detected in an autopsy.

He rang the doorbell.

"That must be the pizza," Brad said to Julia.

Brad opened the front door and was surprised to see an older gentleman as a pizza deliverer.

"Here's your pizza," the man said.

"Thanks," Brad responded with a curious look.

"Sorry it took so long. We're busy tonight. I'm the manager, and even I am out doing deliveries."

"That's okay," Brad said, nodding sympathetically. He handed the man a twenty. "Keep the change…and hire more help."

"Thanks. Will do."

Brad closed the door and returned to the living room.

"Why don't we eat in here," he suggested.

"That's fine."

"I'll grab some plates," Brad said as he headed into the kitchen. As he pulled some plates from the cupboard, the memory flashed into his mind.

It was a very cold, January morning. A foot of wet snow had fallen the night before. Brad was eight years old. He and his four-year-old brother were outside their uncle's house in the backyard making a snowman. At the back of the yard was a large shed which housed an abundance of tools and equipment for furniture making and yard work. Brad plodded across the snow to the shed and rummaged through the tools and equipment. It took several minutes to find what he was looking for—a shovel that he thought would help move the snow easier to build his masterpiece. After he returned back to the snowman, he continued working when he heard his name being screamed out loud—"

"Brad?" Julia called out from the living room. "Could I have a glass of water too?"

"Sure." Brad took a deep breath and emptied his mind of the memory—a habit he had gotten good at over the years.

He returned with the plates and water, opened the pizza box and put a slice onto Julia's plate and gave it to her.

Julia reached for the slice and stopped.

"Is this mushroom?" she asked.

"Yeah."

"Oh no. I'm really sorry, Brad. You couldn't have known. I'm allergic to mushroom. I break out in a serious rash if I eat them. Unfortunately, I can't eat the pizza even if we take them off."

"No problem. But I don't have much here—typical bachelor pad. I do know a great sushi place, however, not far from here."

Within a few minutes, Brad and Julia were in his car and headed to the restaurant. Following close behind was a very pissed-off driver in a black sedan.

CHAPTER 30

After dinner, Julia drove back to the hotel and parked in an area near the front entrance. Although she could stay at her father's house, the hubbub of the hotel felt more comforting and safer. And in light of her recent discoveries, safety was a higher commodity than saving money.

Julia walked hastily toward the front doors with her eyes searching for anything suspicious. As she did, she noticed a black sedan make a u-turn on the four-lane road in front of the hotel and park on the opposite side of the street. It seemed an odd place to stop given there were no buildings across from the hotel.

Her heart beat faster—perhaps she was being followed. She quickened her pace. *Thank God it's well lit here,* she thought, but then realized the light made her an easier target for a bullet.

As she approached the front doors, a man wearing a gray trench coat emerged from the hotel. Julia tightened for a moment. She moved to the man's right, avoiding both his path and eye contact. He passed without any greeting.

Once inside, she ran to the elevators. One of them was open. She ran inside and pressed the *close* button. Just as the doors began to close, a hand shoved in. Julia pressed the button again, hoping the door wouldn't open. No luck. She tensed as the person entered the elevator.

"Just made it," a teenager wearing a jean jacket said, checking her out. Julia paid no attention to him and looked past his shoulder for the man in trench coat. He was nowhere in sight.

When the elevator reached her floor, she swiftly moved down the hallway to her room. She slid the hotel card into the key slot. A red light appeared. *Dammit.* She tried again and the red light reappeared. *Why isn't it working?* She then realized she had put the card in the wrong way. Turning the card over, she reinserted the card, and this time the green light illuminated. She opened the door and quickly shut it behind her, flipping the latch for additional security.

She walked into the bathroom with thoughts flooding her mind.

Am I being followed? They followed my father before they killed him. They must know his car. Could they have been following me ever since I've been in town? If so, they'd know everywhere I've been and who I've talked to...including Brad.

Calm down, she thought as she poured some water over her face. *Don't panic. Maybe I'm being paranoid. Maybe the sedan was lost and pulled over to check directions. The man wearing the gray trench coat could be just another guest in the hotel.*

Julia changed and climbed into bed. While she tried to fall asleep, the driver of the black sedan carefully maneuvered his way to the Prius. With no one in sight, he removed the tracking device. It was no longer needed. Instead, he installed a different device—one that would make sure the car would never be recognized again. And neither would Julia.

CHAPTER 31

*A*t 4:15am, almost as if an angel had spoken to her in a dream, Julia awoke with an epiphany. She sprung out of bed and turned on her computer.

Previously, when she searched the Net for *Meredith Kennedy* and *Washington D.C.*, nothing came up. This time, instead of putting in the nation's capital, she entered the names of cities in the surrounding area and a few other search words.

After several minutes, a helpful site came up. She clicked on it and scrolled down the alphabetical listing.

Bull's-eye!

Julia grabbed a pen and quickly wrote down the pertinent data. *Maybe I would have made a good FBI agent.*

Immediately, she picked up her cell and selected the number still retained on her previous call list. When she heard a recorded voice, she navigated her way through the prompters until a live voice came on the line.

"United Reservations."

"Yes, when is your next flight to Dulles from Denver this morning?"

Within moments, she was booked on the 6:00 a.m. flight. She looked at the clock—4:30 a.m. She needed to hurry.

She phoned Brad. When his voicemail picked up on the first ring, she figured he had his phone turned off—understandably so at this hour. She left him a brief message explaining what she was doing and that she would call again when she arrived in D.C.

Julia took every precaution before leaving the hotel just in case she had been followed. She used the express checkout procedure from her room to avoid going to the lobby. After quickly gathering her belongings, she opened the door to her room and inspected the hallway to make sure no one was in sight. She chose not to take the elevators and used the stairwell that led to the hotel's back entrance.

As she exited the back door, she checked for the black sedan or any dubious onlookers. No one was in sight. The backside of the hotel was not viewable from the front, so if anyone were to be waiting out front, they wouldn't be able to see her as she moved across the rear parking lot.

Julia slipped through a row of trees on the other side of the lot that divided the hotel from a Ruby Tuesday's. A taxi she had just requested was waiting there.

"Denver Airport, please...as quickly as you can," she urged the driver when she got in the cab. Again, she double-checked over her shoulder to see if anyone was following. *All set*, she thought.

The cab pulled out of the driveway and took off for the airport leaving the black sedan stationed in the front hotel parking lot. The driver had maintained a clear view of both the hotel's front door and Julia's car. He hadn't left his post, not even for coffee. Julia was well on her way to D.C. before he'd realize that she wasn't coming out the front door again.

CHAPTER 32

Though best known for the Pentagon and the National Cemetery, Arlington County was one of the most densely populated jurisdictions in the country. With the Metrorail's orange line providing an easy commute into D.C., many city workers lived in Arlington.

Julia got off the Metrorail at the East Falls Church station in Arlington. An escalator led her down to the exit where she pulled out the MapQuest notes she had made. The air was brisk, so she put on some gloves not knowing how long a walk it would be.

She turned left under an overpass and immediately came upon a sign saying "Park, Kiss & Ride." She smiled. Even though she knew it was a commuter lot and a bus stop for children, the name reminded her of her late teens when she and her first boyfriend, JJ Tillman, used to sit in his old beat up Mustang and make out in a parking lot in Denver.

The memory of JJ made her think of Brad. *Brad!* She realized she had forgotten to call him when she arrived at the airport. She had rushed to catch the Washington Flyer Bus to the Metrorail. She decided she'd wait until she was done with this mission. She'd update him then on what she discovered.

At the first main intersection, Julia turned right and walked along a major road until she reached Montana. *This is the street.*

She turned right. The first two houses displayed signs in the front yard declaring, *Vote Kipling for Arlington School Board!* She continued down the road until she found the number she was looking for—4626.

Julia gazed at the modest two-story red brick building. It was a quaint house with white trim windows flanked by black shutters. There was a screened-in porch to one side of the house and a driveway on the other. She was a bit nervous as she made her way up the brick steps leading to the front door.

She rang the doorbell. A woman's voice called out. "One minute! Coming!"

Thirty seconds later, the door opened and a slim elderly woman in her seventies with gray hair and gold-rimmed eyeglasses appeared through the screen door.

"Mrs. Kennedy?" Julia asked.

"Yes?" the woman asked, wonderingly

"Is your daughter Meredith Kennedy?" Julia asked, praying she'd get another yes.

"Yes. And who are you, may I ask?"

"My name is Jane Salter. I went to school with Meredith years ago." Julia cringed a bit having to lie about any close connection with the woman who had killed her father.

"You knew my Meredith?" the woman's voice trembled.

Julia immediately realized that the woman knew her daughter was dead. She had planned two different strategies depending on whether or not the news had reached Meredith's parents. This was the one she'd hoped for.

"I wanted to come by and say how sorry I am," Julia said sympathetically.

"Oh, please come in darling," Mrs. Kennedy said warmheartedly while opening the screen door. "My husband had to do some errands and I was just making some tea. I believe the water is about to boil. Would you like a cup of tea?"

"Well, I can't stay too long but that would be nice. Thank you." Julia was amazed at how someone could be so immediately trusting yet have a cold blooded killer as a daughter—*had* that is.

"Please, have a seat in the living room. I'll be right back."

While Mrs. Kennedy went into the kitchen, Julia looked about the room. The fine, old-fashioned furniture pieces would probably sell quickly in any antique store. Picture frames rested on an old wooden cabinet. In one of them, Julia spotted Mrs. Kennedy with an older gentleman she guessed was her husband. A younger woman stood between them. Julia recognized the woman from the license picture she had seen—it was Meredith.

The kitchen door swung open, and Mrs. Kennedy came through carrying a tray with two cups of tea, spoons, napkins, and a porcelain cream and sugar set. She put the tray on the corner of the coffee table between a pale green couch and a large orange cushioned chair.

"That looks lovely. Thank you," Julia said.

"Please. Take a seat, dear," Mrs. Kennedy ushered to the couch.

Julia sat on the couch while Mrs. Kennedy slowly eased herself into the large chair.

"As you can imagine," Mrs. Kennedy said as she adjusted a pillow behind her back, "we're devastated with the news. She was our only daughter. For many years my husband and I were told we would never be able to have children, and then Meredith came like a gift from God." Mrs. Kennedy poured two cups of tea.

"I can only imagine how difficult this must be," Julia said consolingly, accepting the cup of tea that Mrs. Kennedy extended.

"So you went to school with Meredith. I never met any of her girlfriends from Georgetown."

"Yes. I liked her very much."

"Well I know she wasn't always liked by everyone. I guess the fact that she was so smart and attractive caused jealousy. She was so beautiful from the moment she was born."

"Yes, she was," Julia agreed, trying to give short answers.

"And what she was doing in Denver I don't know. She traveled so much for her job."

"Yes, she did," Julia affirmed but then wondered if she should keep admitting to knowing intimate details about Meredith's life.

"Do you know why she was there?"

"No, I don't."

"She always had to be so secretive about everything. That's the case with so many of these Washington jobs. My husband worked one for forty-three years."

"I know, she never told me details about her work either."

"Working for the government can have its benefits, but I hated not knowing what she did. Too much mystery for my taste. It often felt like we had a spy for a daughter. I guess that comes with being in the Secret Service."

There it was. Just what Julia came fishing for. Mrs. Kennedy had taken the bait and run with it.

"Do you know how she died? I didn't hear about that." Julia was a bit hesitant to ask the question but needed to know what had been communicated. Mrs. Kennedy eyes started to swell. "Yes. The police called and said she—"

Mrs. Kennedy stopped and began to wipe away tears that had fallen down her cheek. Julia leaned forward and grabbed a tissue from a box on the coffee table and gave it to her.

"Thank you, dear." Mrs. Kennedy graciously received the tissue. She took off her glasses and wiped her eyes, then continued.

"They said that she committed suicide. But my husband and I can't believe she would have done that. We think something else happened. She was happy with her job. And even though at times she was lonely being single, she wasn't depressed. She wanted to get married some day. And I know she loved us dearly and felt loved by us. We can't imagine why would she do that."

"What do you think happened?" Julia asked.

"We wonder if she might have been killed given her line of work. But the FBI agent Carlton was emphatic that it was a suicide—there was no other evidence."

Julia froze. She couldn't believe what she heard. *Carlton was involved with this case too!* This confirmed her previous suspicions. *Meredith's death wasn't a suicide—she was murdered!* A cover up had to be happening!

Julia took one last sip of tea and said, "I'm sorry my visit is so short, Mrs. Kennedy, but unfortunately I need to go. I just wanted to express my condolences. Thank you for your time...and the tea." Julia stood up and the two of them made their way to the door.

"It was so sweet of you to stop by. I'm sure you must be very affected by all this as well."

If you only knew, Julia wanted to say but held back. Instead she added, "Yes. This is hard for me, too."

Mrs. Kennedy opened the front door and Julia made her way out. "Take good care," Julia said as she walked down the stairs.

"You too," Mrs. Kennedy echoed, as she waved goodbye from behind the screen door.

As Julia headed back to the Metrorail, her mind raced. *I knew it. Someone didn't want Kennedy alive to talk. Anyone who knew about the tape is being eliminated. Who is Carlton? What is his connection to all this? Is he the executive or the executor?*

Julia's pace hastened. Between the chill of the wind and the anxiety racing through her body, she had to move quickly. This was the Secret Service she was dealing with...they could be on her trail any minute.

CHAPTER 33

"What do you mean she's gone?" the Predator screamed into his cell, nearly slamming into the car in front of him. "What the hell happened?"

The driver of the black sedan hated admitting his mistake but knew the consequences of lying would be much worse.

"My eyes never left the front doors. The car's still there. The hotel said she definitely checked out, and didn't change rooms. She must have slipped out the back."

"Shit! She must have known you were following her. Did you check that lawyer's house?"

"First place I looked after combing the hotel."

"Well change cars and then stay on his ass. If she doesn't reconnect with him by the end of the day, you get that lawyer mouse to squeal where she is—however you need to do that!"

The Predator pressed the end button and then crushed a cigar in disgust. It was time he took matters into his own hands.

* * * * *

While Julia waited for the next train, she called the International Campaign for Tibet. She spoke with one of the organization's directors and arranged an immediate meeting.

She then called Brad to update him.

"What the hell happened this morning?" Brad exclaimed, on his way into the Colorado Athletic Center. He was worried more than angry and relieved to hear her voice.

Julia updated him quickly. "Sorry I took off like that without talking with you first. Like I mentioned in the voicemail, I woke up early and was able to track down Meredith Kennedy's parents' home address in Arlington, Virginia. I decided I couldn't wait—time is running out for the temple. I also figured I could meet with the ICT and give them the tape directly."

"And you thought *I* was the footloose and fancy-free one."

"Well, I was also scared. I think I may have been followed last night. I saw a suspicious-looking black sedan park across from the hotel when I got back last night. But you're not going to believe what I found out."

"What?"

"I just met Mrs. Kennedy, Meredith's mother. I found Meredith's parents' address and pretended I was an old friend of Meredith's from college. Her mother *knew* she was dead. The FBI told her that Meredith committed suicide. But her mother said there was no way that would have happened—she wasn't depressed. Meredith was a Secret Service agent, and a happy one at that. Mrs. Kennedy said there was no evidence suggesting Meredith was killed. But get this. The agent that told them all this was *Carlton*! Can you believe this? Carlton's been involved in my father's case, Senator Green, and now Meredith Kennedy. They're covering this up, Brad!"

"This is nuts," he said in disbelief.

"Someone had Meredith Kennedy murder my father and then killed her to keep all this quiet. This person had Green murdered, too. I'm sure of it. Whoever's doing all this has eliminated everyone who knows about the tape. Something major is going on."

"Julia, you better be careful. You could have been followed to D.C."

"No, I went out the back door of the hotel. No one saw me. I'm sure. But I'm worried about you. Whoever it is may know you and I have met. They probably followed me to your place last night and now know where you live."

"Don't worry about me. My life's been on the line plenty of times...literally. And like you said the other day, they probably wouldn't take either of us out because it would look suspicious if your father's lawyer or daughter showed up at the morgue as well."

"Well, I still want you to be on the look out for this sedan."

"I will. But why is the Secret Service involved?"

"The Vice President could have arranged that," Julia quickly guessed.

"Yeah. Or Ruttlefield. Don't Secret Service agents also protect foreign heads of state on visits?"

"I would imagine so. Why?"

"China's Minister of Commerce doesn't want this tape broadcasted on CNN and the BBC. They've got to have connections with the Secret Service given all their visits."

"And then there's Redman and Ingrols," Julia added.

"Yeah. Come to think of it, I forgot to mention that Ingrols is headquarted in Maryland. A lot of companies set up shop there because there's no corporate income tax as long as you don't transact business in the state. Given how close they are to D.C, who know what kind of connections they have in Washington."

"True."

"Where are you now?"

"At a train station headed into the city to meet with the ICT."

"If you want, I'll come to D.C. to help you."

"Thanks, Brad. That means a lot. I think it's safer if we're not together right now. But how about if I call you when the meeting's over and we'll figure out a plan?"

"No magic disappearing acts this time."

"Okay."

After they hung up, Julia sighed a bit. She really did appreciate Brad's offer. He made her feel safe. But there was someone else

Red Tape 119

who could make her feel even safer than Brad or the ICT. It was a crazy thought, and a long shot, but worth a try. And this person couldn't be farther from D.C. or Denver.

CHAPTER 34

After hanging up with Julia, Brad had a brainstorm while standing outside the gym. He called his dad and got the num-number of a friend whom he had met a few times over the past ten years. Being a prominent attorney, his dad had developed a sundry of personal and professional connections.

Brad wanted to contact retired Secret Service agent Dick McCarthy, who had worked out of the agency's field office in Denver. He explained to his father that a good friend of his was considering a career change and wanted to learn about the Secret Service. He didn't like lying, but at least the second half of that was true. The less his dad knew, the better—that certainly would have been better for Congressman Green.

Brad placed a call to McCarthy. After some brief pleasantries, Brad jumped to the matter at hand.

"I was hoping you could find out some information about an agent named Meredith Kennedy. It's for a case I'm working on. I can't explain why, because the case is confidential." Brad wanted to protect McCarthy. Any exposed details would have the story running through the halls of the Pentagon, not to mention putting McCarthy into the loop—figuratively and, perhaps, literally.

"Sorry, Brad. I need a little bit more reason for giving out agent's information."

"What I can say is we're only looking for some general information...where she worked, her role, and who her boss was."

"Well, I guess that kind of info won't threaten national security. Besides, your father helped me out of a few legal jams. It would feel good to return a favor to his kid."

"I'd appreciate it, Dick."

"I'll make a few calls and see what I can dig up. I'll call you back when I learn something."

"Thanks."

Brad hung up and headed into the gym. As he did, the driver in a blue Mini Cooper kept a watchful eye.

CHAPTER 35

*J*ulia looked up at the flag over the entryway. Though the colors contained red, white and blue, it clearly wasn't American. It was the same one featured in the *Save Tibet* bumper sticker on her father's car.

The International Campaign for Tibet, headquartered in D.C., served several purposes—to advance human rights for Tibetans, to advocate for issues that affect Tibet, and to help protect Tibet's environment and cultural heritage. Many organizations around the world supported the *Free Tibet* mission, but the ICT was the most politically active. In 2002, the ICT influenced Congress to pass the Tibetan Policy Act—a policy to help Tibetans preserve their identity as a people, both in exile and in Tibet. The ICT also helped secure a position within the State Department to support the Tibetan cause. In addition, members of the ICT had been part of a special envoy that had met with representatives from China to explore Sino-Tibetan relations.

As Julia walked up the steps of the ICT, she had no idea she was just blocks from where her father had switched tapes in the Renaissance Hotel. Her copy was now resting safely in her purse.

She pressed the doorbell.

Looking through the door window, she saw a young man approach. When he opened the door, she introduced herself, "Hi. I'm Julia Hamilton. I'm here to meet with Lobsang Tsering. I spoke with him earlier this morning."

"Yes. Please come in Ms. Hamilton. We've been expecting you." The young American gave Julia a welcoming smile as she entered the building.

"I'm Rick—the office manager. Lobsang is still finishing a call. How about a quick tour of our office while you wait?"

"I'd enjoy that." Julia was pleased with the warm reception—it helped calm some of her anxiety.

The ICT building was an old city house that had been converted to office space. As one might expect for a small not-for-profit, the layout was quite modest. The bottom floor contained a library of texts on Tibet, China, Buddhism, and human rights. The main floor consisted of offices for ICT staff. Between the main floor and the second floor hung an enormous twenty-foot *thangka*. Julia remembered seeing one in her father's house; however, this Tibetan wall hanging was five times the size and illustrated many more elegant details of the various *mudras* (or hand positions) of the Buddha.

The second floor opened up to a large meeting space. On the walls were stunning black and white pictures depicting Tibetans and their countryside.

Julia stopped and gazed into the soft eyes of the Tibetans. She couldn't pull herself away from the photos. There was something about them that captivated her, something very familiar. It was almost as if she were looking at her ancestors. The feeling of a deep connection gave her a better understanding of why her father had wanted to help the endangered culture.

After staring a moment longer, Julia was led to a small office where Lobsang Tsering—one of the organization's directors—was hanging up the phone. Lobsang worked on a range of political and cultural matters on behalf of the Tibetan community. He was an integral part of the envoy that had met with Chinese authorities to discuss Sino-Tibetan relations. Though progress was being made between the two delegations, only a meeting between the Dalai Lama and Hu Jintao would truly signify a breakthrough.

"This is Julia Hamilton," Rick said to Lobsang, who rose to greet Julia.

"Good morning," Lobsang stated warmly in very good English with a smile. He came out from behind his desk to shake her hand. He was in his late fifties and was round-faced like many Tibetans. What differed was that he wore an elegant tailored suit that gave him a very polished appearance and fit his slightly heavy body well.

"Thank you for meeting on such short notice," Julia responded, shaking his hand and looking him directly in the eye, being the same height. She then turned to Rick. "And for the tour."

"My pleasure," Rick said as he left the two of them to meet.

"Please have a seat, Ms. Hamilton," Lobsang suggested as he removed folders from a Foreign Relations committee meeting that were resting on the only chair in the room next to his desk.

"Please, call me Julia."

"Okay. And you can call me Lobsang. Please pardon the mess, Julia. We've been quite busy." Amassed on Lobsang's desk and the floor around the office were stacks of papers, books, and boxes.

"I understand." Julia sat in the cleared chair.

As Lobsang went to his seat, he said, "I have cancelled a meeting so you have my full attention. I know you have some very important information, though I am sorry to hear about your father."

"Thank you. He was very supportive of the Tibetan cause."

"And you are most kind to continue the support."

Julia nodded her head with a courteous smile. "As I mentioned on the phone, I have a copy of the tape my father made of the horrific massacre in Lhasa. It includes the presence of the Vice President of the U.S. shaking hands with the Chinese Minister of Commerce while the massacre is taking place, as well as a representative of Ingrols Corporation, Kurt Redman, who murders a Tibetan teenager. There have also been some shocking incidents that have occurred surrounding my father's death."

Lobsang was stunned. "The Vice President was there? I knew the others were meeting at the Barkhor, but I thought the Vice President was in Japan?"

"He was. But on that day he was secretly in Tibet."

"This is even more explosive that I thought." He shook his head.

"I agree. This all must be extremely disturbing for the entire Tibetan community."

"Yes. As if the killings weren't enough. And if the temple were torn down, I cannot begin to tell you the impact that would have on our people. It would be a terrible blow."

"I must admit that I know very little of Tibetan history and the conflict between China and Tibet."

"Perhaps I should give you a brief overview and then we can discuss what to do with the tape?" Lobsang asked.

"Actually, I'd appreciate that."

Lobsang sat back in his chair.

"The invasion happened in 1949. There are varying interpretations as to why. This depends on who you ask, the Chinese historians or Tibetan. In the seventh century, Tibetan King Songtsen Gampo married the daughter of the emperor of China. Chinese historians believe this marriage represented the unification of the two nations. However, the king also married a princess from Nepal showing he had no particular allegiance to China."

"But didn't Tibet exist as a separate country until the invasion?"

"Yes and no. For centuries Tibet had various occupiers. In the thirteenth century, the Mongols maintained sovereignty over both China and Tibet. Yet when the Mongol empire crumbled, both

China and Tibet reclaimed their independence. From China's standpoint, however, the invasion in 1949 was an act of reclaiming what was always theirs."

"So that was their motive…to reclaim what was theirs?" Julia asked.

"The public reason given at that time by Mao Zedong was to liberate Tibet. Supposedly, he wanted to free Tibet from the feudal system it was under and help the people to develop economically. However, Mao and Stalin were deeply passionate about Communism, and wanted its ideology spread worldwide. Tibet was an easy target. Many believe Mao's conquest of Tibet was a way to elevate his legacy and expand the reign of his control and power."

"You said that was the public reason. Were there others?"

"Some say it was a military decision. A representative of the Chinese military once secretly told the Dalai Lama of China's interest to inhabit India. Also, some say that Tibet's environmental resources were a motivator. The Chinese have discovered more than 200 uranium deposits in Tibet. Three nuclear missile sites are situated on the Tibetan plateau and more are likely as China upgrades its nuclear weapons capability. Also, five billion tons of oil and gas have been found in the Changtang region."

"I had no idea of all that," Julia admitted.

"When China invaded Tibet, the Chinese drafted an agreement that forced the Dalai Lama—under duress I must add—to make one of two choices; acknowledge that Tibet was part of China or else the 30,000 Chinese troops, who had already killed tens of thousands Tibetans, would continue their slaughter. The agreement would allow His Holiness to retain political control and Tibetans would maintain the rights to their religious beliefs and customs. His Holiness had no choice but to comply. But, why would there be a need for an agreement on China's behalf if they didn't see Tibet as a separate nation?"

"Good point. Of course, China doesn't see it this way."

"Not at all," Lobsang replied. "And within a few years, the gradual changes of socialism compromised the Tibetan way of life. Tensions escalated on both sides resulting in greater violence by the Chinese. In 1959, His Holiness had no choice but to flee to India to survive. Once this happened, the agreement was renounced by both parties."

"And the Tibetan way of life is mostly gone?"

"Yes. Ninety percent of our monasteries have been destroyed. Sera monastery, for example, which once housed 5000 monks, now holds just a few hundred. The Chinese restrict the number of monks and nuns at the monasteries to keep control on spiritual pursuits. In fact, eighty-five percent of those who escape from Tibet—between two and three thousand a year—do so because they want to be monks."

"So much for liberation," Julia inserted.

"Yes. And all primary schools are taught in Chinese with the exception of a few classes taught in Tibetan. Letters addressed in Tibetan will not be delivered. Buses and street signs are all designated in Chinese. In Lhasa, Tibetans now have just two percent of the housing. Tibetans are told that their homes are unsafe and must be demolished to accommodate the Chinese. They must move or try to flee the country. And yet the Chinese prevent them from escaping. In 2001, 2500 Tibetans were imprisoned after having tried to make the hazardous trip across the Himalayans to reach Nepal or India."

Julia looked baffled. "I'm a bit confused on that one. Why does China make such an effort to keep Tibetans from escaping when they want the territory to be dominated by the Chinese?"

"They're concerned that escapees will reveal firsthand information about the oppressive conditions that exist."

Lobsang took a breath and then continued. "What is sad is that China believes Tibet has autonomy. Hu Jintao made a speech in 2001 to commemorate the fiftieth anniversary of China's occupation of Tibet. He said that people of all ethnic groups are enjoying political, economic, and cultural rights…and have complete control of their destiny. Such propaganda."

"That's absurd given everything you said," Julia stated emphatically.

"Yes. Which is why we keep fighting for our cause."

Lobsang leaned forward. "Why don't we take a look at the tape?"

"Do you have a place where we can view it?"

"Yes, in the meeting room."

Julia followed Lobsang to the meeting room where they viewed the tape. As the massacre unfolded before them, she watched as a grown man was brought to tears.

Lobsang had never witnessed such a horrific scene. And these were his people. Watching them slaughtered was excruciating.

After the tape concluded, there was a long silence.

"Excuse me, I need to take a moment," Lobsang said as he stood and left the room.

When he returned, Julia could see the man's eyes were swelled.

"Let us go back to my office and discuss our next steps," Lobsang said.

Back in his office, they discussed the tape's significance and Julia added to Lobsang's alarm by describing how the original tape was stolen, and how her father was actually murdered, as was Green and Kennedy. She explained agent Carlton's role in the investigations and how the Feds were covering up the murders.

Lobsang was completely bewildered, especially with the Vice President involved. Taking action based upon the massacre certainly fell within ICT's scope but when it came to murder and possibly conspiracy, a higher authority figure would be needed.

Julia made her case passionately. There was one person who would certainly have the perspective and leverage to orchestrate the proper tactics. And a face-to-face meeting, if feasible, would prove much more productive than a phone call to discuss the details of what happened and strategize a future plan.

Lobsang paused for a long moment—he knew it made sense. He knew a private meeting would be desired given the significance of the matter and the objective. He looked down at his watch to calculate time zones.

He picked up the phone and dialed the international number. When a voice came on the other line, he greeted the person in Tibetan and asked to speak with the Private Deputy Secretary of the distinguished leader. By the time the conversation ended, Julia's request had been granted. She was to have a private audience with His Holiness The Dalai Lama. However, she would need to be on a plane to India that night. The plan was in action...her karma continued to roll.

CHAPTER 36

*H*aving completed his workout, Brad sat in one of the leather seats in the lobby of the gym with a protein shake. He was still astounded by the fact that Julia had called him the night before explaining that she was on her way to India to meet the Dalai Lama. *Man, this woman can move.*

Brad took a swig of his shake and pulled out his cell to check his voicemail. There was a message from McCarthy. The man's voice sounded very tenuous. The fact that McCarthy wanted to meet in person in an hour at an unusual location made Brad's heart rate jump to what it had been on the treadmill.

Brad looked at his watch. He needed to leave now. He nearly got brain freeze when chugging down the shake.

* * * * *

The Cherry Creek Shopping Mall was one of Denver's prime holiday shopping locations. Even though it was a weekday, with the retail holiday season soon approaching, the early bargain hunters were already pulling their merchandise from the shelves.

Brad parked in the upper level of the West Deck parking structure. As he entered the mall, he stopped to examine the information map to find his destination. Behind him, a man wearing a blue jacket passed through the first of the two doors of the mall entrance and sauntered over to a nearby trashcan. As the man tossed a napkin into the trash, he watched Brad walk toward the stairs. The man followed behind, keeping him within eyesight.

Brad made his way down the open stairs in the center of the mall. At the bottom he stopped outside the fine Hawaiian jewelry store, Na Hoku. He glanced at his watch—ten minutes before the rendezvous.

Brad wondered if he might get Julia an early Christmas present. He hadn't stopped thinking about her since they met. It wasn't just her attractiveness that stirred him—he'd been with plenty of sexy women, and even rich ones. Maybe it was her grounded attribute, or her zeal for truth. Whatever it was—it had been a while since he felt this kind of interest.

After scanning the glass casings, Brad was drawn to a pair of jade and pearl earrings that he thought would match Julia's green eyes.

"Can I see these earrings?" Brad asked a salesperson, pointing into the glass cabinet.

"Sure," said the salesperson as she removed the earrings and handed them to Brad.

"Pretty pearls," Brad commented. "They're from Hawaii?"

"Actually those are fresh water pearls from China."

Brad cringed at the statement.

"I'll pass," he said, and immediately handed them back to the salesperson. He decided to take that as a cue to not buy anything. Besides, he remembered the line he drew between him and clients; he was right up against it and didn't want to step over.

Brad made his way to Neiman Marcus and the men's department. He selected a few shirts from a rack. The man in the blue jacket entered the department as well, pretending to flip through a rack of shirts.

Brad asked a salesman for the dressing rooms. The salesman pointed to a doorway. As Brad entered the dressing area, there were several enclosed rooms with tall wooden doors extending from the floor to the ceiling so that it wasn't possible to see into them.

Passing the first two doors, Brad stood outside the third. He turned his head to ensure no one was looking. He knocked softly on the door five times. He waited, glanced about again, and then knocked another five times.

The door unlatched from inside the stall and opened a crack. A man wearing a brown tweed jacket and khaki pants peered out. Brad recognized the man's face with very short gray hair. He allowed Brad to enter and then quickly locked the door behind him. Brad placed the clothes upon the metal wall hooks.

"You're being followed," McCarthy whispered.

"What?" Brad was surprised.

"Keep your voice down," McCarthy admonished, keeping his own to a whisper. McCarthy put his forefinger to his lips, and they both paused to listen for any sounds in the dressing area. Only the instrumental jazz music being piped in throughout the store was audible—it was loud enough to block out their whispers.

"There's a man in a blue jacket out there. He's a tail."

"How do you know?" Brad whispered back.

"Thirty-five years of service. That's how."

"Shit!" He noticed the deep contour lines engraved in McCarthy's face. They spoke of countless witnessed scenes that most of humanity only glimpsed in cop movies.

"We'll have to keep this short."

"Okay."

"You didn't tell me she was dead," McCarthy said with a grimace.

"Sorry. I didn't want to answer questions."

"Well, you're lucky I found out from the receptionist at the D.C. office. If it were anyone else, I'd be sucked into this thing like a giant vacuum."

"Sorry," Brad repeated. "What kind of agent was she?"

McCarthy turned his head to listen for any movement in the dressing area. Satisfied it was quiet, he turned back to Brad.

"She was an agent in the D.C. office. She stood some watch posts for the President and Vice President but mainly guarded foreign dignitaries."

"Foreign dignitaries? Would you know if she was ever assigned to protect China's president?"

"Don't know...but come to think of it, I did access her bio in the database and noticed she was fluent in Chinese. She lived in China after college for several years. Why?"

"Like I said, I don't want to get you into this any more than you are."

"You're right. I wanted out of the scene and don't want to be dragged back in. I'm only helping you because you're the son of a good friend."

"Who decides and assigns her posts?" Brad pressed.

"That depends. They're usually handed down through the office head but requests can come from many sources. It depends on the gigs you've done and how close you were to your zero defects quota."

"Is it possible she could've been given an assignment that the head didn't know about?"

"If I were still active, on the record I'd say no. But given I'm not, I can say it's unlikely...but it has happened." McCarthy put his hand on Brad's shoulder. "Here's the thing. I know the receptionist from the D.C. office pretty well. She told me that the official word is that Kennedy committed suicide. But nobody's buying it. In fact, the receptionist told me she put through an unusual call from someone a couple of days before she died. The person seemed quite exasperated when asked some basic questions about who he was and why he was calling."

"Who was that?" Brad asked.

"She didn't remember the name. All she remembered was that the person worked at Ingrols."

Just then, they heard footsteps outside the door. They both silenced. A knock came at their door. Brad and McCarthy remained motionless.

The person tried to open the door but the knob was locked.

A few seconds later, they heard a knock on the door to their left. They listened as that door opened, closed and locked.

Brad looked at McCarthy and pointed back toward the storefront as if to say he got what he needed and would head out. He mouthed the words *thank you* and shook McCarthy's hand.

As Brad reached for the clothes, McCarthy leaned over and whispered in his ear.

"Buy something...and be careful."

Brad nodded.

He opened the door while McCarthy hid behind it. Brad scanned the area. The coast was clear.

He took a few steps and closed the door gently behind him. As he did, the door to the left opened. Brad's head turned swiftly. A kid in his early twenties wearing a t-shirt and jeans carrying a button down, striped shirt walked out of the dressing room. Brad explosively let out the breath he was holding in relief.

Brad walked to a nearby register and bought one of the shirts. As the credit card payment was being processed, he gazed about the area. He noticed the man in the blue jacket pulling a shirt off a rack. Brad quickly turned away, pretending not to have seen him. He thanked the salesperson and departed the store.

As he walked out into the main corridor of the mall, he stopped at one of the chairs. He bent over, pretending to tie his shoes. As he did, out of the corner of his eye he noticed the man coming out of the store. Brad kept his head down. The man walked past him. He waited until the man had walked a little way and then started toward the stairs. He tried not to quicken his pace thinking that might give away the fact that he knew he was being tailed.

At the top of the stairs, he looked back. The man was now coming up the stairs. Brad pushed through the exit doors of the mall and strode quickly through the parking lot though everything in him wanted to run.

When he reached his 4Runner, Brad climbed in, glancing to see the man get into a Mini Cooper parked in the row next to his. A bead of sweat came down the side of his face. He wiped it away and wondered, *was it better to know or not know that he was being tailed?* He didn't have time to ponder the thought.

Brad pulled out of the mall with the Cooper in his rearview mirror. An idea popped into his head and he decided to go with it.

He called a good friend who worked nearby and explained he needed to meet at a local bar/restaurant called Cherry Crickets. He asked his friend to park in the lot behind the place.

The man in the blue jacket followed Brad to Crickets. As he watched Brad park in front, he pulled the Cooper into a spot just down the street where he could keep an eye on the 4Runner. He decided to wait a bit before heading inside—he didn't want Brad to recognize him from the men's department.

Brad went inside Crickets without glancing back. When his friend turned from the bar, Brad greeted him with a pat on the back and after a quick discussion, the two of them left through the back door.

As they did, the man in the blue suit entered Crickets from the front. He inspected the drinkers at the bar but didn't see Brad. He scanned the side booths and tables—not there either. Walking to the back of the bar, he checked the restroom, including each stall. Empty.

It was then he noticed the back door exit. He ran outside, but there was no one in the lot.

"Dammit!" he yelled and ran back inside the restaurant. Walking by a pinball machine, he punched it hard.

How was he to report losing a second target?

CHAPTER 37

For most travelers, the 7500-mile journey from D.C. to India was exhausting and unpleasant. Tight seating, awkward neck positions, babies crying, and frequent flight attendant announcements all made for a very wearing flight. Yet for Julia, these annoyances were merely white noise to the alarming book she consumed during the Lufthansa flights from D.C. to Munich and Munich to Delhi.

Lobsang had given Julia a book entitled, *An Autobiography of a Tibetan Monk*, written by Tibetan monk Palden Gyatso. The book wrenched her heart as she read the chronicles of the monk's horrific *thirty-three* years of imprisonment under Chinese authorities. Palden had been forcefully arrested with thousands of other Tibetans when the Chinese Communist Party fully occupied Tibet in 1959. His *crime* was his continual support for the independence of Tibet and his resistance to embrace the totalitarian ideology.

Confined in labor camps, Palden and other prisoners were coerced to disclose anyone who spoke in defiance of their captors or whispered their allegiance to the Tibetan regime. Guards brutalized them with electric shock guns that pumped 70,000 volts. Attached to their legs were iron shackles and hooked knives that cut to the bone. Cattle prods were injected into their mouths and women's vaginas. Monks were forced to fornicate with nuns. Young Tibetan children were given handguns and then forced to shoot their mothers and fathers. Palden witnessed such barbaric torture until 1992 when he was finally released. He then escaped from Tibet to Dharamsala where he compiled his memoirs to tell the world.

When Julia finished the book, she wearily rubbed her teary eyes. *How could all this still be happening? Why were Tibetans being treated worse than animals? Why was the world standing by allowing it to continue? How could a company like Ingrols be willing to support China in the face of such disrespect for human life?*

Julia leaned back in her seat and touched the *Save Tibet* bracelet. She closed her eyes and her father's face floated to her memory. Usually, just the thought of him elicited a sense of anger. She could feel it now...but with less edge. She felt resolved to carry the baton of his mission. And that made her feel more connected to him.

If only he knew where she was headed...but perhaps somehow he did.

* * * * *

Arriving at Indira Gandhi International in New Delhi, Julia was introduced to India's unpredictable and often inefficient system of operations—if the word *system* could even be used. She made her way through customs with a visa that Lobsang had orchestrated using his connections in D.C. On the other side of customs, a sea of Indian hands and screaming voices accosted her, offering her accommodations and transportation. She held her bags tightly as the natives swarmed her. She shoved one man away when he kept grabbing her arm to get her attention.

Lobsang had instructed Julia that she needed to get to Dharamsala immediately as the Dalai Lama was flying to Mumbai for an important meeting the next day. She would need to take the train to Dharamsala, as the flight to the nearest airport had left before she arrived.

Though she was exhausted, she decided to forego sleep until she was on the train. Her body cried out for a shower, but this too would have to wait.

After changing some money, she found a railway ticket counter located at the airport but was dismayed to see a sign indicating that the office was temporarily closed—it wouldn't be open until the next day. No reason was given. *Welcome to India,* she thought.

She decided to take a taxi to the train station and buy the ticket there. An Indian man seated next to her on the plane had advised that pre-paying for a taxi at the airport would cost less than negotiating with taxi drivers. Also, he mentioned that the pre-paying taxi window outside the terminal door was cheaper than the one inside. Again, *welcome to India*, she thought.

The taxi left the relative cool of the terminal and entered the bright, hot streets. Julia covered her nose and mouth with a handkerchief to escape the toxic fumes from cars, garbage, animals, and urine. Though she had observed these scenes on movie screens, it was something else to experience firsthand.

When the taxi stopped at a light, Julia noticed a retailer come out of his store and empty a bag of trash directly onto the street while a man passing by leaned over, put a finger to his nostrils and blew, sending mucous onto the trash. Julia turned her head in disgust only to find children knocking at the other window begging for anything she might give. She opened the window and gave them each some coins.

Loud horns blasted as cars were stuck in traffic. A cow was passing up ahead. Julia had read about the sacredness of Indian cows. One story she had come upon described a foreigner who was not allowed to enter a holy Hindi temple because it was reserved only for Hindus. As he walked away, a cow was then allowed to pass inside the temple gates.

When Julia arrived at the train station, she was directed to an extended ticket line. The line moved excruciatingly slowly, which even in a non-exhaustion state would be enough to pull one's hair out. Julia was starving but didn't want to lose her place in line.

After nearly an hour's wait, she reached the ticket window. The clerk, in broken English, explained that a railway strike had started and the train to Pathankot, the station near Dharamsala, would not run for a couple of days.

Julia was furious. "But I just waited an hour in this line!" she cried in frustration. "I have to get to Dharamsala by tomorrow morning. I can't wait another two days!"

"Then take bus or taxi," said the clerk without a sign of sympathy.

"How much?" Julia asked in exasperation.

"Bus is 350 rupees. For taxi, talk to driver for price."

Julia quickly calculated the bus amount to be nine dollars.

"How long?"

"Bus take twelve hours...taxi take eight."

Julia walked away, nearly in tears. She was tired, frustrated, and feeling vulnerable in a foreign place. Taking a taxi scared her. Being a young white female, traveling alone through the night with a taxi driver, and arriving somewhere unknown at 3 a.m. didn't seem like a good idea. The bus would arrive by 7 a.m. Though the trip would be longer and more uncomfortable—and among complete strangers—she felt safer among numbers. Moreover, she felt the difference between thirty-five and thirty-nine hours total at this point in her journey was negligible.

Later, she realized, she should have taken the taxi. The ride to Dharamsala was unlike any she'd ever experienced. When she arrived at the bus station, the bus she was to take was by no means a Greyhound. Like most vehicles in India, the paint-cracked sidewalls, rusty bumpers, and worn out tires made the bus look more suitable for the junkyard than a twelve-hour journey.

As Julia stood next to the bus, a man wearing one piece of cloth around his waist grabbed at her bags. Julia immediately clutched at her luggage, demanding he let go. He yelled back at her. After a brief struggle, a monk witnessing the clash, and waiting for the same bus, reassured Julia that it was okay.

"He's the porter," said the monk in English.

She let go of her bags and watched as the skimpily dressed man carried them on his head up a ladder attached to the rear of the bus. He placed them on the roof along with luggage of the other passengers. Julia shook her head and prayed that the bags would still be there when the bus arrived in Dharamsala.

The bus did make a few stops for bathroom and meal breaks. The rest areas consisted of restrooms with holes in the ground and vending machines. The bus also stopped at least thirty times along the main thoroughfare to pick up and drop off passengers. Julia didn't see one bus stop the entire trip—people got on or off at will.

She chose a window seat hoping to sleep but this was next to impossible with the constant sound of blasting horns from the bus and passing cars. Also, the two-person seat soon fit three in order to accommodate all the passengers. People stood in the aisles for hours.

The worst part was in the late evening when the bus climbed sharp bending curves through the mountains of northern India. The road had no guardrails. On one curve, the bus tilted onto two left wheels. Julia gripped the seat in front of her tightly as her body was mashed up against the window from the force of her seatmates. For the first time in a long time she prayed to God. The bus came back to all four tires and survived the journey. Julia later learned that many buses overturned on the treacherous mountain pass.

When the bus pulled into Mcleod Ganj at 7:00am, the center of upper Dharamsala, she descended weary-eyed but glad to see her bags survived the journey. The monk on the bus had suggested staying in the guesthouse of the Kirti monastery given its view and proximity to His Holiness's residency. He gave her walking directions.

The ten-minute walk to the monastery was along narrow, cracked pavement that was poorly maintained—economic resources in Dharamsala were primarily doled out for monk sustenance rather than infrastructure maintenance. Julia passed a few merchant stores as well as roadside beggars who solicited more forcefully upon seeing a foreigner. She gave away what little spare change she had.

The monastery was perched on the side of a south-facing hillside. The mountains to the east and west framed a majestic, panoramic view of the flatlands below, which ran for hundreds of miles.

After Julia checked in, she was directed to her room. It was as she expected—very simple. There was a small bed, desk, chair, and dresser. For an extra three dollars per night, she got a room with its own bathroom—a luxury for many of the guesthouses in town.

When she entered the bathroom, she looked for a shower or bathtub but couldn't find one. It took her a minute to see that the showerhead was attached to the ceiling. She'd have to stand about five feet from the toilet to be directly under the showerhead. A drain was located in the corner.

At this point, Julia was so desperate for a shower, she couldn't wait to wash off the trip. She undressed and turned on the water—only to find it ice cold.

After the disappointing shower, she changed clothes and walked over to His Holiness's residence. She had been instructed by Lobsang to go directly to the residence once she found her accommodation. The residence was located right next to the Tsuglagkhang complex.

The Tsuglagkhang was the most important Buddhist monument in McLeod Ganj. It contained the Kalachakra Temple. This temple was as revered in Dharamsala as the Jokhang was in Lhasa. As Julia passed by the temple, she watched as many Tibetans and monks performed their *koras* around the complex.

As she approached the entrance to the residence, her heart began to pound. She knew what an incredible gift was about to be bestowed upon her. For Tibetans worldwide, meeting His Holiness was one of life's most precious karmic honorable gifts, if not *the* most precious.

At the entrance gate stood several Indian soldiers holding rifles and smoking *bidis*. A couple of Tibetan security guards monitored the grounds as well. Julia introduced herself to one of the guards and explained that a private audience had been arranged for her. The guard took her name and asked her to wait.

A few minutes later, a very handsome Tibetan man in his late thirties, dressed in a business suit, met her at the gate. He was one of several staff members that served the Dalai Lama.

"Ms. Hamilton, my name is Tenzin Takla. I am the Deputy Private Secretary for His Holiness." Julia was impressed with his clear and fluent English.

Julia bowed her head. "It is a pleasure to meet you Tenzin. I have just arrived in Dharamsala. The International Campaign for Tibet in the States contacted your office to set up an audience with His Holiness." She couldn't believe she was even saying these words.

"Yes, I know, Ms. Hamilton. Unfortunately, His Holiness's schedule changed. He had to leave suddenly last night for an urgent meeting in Delhi with the Prime Minister of India and then will be speaking at a scheduled conference in Mumbai. He knows you were coming and asked me to apologize deeply for the unexpected change. He will be returning on Sunday morning and asked if you could stay in Dharamsala until then. He knows you have important information and would most graciously accept meeting with you upon his return."

Julia was dismayed. Today was Wednesday—she'd have to wait several days. She had also rushed to get to Dharamsala, from Delhi, and had endured the painstaking bus ride.

"But as I understand," Julia said trying to keep her composure, "there's a meeting taking place in two weeks to decide whether the Jokhang will be destroyed or not. I have a tape of the massacre in Lhasa which could help prevent its destruction."

"Yes. His Holiness knows of this. He assures that he will be back with enough time to deal with this situation. He will be giving the sacred Kalachakra teachings next week so he will not be delayed."

Julia shrugged her shoulders. "OK then," she said, not wanting to offend the Secretary.

"Where will you be staying?"

"In a guest room at the Kirti Monastery."

"Very good. Please come back on Sunday, and we will arrange for you to meet with His Holiness. Again, please accept our apologies."

Julia forced a smile, though truly she was irritated. She headed back to her room for much needed sleep. She'd never been this tired in her life. If she could, she'd sleep all the way to Sunday.

CHAPTER 38

*I*t was the middle of the night. The man dressed in dark clothes slowly opened the door to Julia's room. He slipped inside and gently closed the door to avoid any disturbance. His black shoes quietly covered the distance to her bed while he clenched a piece of rope in his black gloves.

Julia was sleeping soundly with her body facing the wall. The man leaned over to identify her. He recognized Julia's face.

In one swift move, the man wrapped the rope tightly around her neck.

Julia awoke in shock but began to scream.

The man smacked her across the face.

"Shut up or I kill you!" he commanded.

Julia didn't listen. "Help! Help!" she screamed.

The man gripped the rope even tighter so that it strangled her.

Julia gasped but couldn't catch a breath. She tried to struggle but she was no match for her assailant. Her eyes rolled back. She was dying...

Brad woke up. His heart was pounding. He was completely shaken up by the dream. He sat up and looked at the clock—4:28am. His head fell back onto his pillow. *Thank God—just a dream.*

Brad had spent the last two nights at his friend's house. After he left the bar with his friend, they stopped at Brad's townhouse so he could quickly gather a suitcase of clothes and toiletry items. Not wanting to tell the details of the situation, he made up an excuse that the entire inside of his place was being painted and he needed somewhere to camp for a couple of days. He was going to stay with a casual girlfriend but they got in an argument and she dropped him off at the bar. Brad figured the 4Runner would temporarily get towed and he'd arrange to pick it up shortly.

After lying in bed for a few minutes, Brad couldn't fall back to sleep. The dream stirred up too much anxiety. He got up to check if Julia had received the email he had sent explaining what he had learned from McCarthy.

Using his laptop, he first accessed his personal email. Nothing from Julia. He then checked his business email account. Three emails popped up, but none were from Julia either. The first two were about a case he was working on but the third one immediately grabbed his attention. The subject of the email read *A Secret at Ingrols*. The sender's name was ten scrambled letters.

Brad opened the email and was shocked to read its contents.

> *"Urgent! Must see files on Redman's computer at headquarters! PDF files. Special lock. Files can't be emailed or printed. READ-ONLY.*
>   *ID NAME: REDMAN*
>   *PASSWORD TO COMPUTER: COSTCUT*
>   *FILENAMES: CHINAREPORT9. LHASAOPS.*
> *Do not reply to this email. This is a temporary email address. Get to Redman's computer ASAP! Be careful! Good luck. Sherpa"*

Brad was stunned. He re-read the email a couple of times out of confusion. Questions flashed through his head. *Who was Sherpa? How did this Sherpa get his business email address? What was on Redman's files? How was he to get on Redman's computer?* As quickly as the questions arose, answers followed.

Brad knew that sherpas were tour guides that led treks in the Himalayas. He had watched a documentary once of Mt. Everest treks and the crucial role that they played. Sherpas were often Nepalese but could be Tibetan. Perhaps whoever sent this email was based in Tibet and had a way to access Redman's computer in his China office. Though the email said *see files on Redman's computer at headquarters*, the computers could be networked. But how could this Sherpa have gotten his business email address? *His website,* he thought.

But how could Sherpa have known who he was?

Julia must have been right. Whoever had been following her would know they met on a few occasions. Sherpa must be on the inside. Perhaps Sherpa was someone at Ingrols who had had access to Redman's computer. Maybe the person had stumbled upon Redman's files at headquarters.

Another possibility was that the email was from McCarthy. Though the ex-agent said he didn't want to get further involved, perhaps he changed his mind but decided to be anonymous. Maybe McCarthy had used his connections to get someone to access Redman's files. Thirty-five years of service in the system meant he knew how to work the network.

Brad rubbed his hand through his hair a few times as he contemplated what to do. Part of him wanted to disregard Julia's wishes and call the cops. He had been followed and could be added to the obituary column at any moment. But he wanted to leave that decision to Julia especially, given the fact that she was about to discuss a strategy with the Dalai Lama.

He forwarded Sherpa's email to Julia just in case it hadn't been sent to her. In it he explained a scheme that had just come to him. The plan was dangerous, but at this point, just living was as well.

He picked up the phone to take the first step. By the time he hung up, he had made a reservation just like Mason and Julia had done before him; he was on the next available United flight to the east coast.

CHAPTER 39

I hope you like," said the stocky, middle-aged Tibetan woman in decent English. Learning to speak English was a trademark for maintaining tourism in Dharamsala, especially in restaurants.

"Thank you," Julia said as the woman placed two dishes in front of her. She glanced at the meal she had ordered, which consisted of *momos*—Tibetan dumplings, *tsampa*—roasted barley mixed with butter tea, and *thenthuk*—noodle soup with vegetables. It didn't look terribly appetizing but then she was so hungry, even rare yak would have tasted good.

"You like *tsampa?*" the woman asked.

"Never tried it. It said on the menu common Tibetan food."

"Yes. But not common anymore."

"Why's that?" Julia asked, looking more closely at the woman.

"Hard to get in Tibet now. Mostly Chinese food there." The woman's face was expressionless though Julia could tell what was behind the comment.

In the background, Johnny Cash's voice sang from a boom box situated on a shelf above the cash register. America always had a way of having its presence felt around the world.

The woman pulled silverware from her apron and put it down next to the plates.

"Traveling?" the woman guessed.

Julia wasn't sure how much to reveal. "Yes."

"Many Westerners come here. They are all searching."

"For what?" Julia asked, as she put a napkin in her lap.

The woman pointed to a flyer stapled on the dirty, cracked wall next to the wooden table. It was an advertisement for an introductory two-day program on Tibetan Buddhism.

"Travelers think Tibetans are simple people, living simple path. They shake their heads at us...but with restless hearts. They are lost. Attend this program. It will bring you home." She smiled and walked through a burgundy drape that led to the kitchen.

A bit confused, Julia looked up at the flyer. It was a brief description of a program being held at Tushita—the Tibetan meditation center located on a hilltop above Mcleod Ganj. The topics included the Nature of Reality and Mind, Understanding the Eightfold Path to Ending Suffering, Working with Negative Emotions, and Cultivating *Bodhichitta*—developing an Awakened Heart of Compassion. The bottom read, *"Be prepared to investigate your view of Reality.*

It was this last sentence that churned Julia's mind about her spiritual view—or lack thereof. As a child, Julia hadn't been exposed to any religious affiliation. Her father was Catholic by birth but had rebelled against the church and its indoctrinations. Mason believed that control and order by any establishment squelched, not bolstered, free spirit. During his work with Amnesty International, he often ranted that the humanitarian aid sponsored by the church wasn't really about saving people's lives...it was about people being *saved*. The few times Julia broached the subject of God, he encouraged her to discover her own view. She became more of a hard facts warrior and left the seemingly amorphous spiritual path to others.

But Julia was intrigued by the Tibetan woman's comments. As she continued to read the flyer, surprisingly, an urge came to attend the course. Learning about the Tibetan teachings would provide insight into their journey and help prepare her for meeting with the illustrious spiritual leader. Besides, she now had a couple of unexpected days on her hand. And though signing up for a program on Buddhism was the last thing she had planned on doing, there was hardly anything about what happened the last couple of weeks that she had anticipated.

CHAPTER 40

The bell rang. It was time to go in. With her hands snuggly fit into her coat pocket to fend off the cool mountain air, Julia and twenty other students entered the main meditation hall of Tushita to receive the introductory talk.

Inside the dimly lit building, thirty or so *zafus*—meditation cushions—were spread out around the floor. To the left was a platform from where the teachings would be given. At the back of the platform stood a large statue of a golden Buddha.

A few paces inside, Julia stopped. She stared as a few of the students in front of her prostrated three times in front of the Buddha.

Was this mandatory? It didn't feel right to her.

She walked past them and took a seat in the back. A few others took seats near her without prostrating either. Her tension eased. *Good, I'm not the only one.*

The hall was adorned with many Tibetan *thangkas*. On the platform in front of the Buddha were three seats. The middle was a large red and yellow embroidered chair situated behind a small table covered with a white cloth. The seat was reserved for the Tibetan Geshe—an elderly Tibetan monk who was an expert on Buddhist scriptures.

Just to the left of Geshe's chair was a smaller chair to be used by his interpreter. To the far right of the platform was a large *zafu* alongside a large meditation bowl. This was reserved for the western monk who co-taught the program. With most of the students being foreigners, a western monk helped make the teachings germane to the western mindset.

After the students were seated, the western monk, looking about thirty years old dressed in traditional maroon and gold

Tibetan robes, slowly entered the hall. He stepped onto the platform and mindfully took his place. Once he settled, he murmured a brief prayer in Tibetan and then addressed the group in an English accent.

"Welcome to Tushita. We are pleased to have you here. My name is John, and I will be helping to teach this course along with the Geshe. As you know, this course is an introduction to Buddhism. In our brief time together, we will present many concepts of the Buddha's teachings...but remember this is merely an introduction. The teachings contain many subtle layers that require deep investigation in order to fully understand their true meaning."

John looked down for a moment. As he reflected on his next comment, Julia continued to gaze at him. She liked his presence. There was something genuine about it.

"Buddhism is about seeing things the way they really are. It's not about faith in some supreme being. It's not about opinions or beliefs. It's about seeing into the nature of reality and then abiding in that nature. Throughout this course, listen with your whole being...not just your mind. What we will speak about is not just for intellectual understanding but for experiential knowing. Do not believe anything that I say. The Buddha said *be a lamp unto yourself*, meaning examine the teachings with your own direct experience. Question everything. Discover for yourself what is really true."

Julia appreciated the fact that no dogma would be imposed upon her. She felt a wave of relaxation carry through her body.

"For those new to Buddhism, all sects of Buddhism refer back 2500 years to the teaching of the Shakyamuni Buddha, originally known as Siddharta Gautama. When you see monks prostrating in front of the Buddha, they are not praying to a statue. They are honoring the teachings the Buddha set forth and the enlightened understanding he realized."

With John's explanation of the prostrations, Julia felt a bit more comfortable with the ritual she had witnessed. It helped knowing the custom was out of respect for the teachings rather than a bowing to a statue.

"The term Buddha actually means the awakened one…awakening to our essential nature. We will conduct a few meditations to help you experience this nature directly as, ultimately, the intention of Buddhism is to realize enlightenment…a direct experience of our Buddha nature. And, as particular to the Tibetan Buddhist path, we are here to cultivate the way of the bodhisattva—which is to become enlightened in order to assist the enlightenment of all sentient beings."

John took a sip of water from the glass resting on a table next to his cushion and continued.

"Let me begin by asking what is the core motivation common to all human beings regardless of race, gender, age, religion, or geography?"

John let the question sit with the group.

"We all want to be happy," he answered. "But what does it mean to be truly happy? I am not speaking about the happiness that comes from an experience like winning at sport, buying a new car, or getting married. These experiences come and go. People then become unhappy when they lose the next game, wreck the car, or have problems in their marriage. I want to explore a happiness that is beyond any experience in life…a happiness that can exist even in difficult situations. The Buddha taught how to end our suffering and abide in this profound happiness."

John took another sip of water and continued to address the group.

"There certainly are aspects of life that cause physical pain such as injury, disease, and old age. But *psychological* suffering is different and unnecessary. In this course, we explore the reasons for the psychological suffering. The three main causes of suffering are *greed*—not getting what we want, *hatred*—having aversion to what is happening, and *ignorance*—not understanding our true nature. Let us explore this last topic first, as it is the root of the others."

Julia repositioned herself on her cushion. She was curious what was meant by *true nature.*

He continued. "What is this thing we call John, Sarah, Gareth, or what we refer to as me or I? What are we really? What is our true nature? The core tenet spoken by the Buddha is *events happen, deeds are done, but there is no individual doer thereof.* Here's an example of this teaching."

John paused for a moment.

"Imagine an empty piece of land. Now imagine all the parts it would take to build a house were dumped on the land—the wood, the nails, the roofing, the cement, the dry wall, the wiring, the appliances, the pipes...all the parts. Let me ask, would you have a house?"

Of course not, Julia thought.

"Of course not," John stated. "Now if you took all those parts and rearranged them so that the cement created a foundation, the wood stood upright with nails binding them together, the dry wall was hung, the roofing was lodged on top, and the plumbing and wiring were positioned in their respective places. Would you now have a house?"

Yes, Julia murmured, not knowing if the question was again rhetorical. Heads nodded throughout the room.

"Yes. Of course," John reiterated. "So what is the difference between the two scenarios? The parts don't change. All we have done is rearrange them. In the second scenario, however, we have added a label to the parts. House is merely a label for the parts organized in a certain way. The label is a concept added by the mind that gives identification to the arrangement. Naturally, labels certainly facilitate ease in communication. Imagine rather than using the word *house* one always said *look at that combination of wood, nails, dry wall, cement, roofing, electricity and plumbing*."

The group chuckled.

"But labels are just labels. There really is no *house*—there's just a composite of parts we call *house*. Now suppose a hurricane comes through and rips off only the roof of the house. Would you still have a house?"

John paused for a longer moment waiting for a response. After a long silence, one of the attendees spoke out, "Yes."

"Most people would," John affirmed. "Most would call it a house but would say it needed a new roof. Now imagine the hurricane ripped off just a quarter of the house on one side. Would you still have a house?"

The same person said, "Yes."

"I agree. At what point, however, do we say there is no house? When one-half is gone? Three-quarters gone? Completely demolished? Can you see how the mind adds the label of house at some point or removes the label at some point?"

Most of the group, including Julia, again nodded their heads.

A guy with long hair, wearing a ragged white t-shirt and brown baggy pants raised his hand and spoke with a French accent. "How does this apply to us as human beings?" The tone could have been taken as challenging but was inquisitive.

"Spot on...right where I was headed," John responded. "What if human beings are exactly the same? We are made up of parts. We refer to these parts as the Five Aggregates: Material Form, Feelings, Perceptions, Mental Formations, and Consciousness. We then add the label of names like John or Sarah. Over time we learn to identify with our names as who we are. But like in the house metaphor, what if our name, or what we commonly refer to as *me,* is just a label that we add on to the five aggregates. If we look deeply into our direct experience, can you actually find a *me*? Or is *me* a label of all the parts like the concept of house? Is there really a *me*? Perhaps this will get clearer as we explore different parts of our being which are commonly mistaken for what we are. For example, are you your thoughts?"

John watched the attendees shake their heads indicating no.

"No. Thoughts come and go but something seems to continually exist whether thoughts are present or not. What exists when thoughts aren't present?"

John paused again for several moments to let the question sink in.

"We'll come back to this. Are you your feelings? No...feelings come and go, too. We have feelings but we aren't our feelings. Yet we talk as if we are our feelings. For example, we say *I'm angry* or *I'm glad*. But the truth is I am not anger. There is a feeling of being angry. Likewise, I am not gladness. There is a feeling of being glad. But as we know, feelings come and go. Similarly, are you your perceptions? No, these, too, come and go. What about your personality? Are you your personality?"

Once again, John waited before continuing.

"You may have different qualities that reveal themselves at various times. Sometimes you might be friendly. Sometimes you might be aloof. But these qualities come and go as well. So when we look closely, we see that we are more than our personality. Now, are you your body? This gets trickier. Like in the hurricane example, if you lost your legs, would you say you still exist?"

"Yes," Julia stated out loud.

John smiled. "Of course. If you lost your arms as well, you would also say you still exist, yeah? As in the house example, how much of the body would have to be destroyed until we say there is no body?"

"When the heart stops beating!" the Frenchman called out.

"Okay. Is there still a body though when the heart stops?" John challenged back.

"Yes," the Frenchman conceded.

"Now we would say we need the heart to function in order to be alive but are you your physical heart?"

"What about consciousness?" the Frenchman asked. "Are we our consciousness?"

"What happens when you sleep?" John replied. "Are you conscious of what is happening around you?"

"No," the Frenchman responded.

"But do you still exist?" John asked.

"Yes."

"So what is it that continues to exist? The Buddha taught that *events happen, deeds are done, but there is no individual doer thereof.* Look closely within your own experience. See if you can find a doer...a thinker...a feeler...or this thing we call *you*. Let me use a different metaphor. What if you were like the character in a dream or film? When you watch a good film, you get immersed in the story. The characters seem real. The projector projects images onto the screen—such as someone being chased or being murdered. As you watch, you actually can feel deep emotions such as terror or sadness, and yet you know the film isn't real. At the end of the film, the actual physical screen is not affected by what takes place on it. What if ultimate reality is like that? What if your true nature is a silent aware presence that goes beyond all your senses and experiences, and functions like the movie screen? And all the experiences you have, internal and external, are just projections on this constant aware presence?"

Julia tensed up a bit upon John mentioning the examples of being chased and witnessing a murder. She was amazed those were the examples he used. Though she made sense of what John was saying, she was still perplexed. Life seemed very real. Her father's death certainly felt real. Her anger felt real, though more diminished at this point. What did John mean by these experiences weren't ultimate reality? Was she truly living inside some dream world? Was life like a dream of some divine director and people were the characters in the movie?

As the talk ended, Julia's head was spinning like a shaken up snow globe. There was truth to the sentence in the flyer she had read; her view of reality was being turned upside down. She had never looked at the question *what am I* this closely. John met any answer that came like a gardener pulling out the root of a weed. She was left with only one truthful response...

She didn't know.

CHAPTER 41

Whatever you're into, Brad thought, as he pushed the gray button to recline his window seat while the plane cruised at 41,000 feet.

Before getting on the plane he had received an email from Julia describing her precarious journey to Dharamsala and that her meeting with the Dalai Lama had been postponed a few days. She also mentioned she was going to take a course on Tibetan Buddhism to learn more about the spiritual ground upon which the culture had been built. If he had been given that free time, he would have gone trekking himself.

He closed his eyes to capture some desperately needed sleep, yet his mind drifted to his impending task. He knew sneaking into Ingrols and getting on Redman's computer was incredibly risky. But it was the threat of danger that always gave him a rush. *What's the worst thing that could happen,* he often told himself when his life was on the line. *I'll die. So what?*

As he leaned his head against the cold window, he drifted into light sleep. There he stood that January morning, shovel in hand. He was working on the snowman when he heard, "Brad! Brad!" He turned his head and saw the tool shed on fire. He began to run through the snow but his legs sank into its heavy depth. He fell face first. *Hurry*, he screamed to himself. *Don't let it be too late!* He picked himself up but after a few strides, he fell again. He looked up and saw the blaze had quickly spread throughout the shed. He heard his name being called even louder. "Brad!! Help!!"

Just then, the plane hit some turbulence and jolted Brad from the haunting image. He shook it away as he had done many times before. Firmly, he began to think about the slopes—it was the one thing that worked whenever the nightmare arose.

* * * * *

The Predator paced back and forth in his office restlessly chewing on his cigar. He was expecting a call from a contact that might be able to detect Julia's and Brad's whereabouts. It was time to end their detective stints regardless of the media consequences.

He looked at the date on his watch—one week before the WHC meeting. The Jokhang would be demolished the day after the vote. His position came with the power to make things happen fast…if only he could speed up the hands on a clock as well.

CHAPTER 42

The second day was Tibetan meditation. At first Julia was nervous because just the words *Tibetan meditation* conjured up images of going into some altered, transcendent state resulting in a wacky experience. She had never been exposed to meditation other than closing her eyes for thirty seconds in a beginner yoga class in Mill Valley. Though she was comfortable being outdoors, it was a different story when it came to exploring the doorways into her persona. Like most people, she felt it was safer to move about one's living room than to explore the dark shadows of one's basement.

Julia sat closer to the front. Though anxious, she was looking forward to hearing John speak again. She had liked the traditional teachings given the previous day by the Geshe, but she was particularly drawn to John's approach. She felt that John communicated the teachings with a contemporary simplicity that resonated with her. She also found his relaxed presence very calming.

John began the meditation practices with an analogy that put into context the teachings he was about to explore.

"*How big is your box?*" John began. "Let me explain. Imagine a glass of water filled to the brim with no room to hold another drop. Now imagine taking this glass of water and pouring it into an empty bucket where the water only fills the bottom of the bucket. There'd be much more space to hold that water. Now imagine you could pour that water into the Grand Canyon. The water would seem like a drop of rain in the massive gorge. Most people are like the first glass of water—they can only hold so much. Their minds and bodies are so full of reactive thoughts, emotions and fixed agendas that they are like walking clouds ready to burst. They can't absorb any more. When they bump up against circumstances that don't go according to their wishes, they burst and suffer. One of the main purposes of meditation is to become aware of the deep canyon-like spaciousness that exists within our being. It actually *is* our being. The more you tune into this deep spaciousness that you are, the more expansive you are, and the easier you can *hold* whatever happens in life. You're able to go through life with more ease because you're less reactive, less affected by what happens. In meditation, we come to this spaciousness by first clearly seeing what is actually happening in our direct experience and allowing the experience to be exactly what it is…without judging it and without changing or manipulating it. By simply witnessing our experience and not getting consumed by it, we become more like the big sky that holds the clouds rather than the clouds themselves. From the vantage point of the sky, the sky is not injured by the passing clouds, just like the screen that is not affected by the film that appears on it."

After John explained a few more details of meditation, the first one began.

Am I doing this right? I wonder what will happen? Perhaps I was crazy to sign up for this course. Oops…there I am thinking about not thinking. He said try not to get lost in thinking.

She was amazed that she couldn't stop her mind even if she wanted to—it seemed to have a mind of *its* own.

The next meditation involved dealing with anger. The group was asked to imagine a situation in the past that elicited anger. Julia immediately thought of that dreadful day when she discovered the letter about her mother. It didn't take much for the anger towards her father to make her tense. As she replayed the incident in her mind, she got so caught up in the images that she missed the series of instructions on how to actually deal with the anger. When the bell rang to end the session, Julia realized she had spent the entire time engaged in thought and fueled with anger.

Upon leaving the meditation hall, she saw John walking through the garden outside and quickly caught up with him.

"Excuse me, John. Do you have a minute?" Julia asked.

John stopped and turned. "I've got a quick one before I need to meet with the administrator."

"Well, I don't know how to say this other than to just say it. My father was murdered about a month ago and there's a lot of anger that's... arising... as you say."

"I'm terribly sorry to hear that," John sympathized.

"Thanks. During the last meditation, I was feeling some strong rage that I have felt toward my father for quite some time. My mind got so agitated that I missed your instructions. I was hoping you could give a couple of quick tips to help me get rid of the anger."

John rested his hand on a wooden bench in the garden.

"There are many levels to working with anger. The first of which is to truly feel into it and not try to get rid of it. It's important not to resist the anger, for what we resist persists."

"What do you mean by feel *into* it?"

"Close your eyes for a moment."

Julia let her eyelids close.

"Imagine sitting on the shore of a lake and looking at the water. You notice the water is there but you don't actually experience the water. Can you do this?"

It took a second but Julia was able to do this. "Yes," she said.

"This is like being aware of an emotion but not quite feeling it. Now imagine walking into the lake—actually going into the water. Imagine what it feels like to be in the water. Can you imagine feeling it?"

"Yes."

"OK...you can open your eyes. Most people don't actually feel their emotions, if they are aware of them at all. By truly experiencing the anger, or any emotion for that matter, you allow the emotion to take its natural course. Like everything else in life it will come and then pass. However, if we judge it, analyze it, resist it, try to get rid of it, or even wallow in it, it will last longer. Be like the sky and let the anger be a dark cloud passing through. It won't last as long...and you'll also probably uncover even deeper emotions."

"Deeper emotions?" Julia inquired.

"Yes. Anger is almost always a mask for a deeper emotion...most often some kind of hurt. By sitting with the anger, you might recognize something else you're feeling. Have you fully explored your feelings since your father's death?"

"Not fully," she admitted. "I've been so busy in dealing with the aftermath of his murder that I haven't taken the time to really feel my emotions."

"That's a good place to start. Like the old cliché, the only way out of the pain is through it. Otherwise, the anger will continue to eat at you. Anger is our worst enemy. It leads to judgment, hatred and all the violence in the world. And as we discussed, the Buddha taught that events happen, deeds are done, but there is no individual doer thereof. Once you recognize that your actions and those of others are a function of karmic programming and conditioning, this will help you to accept and forgive your father, as well as his murderer. It is only compassion and forgiveness that leads to peace in the heart...and eventually the world."

John looked at his watch. "I'm sorry, but I must meet with the administrator now. Again, I am sorry about the loss of your father. I wish you well."

"Thank you," Julia said.

John smiled, nodded, and headed off down the path through the garden.

* * * * *

Julia sat alone on a bench in the garden. The other participants had left the area. Closing her eyes, she reflected upon her relationship with her father. Within minutes, a subtle tightness began to stew in her gut.

She thought about what John said—*go into the water*. She tried to bring awareness directly into the sensation. She felt the anger and did her best to imagine going into it. As she did this for a couple of minutes, surprisingly, the tightness slowly began to loosen. It was then that a childhood memory arose of her walking hand-in-hand with her father through the streets of Disneyland. She remembered him taking her into the Haunted House. They rode the carriage as it swerved, tipped, and glided through the scary mansion. He held her tight as ghosts appeared unexpectedly around each corner. She remembered feeling safe in his arms.

As the memory faded, she realized that the anger had given way to a profuse heaviness. Julia let herself sink into the heaviness as it pervaded her entire body. After several minutes of truly feeling the heaviness and allowing it to be there, a realization popped in her mind like a champagne cork.

That's wild. The emotions are shifting on their own without my doing anything to them.

The anger had come without trying to make it appear. It loosened without her trying to loosen it. The anger had transformed into a heaviness by itself. Even the realization that emotions were shifting by themselves had popped into consciousness on its own accord.

Julia then recognized that this was the same with all thoughts—they just came to her. It seemed like *she* was thinking the thoughts, but in actuality, thoughts just flashed in her head. Perhaps all of life was like this for everyone—a string of seemingly spontaneous thoughts, decisions, and actions.

Maybe that was what the Buddha meant by events happen, deeds are done but there is no individual doer thereof. Given people's genetic makeup, childhood upbringing and societal conditioning, they were always making the best choice they could in the moment, not that these choices were necessarily good, ethical, or even lawful. And, if this was true, then this was the case for her father. He couldn't help himself from deciding to cover up her mother's existence. He was doing the best he could…at that time.

For the first time, Julia felt acceptance and compassion for her father and could honestly forgive him. She felt the deep love for him that she had felt as a child. As this happened, the heaviness burst open—tears of forgiveness rolled down Julia's face.

Ten minutes went by while Julia cried. Pulling some Kleenex from her backpack, she then noticed the box of her father's remains that she had been carrying. For weeks, she had wondered what to do with his remains. A decision came to her—Tushita would be the perfect place. Her father would have cherished the notion that his ashes were spread across such a paramount Tibetan location.

Julia pulled out the box. With her tears still falling, she walked over to a beautiful patch of flowers. She released his remains and watched as the ashes dispersed in the air. A wave of peace came over as she looked up and saw that the sun was setting beautifully in the background over the Himalayas.

CHAPTER 43

*B*rad entered the front doors of Ingrols headquarters located in downtown Dover—the capital of the First State. It was just after 8pm on Friday, which meant any usual late night worker-bees were probably home with a loved one, or on the town trying to find one.

Carrying his black leather briefcase, Brad was dressed in a sharp Hugo Boss gray pinned-striped suit. There was no need for an overcoat tonight—unusually mild temperatures had blanketed the east coast.

Inside the building, a manned security podium was set on the left side of the lobby. It was between the front doors and the bank of elevators.

As he walked into the lobby, Brad headed straight for the elevators. He took a quick glance at the security guard on duty. The guard, reading the newspaper, looked up over his black-rimmed reading glasses and noticed Brad in stride.

Brad immediately waved and said, "Hey, Joe. Sorry to hear about your dad." He then turned his head away and proceeded directly toward the elevators as if he were an employee. The guard hesitated a moment but then waved and went back to reading his paper.

Brad had learned the guard's name from an employee the day before when he scoped the scene. He had also discovered the man's father was in the hospital for a triple by-pass.

Once inside the elevator, Brad breathed a sigh of relief. He would have expected better security from a downtown city location so close to the nation's capital. Evidently the Department of Homeland Security's mission hadn't penetrated as widely as the government propagandized. Then again, the Ingrols office building wouldn't be high on a list of targeted sites for a terrorist attack.

Brad pressed the button to the 9th floor. He had earlier made a phone call to Redman's assistant explaining he wanted to drop off a package for him. Brad received an early Christmas gift when he learned Redman was out of town for a few days and that he could drop off the package with the receptionist on the 9th floor.

The elevator doors opened to a small foyer with a large sign on the wall—*Ingrols Executive Offices.* To either side of the unattended receptionist's desk were glass doors. Brad strolled across the white marble floor to one set but found them locked. He peered through but saw no sign of life. He checked the other doors but they were locked as well.

As he contemplated his next move, a cleaning lady came into view through the doors. Brad waved and pointed to the door to imply he needed it opened. She complied.

"Thanks," Brad said as she opened the door. "I left my badge in my office."

Brad quickly flashed his driver's license to give the impression he was an employee and then stuffed it back in his coat pocket. The woman smiled and nodded. Brad assumed she didn't speak English, so he just kept walking as if he knew where he was going.

The floor consisted of a maze of offices. Finding his way through to the far side, Brad passed several executive offices with engraved nameplates on each door. Within two minutes he found Redman's name. He scanned the area to ensure it was vacant. He then twisted the door handle. It was locked.

"*Dammit!*" he said under his breath. *Now what?*

An idea came to mind. He knew it was risky but it was his only chance.

He retraced his steps and tracked down the cleaning woman.

"Se hablas espanol?" he guessed, approaching her.

The woman smiled. "Si Senor."

"*Es possible abre' mi puerta? Mis llaves en la oficina.*" Brad did his best to recall the language that he learned at CU and practiced from time-to-time with a ski buddy from Spain during his Aspen years. He had asked the woman if it was possible to open his door as he left his keys in the office.

"*Seguro,*" she said smiling back affirmatively, appreciating his ability to speak her language.

The cleaning lady followed Brad back to Redman's office. As she opened the door with her master key, again Brad looked over his shoulder for any observers. The coast was still clear.

"*Muchas gracias,*" Brad said in a low voice as he slipped by her into the office. He closed the door and then locked it as she walked away.

Phew, he thought. *She didn't know Redman's face...though I'm sure Redman wasn't the type to make small talk with janitorial staff.*

As Brad scanned the office, he could scarcely see the contents in the dimness. He didn't turn on the light in case someone walked by.

The room was immaculate. The desk was clear with the exception of a few files neatly stacked to one side and a computer monitor on the other. The rest of the office was sparse—there were no family pictures or personal artifacts on the wall or the desk. An antique bookcase hugged one side of the office displaying titles related to China Economics, International Trade, and U.S. International Business Regulations.

Brad didn't waste time. He moved swiftly to the desk, sat down in the chair, and booted up the computer. While waiting for the desktop to appear, he touched his forehead and realized it was covered with sweat. With no handkerchief or tissue in sight, he wiped his forehead with the sleeve of his suit jacket. As he pulled his arm down, his elbow banged the edge of the desk and made a loud sound.

"*Shit,*" he thought. He needed to be more careful. He listened for any movement outside the office. Nothing stirred.

As the desktop appeared with a picture of modern Shanghi, so did a window asking for an ID name and password. Brad reached into his coat pocket and pulled out the information from Sherpa's email. He typed in *Redman* for the ID name and *Costcut* for the password.

"Yes!" Brad murmured quietly, as the computer accepted the two codes.

At that moment, he heard footsteps outside the door. He froze. Holding his breath, he listened carefully.

He knelt down behind the desk and after a few moments of silence, the footsteps walked away.

Brad slid back on to the chair and searched for the file CHINAREPORT9. A .pdf file immediately surfaced and he opened it. It was dated July 25th, a few months prior to the Lhasa massacre.

The title page read *CHINA OPERATIONS: MAJOR CRISES.* An auditor, contracted by Ingrols to inspect its Chinese factories, had submitted the report to Redman. Ingrols and many other international companies doing business in China hired auditors to ensure quality control of products, production guidelines, and compliance of labor laws. Conditions varied from factory to factory. Those owned by Taiwanese tended to be first rate. Chinese owned factories, however, were generally more primitive.

Brad's eyes widened as he read the Executive Summary. The document highlighted three flagrant crises within Ingrols' operations in China. The first was the physical abuse of employees that transpired in several factories. Workers were beaten by factory managers for not working fast enough or for refusing to work extra hours. In one small factory, a factory manager smacked a worker for not meeting a stringent Ingrols deadline. The worker slipped and hit her head on a machine, dying instantly. The official report from the factory was that the worker had died accidentally on the job.

The second issue was a series of labor law violations. These violations were comprised of workers being paid less than minimum wage, not being paid for overtime, locked in the factory to work extra hours, and forced to work in extremely cramped spaces without air conditioning. The auditor warned that should the violations reach the public domain, Ingrols would fall to the mercy of international labor laws and be sued for millions.

The auditor also strongly admonished *against* building an Ingrols factory in Tibet. Trying to get UNESCO to remove the sacred Jokhang temple from the protected heritage list would ignite enormous outrage from the Tibetans and surely create massive protests. Tibetans certainly would not take factory jobs in opposition. Though the factory could be employed with Chinese workers, the disastrous press would cost much more than the potential profits. This was a Titanic in the making.

Brad reached into his briefcase and pulled out a portable document scanner. Within minutes, he scanned each page of the detailed report, clearly ignored by Ingrols management.

He then located the second file—LHASAOPS. Brad read the document, which was a letter Redman had written to Liung Xilai, the Minister of Commerce on October 7th—three days *after* Mason was killed. Brad's jaw dropped as he read a few key sentences.

"*The Tibetan protest problem was taken care of. We've recovered the tape. The infiltrator will no longer be an issue as he's been put to rest. We will continue to develop the factory in Lhasa. Deposit my funds as agreed.*"

Brad was stunned. There it was in black and white. Julia was right all along. Her father had been murdered—here was a document incriminating the source.

Brad could only imagine the impact to both Ingrols and China if the media got hold of these files. Between these two documents and Mason's tape, there was enough evidence to send Redman to jail for life and bring Ingrols to its knees. The UN, WTO, and media would have a field day with China. And with the Vice President supporting it all, the administration would face one of the greatest scandals in history.

Brad quickly scanned the second document, stashed all the copies in his briefcase, and then shut down the computer. He walked to the office door then stopped to listen for anyone nearby.

He slowly opened the door. With no one in sight, he swiftly made his way to the elevators and back down to the lobby.

As he walked across the lobby floor, the guard was still at his station reading the paper. Keeping his eyes fixed ahead, Brad gave a quick wave and said, "All the best to your dad, Joe."

"Hey you!" called out the guard.

Brad kept walking to the doors as if he didn't hear him. When he reached them, he found them locked. He looked back and saw the guard staring at him.

"Hey you! I said. I thought I recognized you before but I don't. Come here!"

Brad's heart started to beat faster again. He looked for another exit but there wasn't one.

He turned and tried to the push the doors harder. They wouldn't budge. The guard stood up.

"Hey! Stop right there or I'll call the police!" the guard yelled. He came out from his desk. Though he was overweight and moved sluggishly, Brad guessed he probably once benched three hundred.

As the guard reached for a gun by his side, Brad noticed a red button to the right of the doors. He whacked the button with his palm and heard a click. Another strong push and the doors flew open.

Brad raced out of the building and bolted down the sidewalk. The guard banged his way through the closing doors but quickly realized he was no match for Brad's speed. He ran back to his station and called the cops.

Darting through downtown Dover, Brad kept the briefcase securely to his side. He passed several legislative buildings when he saw an empty taxi approaching. Brad flagged it down and quickly jumped in.

"Where to?" said the driver in a croaky smoker's voice. Brad tried to catch his breath when he heard sirens shrieking in the background. *He must have called the cops,* he thought. Seeing a cop car approaching, Brad slid down in the seat behind the driver.

"Where to, Mister?" the driver urged again, more annoyed.

"The Malcolm Hotel," Brad answered. He had checked into the hotel that afternoon.

Upon reaching his hotel room, Brad affixed the latch on the door and drew the curtains on the window. He then sent Julia an email explaining the documents on Redman's computer. He included the phone number of the hotel and told her to call or email him immediately.

Afterwards, a swell of satisfaction for what he accomplished brought a smile to his face as he lay on the bed, arms behind his head. And he was certain his tracks couldn't be traced to the hotel. Danger was out of sight—*at least for tonight.*

CHAPTER 44

Julia woke up early the morning after the course feeling as lucid and alive as she could ever remember. The sheets on her bed felt softer, the air smelt cleaner, and the sound of a monastery bell lingering in the background had a more distinct tone to it. All her senses felt more present.

Though the course had been just a couple of days in length, it had a transformational effect. Just like clearing out a storage closet of collected debris, Julia felt as if emotional junk stored in her body had been emptied out. For the first time since her father's death, the thought of him didn't bring forth a clenched tightness or anger.

Julia stood in front of the bathroom mirror. Never in her wildest dreams would she have thought that she'd be meeting one of the world's leading spiritual ambassadors. She inspected her outfit—a beige sweater, white blouse and green khaki pants. Western visitors were not expected to wear formal attire when meeting with His Holiness in Dharamsala. Nonetheless, Julia wanted to look respectful. She placed her hair back in a bun and moistened her lips with lip balm.

Walking out of her room, she stopped to take in the magnificent sight of the northern India Shangri-La. It was a particularly clear, brisk day. The higher altitude of Dharamsala could reach below freezing during the winter months. Although it was just a three-minute walk to the Dalai Lama's residence, she was glad she was wearing the sheep wool Tibetan sweater that she had purchased from one of the merchants in Mcleod Ganj.

Julia's thoughts turned to Brad. She wished he were standing beside her soaking in this unique experience. It felt good, and unfamiliar, to be missing him. She hoped he was safe.

Passing through the Tsuglagkhang Complex, Julia noticed a much larger crowd of Tibetans and monks than the previous time. A public audience with the Dalai Lama was to be held later that afternoon. Several hundred would line up in a wedding reception-like procession just to receive a brief blessing from His Holiness. People were already gathering, much like die-hard fans before a big game.

As she approached the gate to the residency, Julia's heart raced. She first passed through a set of metal detectors and then was patted down by a Tibetan guard. She was asked to wait in a small room at the guard station.

After fifteen minutes, a familiar face appeared. It was Tenzin Takla, the Deputy Private Secretary. He escorted her to a waiting room within the residency where there were several elderly Tibetan monks also expecting an audience with His Holiness.

Throughout the room were cabinets encasing many awards and gifts His Holiness had been granted from around the world. The walls were covered with several pictures of the Dalai Lama with distinguished world leaders. And, in tradition, exquisite *thangkas* hung throughout.

Tenzin guided Julia over to a seat next to one of the elder monks.

"Thank you," Julia said to Tenzin with a smile. She bowed her head in respect and took a seat. Tenzin bowed in return and left the room.

Once settled, she glanced briefly at the monk. As their eyes connected, she nodded her head. The monk smiled and reciprocated the gesture. Something in his smile made Julia feel deeply connected to him without even knowing his name or story. There was such an authenticity about his presence.

In preparation for meeting with the Dalai Lama, Julia had learned a few tips on proper protocol from John. In her right hand was a *khata*, a special white prayer scarf. The khata, in Tibetan custom, was offered to someone at the start of any meeting or relationship. It indicated the good intentions of the person offering it. Khatas were also offered to religious images, such as statues of the Buddha, to great lamas, and to representatives of the government.

Julia neatly folded the khata and then closed her eyes. Though her heart was still racing, she felt a deep underlying calmness from having participated in the course. She relaxed into this presence and practiced some of the meditation she had learned.

Five minutes later, the door opened. A short Tibetan man dressed in a brown suit entered the room. It was His Holiness's Personal Secretary. He scanned the room until his eyes fell upon Julia. He waved for her to come forward.

Julia was led to a good-sized room, a den of sorts, where His Holiness often conducted his private audiences. Unlike the Oval office, this room was simple and unconventional with the exception of a few elegant thangkas. In a corner were two large Indian style chairs and a small end table covered with a cloth and a plain lamp. Julia was guided to the chair on the right reserved for guests and asked to wait while the Personal Secretary temporarily left the room.

Her heart was beating fast. She imagined the Tibetans still imprisoned who withstood years of torture and abuse, because they wouldn't renounce their reverence for His Holiness. They prayed everyday for the opportunity to some day be in his presence again. And here she was. She felt somewhat undeserving...who was she to have this grand opportunity?

In a few minutes, His Holiness entered the room accompanied by his Personal Secretary. The contrast of his physical presence was intriguing. On the one hand, like most of the elderly monks in the waiting room, he had rounded shoulders, poor posture, and wore Tibetan monk robes and glasses. He tottered a bit as he approached her with his back slightly bent. But despite his hunched appearance, there was an immense energy lift as he entered the room. Whether it was from the glow of his presence or her exhilaration to see him, Julia couldn't tell. All she knew was that she was now in the company of a holy man.

Julia immediately arose in a bowing posture, trying to keep her head down below his—another proper protocol she had been advised. Then, whilst keeping her head down, she extended her arms with the khata outstretched in her hands as an offering. In custom, the Dalai Lama took the khata from her hands and placed it back around her neck. Julia felt the silk touch softly against her skin.

His Holiness touched the top of her head. "Please, sit," he said in English.

Julia sat back down in her chair while His Holiness took the chair to her right. He slipped off his sandals and proceeded to sit comfortably cross-legged on the chair. Though Julia didn't feel comfortable doing the same, she shuffled in the chair and crossed her legs.

"Welcome to my home," he said with a smile.

Julia's entire body softened feeling his warmth. It was like he wore his heart on his face.

"Tashi Delek," Julia said using the common Tibetan greeting she had picked up, bowing her head slightly as she said it.

"Very good," he added with a hearty chuckle. His laugh was infectious. It made Julia relax even more.

"Thank you so kindly, Your Holiness, for meeting with me. This is such an incredible honor."

His Holiness nodded as his eyes momentarily shifted down. After a brief pause, he looked up and spoke.

"I understand you have tape of killings in Lhasa your father videotaped." His English was decent, though at times broken.

"Yes," Julia said.

"I also heard about your father's death—Lobsang at ICT explained. I'm very sorry to learn about this. Very sorry."

"Thank you, your Holiness."

Julia sensed something unique about His Holiness's compassion. Others had expressed their sympathy but there was something in his tone that made her feel like he knew her emotions intimately.

"I am told your father was very good man. Big heart."

"Thank you. My father was a deeply committed humanitarian. He was very passionate about supporting the Tibetan people."

"We very much appreciate the support of so many dedicated Americans."

His Holiness paused and then said, "I understand you took Buddhism course at Tushita?"

Julia was surprised by the change in topic, but even more so that he knew this.

"Yes."

"What did you think?" he asked.

Julia had not anticipated talking about her experience of the course.

"It was...it was...very good. I learned a great deal about Buddhism and in dealing with...overcoming...well, working through anger." Julia felt like a ditz for not being able to form a clear sentence in front of the world leader. Americans were already branded with being loud, unintelligent, babbling fools. Stereotypes got established for a reason—and she didn't want to add credence to this one.

"Tell me about your working through anger, if you don't mind."

Julia was surprised. This was one of the holiest men on the planet, with an extraordinarily demanding schedule, and yet he was taking the time to ask her questions about her experience at Tushita.

"Well, I've been angry with my father for quite some time based on something he did a long time ago. I'm also angry with his murderer. I imagine you heard through Lobsang that my father was killed."

"Yes. I did hear the details of your father's death. I am very sad to hear about your father dying this way, particularly because it happened in connection with supporting Tibet."

"Thank you. The teacher at Tushita encouraged me to feel into the depths of my emotions. I've been able to go deeper into my anger with my father. It's been difficult but cathartic. I haven't really sat with my anger toward my father's murderers. The teacher mentioned having compassion for one's enemy. This doesn't seem possible for me...at least not yet."

"This is not easy."

His Holiness took off his glasses and wiped his eyes—not because they were teary but at the age of over seventy, they watered frequently. He put his glasses back on but before he continued, a knock came at the door. A Tibetan man entered in a bowing position with some *po cha*, Tibetan butter tea, and placed it on the table between them. When he was done, he walked away backwards remaining hunched over. His Holiness nodded his head in a slight bow and said, *"Tudiche."*

After the man left the room, His Holiness motioned for Julia to take some tea.

"Thank you," she said.

Julia took a sip and found the tea to taste a bit rank but she nodded her head to indicate her gratitude.

His Holiness took a sip and then spoke.

"I asked you about your retreat experience at Tushita and your anger for a reason. I believe every situation in life is an opportunity for..." he paused trying to find the right words, "spiritual maturity. Though we will discuss actions to take with videotape, as a Buddhist monk I believe what is most important is to explore our deepest motivation underneath our actions. We believe if one acts from anger, this will inevitably lead to more suffering. This has been very important in my relationship with China."

As he spoke, Julia realized that she hadn't examined her motivation that astutely.

His Holiness continued. "Perhaps if I discuss my relationship with China this will help our discussion of what to do with videotape."

"I'd very much appreciate learning about that," Julia said.

"Let me first say my relationship with China is very complex...and not easy to explain in very short time. This is because one needs to understand—deeply understand—the subtle Buddhist teachings to fully comprehend my view. You received an introduction to teachings on interdependence, true nature, and compassion. However, it takes many years to truly embody these teachings."

His Holiness took a deep breath. Julia could see the man was very mindful about each word he chose as if he were picking ripe fruit.

"All human beings want happiness. In this way, we are all same. But people have different interpretations of ways to achieve happiness. I completely disagree with the Chinese in their possession of Tibet and the violent, unjust manner in which they have destroyed our people and culture. But we are same in wanting happiness. When people have different views, how to come up with solution? First of all, violence is not the way. Violence only provokes anger, hatred, and more violence. We are against violence of any kind. Not only do we Tibetans not want to act violently, but we do not wish to provoke it either. I encourage Tibetans in prison in Tibet to renounce their relationship with me, as I do not want them harmed or to provoke aggression of Chinese. It is what is in one's heart that matters. World peace will come, I believe, when each person has inner peace. I believe in inner disarmament. For humanity to live in a world free from hatred and violence, we must cultivate their opposite motivations—compassion, love, tolerance and patience."

Julia nodded. "My father often quoted Martin Luther King who said hate cannot drive out hate...only love can do that."

"Yes. This is the only way for peace in the world."

"I was wondering, if you don't mind me asking, do you have anger towards China given all they have done to you and your people?"

"These days, anger, hatred, they don't come. Little irritation sometimes come in situations. But in my heart, I never blame and never think bad things against anyone. I always think he or she is a human being who wants happiness. Me, same. I do not have anger against Chinese. At beginning, yes. I was fifteen. But I have learned that anger only upsets my own peace of mind...my happiness. I not let them do this to me. If I forgive, my mind becomes calm. I tell you short story. I once spoke with a monk, Lopon-la, who was put in prison by Chinese for eighteen years. When he finally free, he came here to India. He told me Chinese forced him to denounce his religion. Many times. I asked him if he was ever afraid. Lopon-la said to me, *Yes, there was one thing I was afraid of... I was afraid to lose compassion for the Chinese.* I was very inspired by this. No matter how much they tortured his body, his mind was always a safe place for him. I am convinced the power of forgiveness helped him survive all those years."

"That's quite a story," Julia said, amazed that a human being could respond to a situation that way.

"Yes. When we have anger, the best part of the brain does not function well. We make bad judgments. When we act from anger, we cause harm to others—physical or verbal. This is not helpful. We must learn to cultivate compassion so we do not use violence or force but respect and dialogue to resolve our differences. We must make distinction...actor and act. We have to oppose bad actions but that does not mean we must be against the person or actor. There is always the possibility the person someday be friend. This is why I often say that my religion is kindness. And so I try to cultivate compassion for the Chinese. I think if I were them, and had their circumstances, I might act this way too. This helps cultivate forgiveness. Then the wisdom of interdependence is very important. Everyone and everything is deeply interconnected. Destruction of your neighbor is in some way destroying yourself. Our interest is connected to their interest. Our future depends on them...so taking care of them is taking care of ourselves. We will always be neighbors with China whether or not we have autonomy. So I send them positive emotions like happiness and affection. I wish them peace in their heart. This brings goodwill feelings toward China and helps me have open heart. I believe in time their hearts will open too."

"I should apply this to my situation."

"It may take time. See your enemy as your teacher. It is best to work at developing more patience, tolerance, and compassion in situations with conflict."

"But as I understand, it seems that you don't believe in being completely passive either."

"Yes. For us Tibetans-in-exile, we stand up for our principles and speak out against the violent and unjust actions of the Chinese. We have tried to gain support. We have needed—and still need—the help of U.S. and our international friends to shift the minds of the Chinese."

"It is remarkable the resilience you have had to sustain this effort for so long. As I understand, China has been reluctant to even meet with you."

"Yes, the Chinese government for many years have repeatedly said that the door to dialogue and negotiation is open so long as I make a public statement saying that Tibet is and has always been part of China and that I accept that the PRC as the sole government representing the whole of China, including Taiwan as well. Also, they require that I abandon any proposition on the independence of Tibet."

"But Lobsang told me that you are not seeking complete independence but some sort of autonomy?"

"Yes. I have stated on many public occasions that I am not seeking complete independence of Tibetans...autonomy, but not a separate nation. Yet, China refuses to acknowledge my public declarations. They claim I am *separatist* and that I try to split up the motherland for my own political gain. I have said publicly I would not play any role in a future government of Tibet and would only remain as a public figure to offer advice to the existing government if needed. To prove this even further, in 2004, I handed over all my residual powers to the Assembly of Tibetan People's Deputies, which they accepted. This closed the long history of the Dalai Lama rule."

"So you want autonomy but not independence."

"Yes. There can be sovereignty over land without complete sovereignty over people. One country with two systems such as the relationship between Hong Kong and China or Scotland and the U.K."

"Well hopefully this tape can be used as leverage for gaining some kind of dialogue between you and China to discuss Tibet."

"I hope so too. A dialogue with China is our only hope to protect and preserve the Tibetan culture and to honor our right to express our spiritual views and perform our religious practices. Tibet could still be under the sovereignty of the People's Republic of China. Yet, as part of our autonomy, the Tibet region would be a zone of peace, with no violence of any kind. Hopefully, through dialogue we can arrive at a solution satisfactory to both parties. I have deep appreciation for those in U.S. government who helped organize dialogues between Tibetan representatives and Chinese officials. Progress is being made. Yet the American corporate community..." he paused again searching for the right word, "still colludes with China. Companies turn their eyes away from human rights because their eyes light up with dollar signs when they look at China. Greed, in addition to anger, is the other culprit for suffering in the world. But I, and many in the Tibetan community, believe one day our time will come. People did not believe the Berlin wall would ever fall or the Russian Totalitarian regime could change. We keep hope alive."

His Holiness stopped at that point. He took a sip of tea, as did Julia.

"There is a lot more that I could say but that is enough for now. Let us now talk about videotape and what can be done."

For the next ten minutes, they discussed the pressing concern of the Jokhang and how to best use the videotape. Julia had made a few copies in D.C. prior to leaving on the trip. She gave one to His Holiness. He accepted it but chose not to watch the bloody sights—he had heard enough details from Lobsang and didn't want the images imprinted in his memory.

He advocated a two-pronged strategy for moving forward. Listening to his plan, Julia was amazed not only by his benevolent motivation but his shrewd tactics as well. For a man of spirituality, he was clearly adept at international politics.

Julia was both honored and surprised that His Holiness recommended that one of the strategies involve action on her part. The tape and murders needed authentication—and she was the only one that could provide that. He outlined the steps he thought she should take but emphasized, once again, that she continue to monitor her motivation. They both agreed that action had to be taken quickly before time ran out on the Jokhang.

His Holiness's Personal Secretary then entered the room. The Dalai Lama nodded in the Secretary's direction signifying the meeting was concluding. As they both stood, Julia remained in a bowing position. His Holiness put both hands on top of her head and murmured a Tibetan blessing. When he was done, he removed his hands. Julia looked up to see him leaning forward with hands together in a prayer position.

"Thank you so much for this opportunity. I have so much admiration and respect for you." Extreme gratitude glowed from Julia's eyes.

"Thank you, Julia," the Dalai Lama replied. "It is I who am grateful for your fortitude. May you be happy and at peace."

With that, His Holiness's Personal Secretary then escorted Julia out of the room.

Outside the residency, Julia walked in a daze from the powerful transmission she felt from being in His Holiness's presence. She marveled at everything about the man and felt completely committed to do whatever she could to help him and his people.

Julia maneuvered her way through the waiting crowd that had grown significantly larger during her time inside the residency. She headed directly to the Cyber Café at the Green Hotel, which had Internet access. She had to send Brad an email immediately to update him on her conversation and plan of action.

Logging on, Julia found Brad's emails. Her mouth dropped when she read the line from Redman's file, *the infiltrator would no longer be an issue as he's been put to rest.* The words of His Holiness echoed in her ears. *See your enemy as your teacher.*

She quickly emailed back, thanking Brad for taking the huge risk. She explained what His Holiness had recommended and mentioned she'd get a taxi to New Delhi right away—no bus this time. She'd call when she reached the airport to let him know the soonest flight she could get back to the States. She sensed something major was going to happen...if it hadn't already.

CHAPTER 45

Stretched out on the hotel's king sized bed, Brad was engrossed in ESPN's match up analysis of the Broncos/Redskins game being played at RFK stadium later in the afternoon. The Broncos were leading the AFC West while the Redskins were heading up the NFC East. The game was being headlined as a battle between the two most likely Super Bowl teams. Brad salivated at the possibility of his team triumphing through the playoffs and making it to the big dance. He thought of Prince's song "1999." It would be great to party again like it was 1999—the year the Broncos last won the Super Bowl.

Brad had spent the day before, Saturday, dealing with important client matters. He had time to kill since receiving an email from Julia explaining she would call him the following morning.

The phone rang. Brad looked over at the clock. It was 8:30am—right on time.

Brad cleared his throat and picked up. "Hello?"

"Brad?" Julia said enthusiastically, standing at the airport phone in New Delhi after an all day taxi ride that was much easier than the bus journey.

"Hey there," Brad said, glad to hear her voice again. He clicked off the TV with his remote. He sat up a bit in his bed so he could talk and hear more easily.

"Can you hear me okay?" Julia asked.

"Like you were next door. You okay?"

"Yeah. And thank God you are. I can't believe you got those documents. You're an angel. But please be careful. There's no telling if these people followed you.

"Don't worry. I'm a walking security camera. They've got no idea I'm here."

"Still, keep an eye out."

"I will. And I'll call Coleman's office first thing tomorrow. When are you getting back?"

"There's a flight arriving into Dulles at 6 p.m. your time tomorrow. That'll still be Monday with the international dateline. Can you meet me at the airport?"

"Like a receiver catching a pass in the end zone."

"Thanks, Mr. Football. Maybe you can set up a meeting for Tuesday morning—if I'll even know what morning is with all the time zone changes. But there's no such thing as time anyway. Time's just a concept," Julia added flippantly.

"What's that supposed to mean?" Brad poked.

"The past and future are just thoughts. There's only the present moment. So much to explain," Julia said in a lighthearted tone.

"I can only imagine," he replied. "I'll see you tomorrow night, Ms. Buddha. At 6 p.m. *Dulles time!*"

"Very funny," Julia sneered.

"Get some sleep…you're gonna need it."

"I will. And Brad?"

"Yeah?"

"I…really can't wait to see you."

"Yeah, yeah, yeah. You just can't wait to get your hands on the merchandise, huh?" Brad paused. "The documents that is…"

"Bye, Brad," Julia snickered.

* * * * *

After they hung up, Brad switched hotels to the Doubletree in D.C. to be closer to both the airport and the office of Senator Marjorie Coleman. As part of His Holiness's strategy, the Dalai Lama had asked Julia to immediately contact Congresswoman Coleman—a strong Tibetan ally—and get her a copy of the tape. As House Minority Leader, Coleman would not only have the influence to act expeditiously but would also arrange appropriate security for Julia and Brad. Coleman was the most zealous defender of the Tibetan mission in the U.S. Administration. She had been instrumental in helping to create the role of Special Coordinator for Tibetan issues, a U.S. Governmental position serving under the Secretary for Global Affairs that helped promote dialogue between the Chinese Government and the Tibetan Government in-exile.

After checking into the hotel, Brad headed to a 24-hour FedEx Kinkos where he signed onto a Macintosh at the self-serve computer station.

Connecting a USB cable from his scanner, he downloaded the pictures taken of Redman's files. He double-checked their clarity. The scanner had worked perfectly.

After the documents printed, he made a CD copy and then dragged the downloaded files to Trash and emptied the file. He logged off and walked over to the cashier to pay cash for the transaction.

As Brad handed over a twenty, the cashier gave him a dubious look. "You're here in D.C. on some covert mission, aren't you?" The cashier rang up the job.

Brad froze. "What?"

"Maybe I should call the cops. Those are stolen documents, aren't they?"

Who was this guy? How the hell...!?!?

"You're from Denver, right?" added the cashier before Brad could say anything.

"How'd you know?"

"Right there on your briefcase." The cashier pointed to Brad's business card in a bag tag hanging from his briefcase. "I saw you make copies...probably some secret plan to screw the Redskins. Well, it won't work. They're going to kick the Bronco's butts today." The cashier smiled as he handed Brad his change and a receipt.

"Not with the stolen playbook I've got," Brad jeered, relieved as he left.

CHAPTER 46

*B*rad maneuvered his way to the front of the line and positioned himself directly outside the customs door against the steel gates that kept away the eager crowd. One by one, travelers came through *Declarations* with trolleys carrying piles of luggage.

Brad was pumped. He was excited to see Julia. Not only that, he was still on a high from the Broncos pulling out a one-point victory on a Hail Mary pass the last play of the game.

He noticed her as soon as she emerged through the doorway. Despite her weary appearance, she radiated a presence even more beautiful than he remembered. He raised his hand in the air to catch her attention.

Julia immediately smiled and quickly wheeled her trolley over to him. Though the gate was between them, Julia leaned over to give him a hug.

"Hi," she said as they embraced.

"Welcome back," Brad said into her ear.

Julia didn't want to let go, but did.

Brad flashed his handsome smile. Julia was so glad to see it.

"How was the flight?"

"Good…didn't sleep much, but that's all right."

"Well, you look great."

"Thanks."

"Something happened over there. Did they do some kind of Tibetan Voodoo Dance or something?"

"Did they ever," Julia grinned. She gazed into his eyes for a moment, and they maintained eye contact until a bit of embarrassment set in. He then looked to his left and pointed to the end of the gate.

"I'll meet you down there and we'll catch a cab to the hotel."

* * * * *

On the ride to the Doubletree, they held off heavy discussions to let Julia settle and to keep the details away from the ears of the cab driver.

At the hotel, Brad took Julia's bags into the lobby and went to at the registration desk. He had considered getting one room for the two of them but didn't want to push things too fast. He was dangerously close to crossing over his line.

"Listen," Brad said as they waited to be helped by a front desk attendant, "I reserved you a room…adjacent to mine."

Julia had thought about this moment too. She decided she'd let Brad decide yet secretly hoped they'd room together.

"That's fine," she murmured.

After checking in and freshening up in the room, they met for a quick bite in the hotel's dining room. Once seated at the dining table, and having received their drinks and light sandwiches, Brad filled her in with what he'd done.

"I called Coleman's office today and spoke with her Chief of Staff—a guy named Chelmsford. He said to call tomorrow morning and they'd usher us in right away to meet with the Congresswoman." He took a swig of his Sam Adams Ale.

"Thanks," Julia said, sipping red wine. "The Dalai Lama mentioned she's the best supporter on the Hill. Given she's the House Minority Leader, she'll have huge impact with a press conference."

"And with the low approval rate of the administration, they'll have to support the Dalai Lama to keep their numbers from going further into the cellar." Brad took a bite of his turkey sandwich.

"From what I've read, she's very savvy. I'm sure she'll know how to twist the right arms with all the evidence we've got."

"And I made copies of everything to give to her." Brad took another swallow of his beer. "It also sounds like the Dalai Lama has his own muscle power."

"I guess the Director-General of the WTO is a big supporter. With a gift of fate, there's a Ministerial Conference of the WTO scheduled in Geneva next week. His Holiness is sure when we go public with we've got, he'll get the support he needs from the WTO members for a mandated dialogue with China. He's confident that his connections with the UN Security Council will result in getting their backing. He also has some way to get Saudi Arabia to back him. They're the second largest supplier of oil to China. Cutting off China's oil supply will make China's knees buckle. Money does drive politics."

"And with a media blast, all of this will be a full force blitz. China and Ingrols are bound to get sacked."

"Still got the Broncos game on your mind, I see," Julia teased.

"Celebrate while I can," Brad grinned.

Once they were done, they headed back up to the rooms. They stopped outside Brad's door. An awkward tension filled the air between them. Julia was curious whether he'd make an invitation into his room—but she wasn't about to suggest it.

Should I ask her in? Brad thought. *She's probably tired from the travel and still a bit vulnerable from everything. Not right yet.*

"Well, let's call it a night," Brad finally said. "You've had a long journey and could use a good night sleep...actually we both could."

"Yeah, I really could," Julia replied, not knowing what else to say.

Brad leaned over and kissed her on the cheek. They both said good night and went into their respective rooms.

Once in bed, Brad was so overtired he couldn't fall asleep. He looked over at the adjacent door and saw the light still on in Julia's room. Perhaps he could knock on the door and check on her... sort of dip the foot into the pool and check the temperature.

He got out of bed and walked over to the door. He was just about to knock, when he hesitated.

Let her get some rest. She'll need it for tomorrow.

Brad turned and climbed back in bed.

Julia thought she heard footsteps approaching the adjacent door. For a moment, she was hopeful. She listened closer. Nothing.

Reluctantly, she leaned over and turned out the light.

CHAPTER 47

I found her," the Predator said arrogantly into his cell.

"Where is she?" asked the man in the black suit, wanting a chance to redeem himself after the fiasco of Mason switching tapes on him.

"Somewhere in D.C.—just back from India."

"What was she doing in India?"

"Who knows but you've got twenty-four hours to kill the bitch."

"But how—"

"Check every damn hotel in D.C. if you have to. The WHC meeting is in three days."

"Twenty four hours? But sir, D.C. is a large—"

"TWENTY-FOUR HOURS!" the Predator barked.

The phone line went dead. Dirk knew he'd better find her fast. Otherwise he'd be cut off the same way.

CHAPTER 48

I might need another one of these," Julia said holding a cup of coffee as she and Brad walked into his room. It was her second. They had just finished breakfast in the hotel restaurant and came up to the room to make the call.

"Yeah, we need that brain working so drink up." Brad closed the door behind her. "I'm gonna call Coleman."

"Okay. I'll be in the loo," Julia grinned.

Brad phoned Congresswoman Coleman's office to set up the appointment.

When Julia emerged from the bathroom, she saw Brad shaking his head dejectedly.

"What's going on?" she asked.

"We've got to wait until tomorrow. Coleman had a family emergency. She'll be out all day today and can't be reached. If she calls in, the office will relay the message and try to reach us on my cell. Otherwise we're to call first thing tomorrow."

"But the WHC meeting is scheduled for Thursday. Today's Tuesday...that doesn't leave us much time," Julia stressed.

"I know."

Julia changed her tone. "Well, who knows what's good or bad. Let's roll with it."

"Here we go again, Ms Buddha." Brad rolled his eyes, agitated that the meeting had been delayed. He turned on the computer to check email.

Julia started to open the door connecting the two rooms. She turned her head over her shoulder and said, "At least I'll have a day to get a clean outfit. Everything I own smells like I've been living behind an exhaust pipe. I don't think—"

"Julia!" Brad interrupted urgently.

"What?"

"Come look at this. Another email from our Secret Santa."

Julia hurried over to the desk and peered over Brad's shoulder. She read the email:

There are more vistas on the trail. Don't stop. Connect all the dots on the map. Even if you're blind, keep trusting. Sherpa

"Is this the same person who emailed you before?" Julia asked as she reread the email.

"Yep."

"The last one was so specific. Why the code?"

"Don't know. Maybe it was sent from a traceable location." Brad reread the email again as well.

"What dots do we need to connect?" Julia asked as she continued to look at the screen.

Brad turned toward Julia.

"I'm guessing there's some connection between our suspects. We've got to find out why the Vice President was in Lhasa and what his connection is with Redman and Ingrols."

"Do you think Ruttlefield's involved too?" Julia wondered.

"Probably by now."

"See Brad, who knows what's good or bad. You wouldn't have checked email if we had the meeting with Coleman right now. This message could be an important clue as to what's going on."

"Perhaps," Brad agreed as he wrote down the message on the hotel's note pad. "In either case we've got twenty-four hours to piece this puzzle. Coleman's gonna want facts, not just presumptions."

"And how exactly do you think we're going to solve all this in twenty-four hours?" Julia challenged.

"Well, I know where we should start."

Brad shut down his computer and got up from the chair. "Let's go," he said, removing his coat that was hanging on the chair.

"Where to?" Julia asked.

"Where else can you find access to public information?"

"The library?" Julia guessed.

"Good...it only took two cups. You might not need another one." Brad slapped her on the butt as he walked by her.

"What about the tapes and documents?" Julia asked.

Brad turned and reflected for a second.

"I don't think we should carry them with us," he said. "If something happens to us, they'll be stolen and destroyed."

"Good point. There's a safe in the closet. What about in there?" Julia suggested.

"Too obvious. If these people track us down somehow, they'll get into the room."

"In the mattress?"

"I've got a spot."

Brad took the tapes and documents into the bathroom. Julia followed him in.

To the side of the sink was a tissue emerging from a tissue box encased in the wall. Brad removed the casing and pulled out the rectangular tissue box. He carefully folded the Ingrols' documents and put them, along with the tapes, underneath the remaining tissues in the box. He then placed the box back into the compartment, affixed the casing, and pulled the top issue through.

"Not bad for only one cup," Julia said, as she returned the slap to his butt and headed out of the bathroom.

CHAPTER 49

Just a ten-minute cab ride from the Doubletree, the Martin Luther King, Jr. Memorial Library was located on the corner of 9th and G Street. Open seven days a week, with 400,000 square feet of floor space, the central city library was renovated in 1972 and contributed greatly to the old downtown business district by infusing its logo upon Washingtonians and visitors...*engaging minds, expanding opportunities.*

Julia stared at the black steel, brick and bronzed-tinted glass building as Brad paid for the taxi. She was amazed by the serendipity of circumstances that had unfolded. Having just been in the presence of one of the world's greatest leaders of non-violence, and having just mentioned the MLK quote her father often cited, here she now stood outside a building named after the illustrious promoter of peace and equality.

"Isn't it interesting," Julia said as they walked toward the front door, "that we all worship such nonviolent heroes as Martin Luther King, the Dalai Lama, Gandhi, and Mother Theresa. And yet, I just read that the world currently spends the greatest amount of military spending in history...over three *trillion* dollars. The U.S.'s military budget is twice that of any other nation."

"Crazy, isn't it?" Brad said opening the door.

Julia passed through. "And the President just attended Gandhi's memorial in India and recently gave the Dalai Lama the Congressional Gold Medal. He then went back to his office and doubled military spending in the Middle East."

"Reminds me of the bumper sticker I just saw...Who Would Jesus Bomb?"

As they passed through the library's security area, Julia and Brad placed their jackets through the X-ray conveyor belt.

In the main hall of the library was a huge mural depicting Dr. King's life. Stretching over one hundred feet long, the mural displayed scenes from a half-century ago with signs that read *Colored Need Not Apply, White Only,* and *Colored Entrance.* The images brought an ache to Julia's heart. They reminded her of Palden Gyatso's book that she had read on the plane to India and how the Tibetans were also treated like slaves...even still today.

Brad and Julia walked over to the large information desk in front of the mural.

"Excuse me," Brad said to the library assistant. "Where would we find the business research area?"

"I can only tell you if you promise to give me a stock tip based on what you find out," said the librarian with a smirk.

"Sell short on Ingrols," Brad impulsively replied.

"Well, in that case," said the librarian with a giant smile, "it's over there." The man pointed to the Business & Technology Center to his right.

"Thanks." Brad and Julia headed that way.

* * * * *

"I found them," Dirk said into the phone.

"Where are they?" the Predator demanded.

"At The Doubletree on Rhode Island. I'm headed there now."

"When you find them, follow the plan."

The Predator hung up and blew a smoke ring in the air. With these problems out of the way, he was just two days away from a done deal.

CHAPTER 50

*I*nside the Business & Technology Center, Brad and Julia split up their research. Since Brad had already begun investigating Ingrols, he decided to continue searching for information about the company and Redman. Julia would explore any possible connection between Ruttlefield, Ingrols and the Vice President.

After working on her workstation for almost an hour, the most detailed information Julia was able to dig up on Ruttlefield was his biography. He had been appointed by the President two years ago to his current role as U.S. Trade Representative. Previously, he had served in the House as a Representative from Virginia. He worked on several committees including the House Ways and Means Committee and the Subcommittee on Trade. Prior to being elected to Congress, he was a managing partner at Dreyman, Crowley and Ross, a long time established and prestigious D.C. law firm where he specialized in international trade law.

Brad walked over to Julia's station to compare notes. He leaned over her shoulder.

"Whatcha got?" Brad whispered, keeping his voice down so that he didn't disturb other researchers in the room. He also liked having a good reason to get close to her.

"Not much…just his background. Couldn't find any connection between them all," Julia whispered back as she finished scrolling through another Web page. "What about you?"

"No connection either but I found more scoop on Ingrols in China."

Brad began to read from an article he had printed. "*Ingrols won two lawsuits involving labor law disputes in China that saved them millions. Attorney Robert Crowley says that Ingrols was vindicated in both situations and was the true Jolly Green Giant standing for goodness in fair trade."* Brad shook his head. *"Jolly* and *goodness* my ass. And Green as in filthy rich green," Brad scorned.

"Wait!" Julia blurted. She then whispered, "Let me see that."

Julia snatched the article from Brad's hands.

"What?" Brad asked still standing over her shoulder.

"Hold on."

Julia fingers typed feverishly until she brought up Ruttlefield's background profile once again. She then looked at Brad's article. Her eyes lit up when her suspicion was confirmed.

"The attorney's name in your article was Robert Crowley."

"So?" Brad asked as he peered at her screen.

Julia pointed to a passage on the screen. "Ruttlefield used to be a managing partner in D.C. for a prestigious law firm Dreyman, Crowley and Ross. I wonder if Robert Crowley is the Crowley in Dreyman, Crowley and Ross?"

"Damn, you're good."

Julia looked up at Brad. "Do you think Ruttlefield was involved somehow in these suits?" Julia suggested, her eyes wide.

Brad patted her on the back. "Those dots just might connect."

CHAPTER 51

"May I help you?" asked the hotel clerk at the Doubletree.

"I'm a relative of Brad Benson," Dirk said. "I'm supposed to meet him here. Can you tell me what room he's in?"

"I'm sorry, sir. We're not allowed to give out that information...even to family. Security purposes. I'm sure you understand."

"Can you dial his room to see if he's there?

"Let me check." The clerk retrieved Brad's room number and dialed the room. After several unanswered rings he said, "There's no answer, sir. Would you like to leave a message?"

"No, I'll just come back later."

"That's fine."

As Dirk started to walk away, the clerk called for his attention.

"Excuse me, sir."

Dirk turned back around.

"I just remembered that Mr. Benson called down a couple of hours ago and asked for the nearest library. Perhaps he and the woman he was with headed that way. It's the MLK library at 9th and G. You might catch them there."

"Thanks. I'll do that."

Dirk walked out of the hotel smiling as he thought about the clerk's choice of words.

Outside, he pulled out his cell and dialed the number.

"They're at the MLK library. On my way."

* * * * *

An elderly man sitting at the workstation next to Julia's got up and left the room. Brad immediately switched seats so he could work next to Julia. Brad then searched through past articles of Delaware's Dover Post until he hit a gold mine.

"Julia. Look at this," he whispered loudly.

Julia leaned over the wooden divider separating the workstations. She couldn't believe what they were reading.

"Burton D. Ruttlefield, lead attorney for Ingrols Corporation, successfully represented two cases for Ingrols, the international retail giant. In addition to vindicating Ingrols for a child labor scandal in Beijing, Ruttlefield was able to gain a $100 million dollar settlement for Ingrols with competitor Silipon Stores for patent infringement. Ruttlefield is a managing partner for Dreyman, Crowley, and Ross.

"I knew it," Julia stated, trying to keep her voice down. "Let's print that out."

"Already did." He had also emailed the link to his email account.

"I'll bet he made a fortune for the firm," Julia asserted.

"And it's possible he's a healthy stock owner of Ingrols," Brad quickly replied. "We need to find that out."

"Maybe there's even another dot," Julia said. "Let's keep looking."

CHAPTER 52

Standing outside the front door to the MLK library, Dirk looked through the window and saw the security metal detector. He needed a plan B. To his right was a trash bin. He walked over and found an empty brown paper resting on top.

Scanning the area, Dirk removed a revolver from the confines of his jacket and inserted it inside the brown bag. As long as the city waste truck didn't empty the trash in the next ten minutes, his weapon would be fine.

Entering the main hall of the library, he pulled out photographs of his two targets. To his left was a sign that read *Business & Technology*. This would be as good a place to start as any.

* * * * *

"Anything?" Julia asked peering over the divider again.

"I checked the Vice President's and President's public tax return for the past five years but no connection to Ingrols showed up. But that doesn't mean anything. Any stocks they own personally would be put into a blind trust because once they take office, legally they must have someone else control their investments. Otherwise they could be held liable for—"

"Hold on!" Julia interrupted in a loud whisper, putting her hand on his arm. "Did you say *blind trust*?"

"Yeah, why?" Brad whispered and motioned his palm downward to suggest she keep her voice down.

Julia whispered back. "In Sherpa's email, it said, *even if you're blind, keep trusting*. Do you think that meant to look for a blind trust?" Julia's intensity pierced through him.

"Wow. Was that second cup this morning a triple espresso? I'll bet you're right on the money…literally."

"But how do we find out if any of them are invested in Ingrols?" Julia pressed.

"I don't know. But you just gave me another idea."

* * * * *

Dirk slipped quietly into the Business & Technology Center. Standing inside the door, he scanned the room. Several computer stations were situated directly in front of him. He inspected the occupiers—no matches.

He then noticed a man and woman sitting side by side at workstations with their backs toward him. He made his way behind bookshelves to get a better look. Glancing at their faces through a space in the shelf, he pulled out their photographs. Bingo!

Picking out a book from the shelf, the man made his way to an empty workstation behind them. Though his back was toward them, he could easily eavesdrop.

"Julia, what's the Vice President's wife's name again?" Brad asked, a bit embarrassed that he had forgotten.

"Colleen. How come?"

"Let me check something."

Brad typed *Colleen Langstrom* into a search engine. The Whitehouse website came up describing the Second Lady's Biography.

Brad scrutinized her background. There was some narrative of her stance on children's education and improving America's School Systems. She had also written articles for education journals.

As Brad read further, something caught his attention. In addition to references about her teaching history, there was a sentence describing that she was the only one of three siblings who didn't pursue a career in the retail business.

Brad plugged in some other key words, *Colleen Langstrom maiden name*. Intuitively, he knew he was onto something. Up came a site that read, *"...Colleen Langstrom's maiden name is Pratt..."*

He then entered *Pratt and Ingrols*. His jaw almost hit the table from when he read.

He leaned towards Julia and whispered. "You're not going to believe this."

Dirk leaned back a bit. Despite Brad's attempt to whisper, Dirk was close enough to capture everything that Brad had discovered.

CHAPTER 53

*B*rad and Julia printed out their discovery. The dots they had connected were more like enormous boulders. If this information were to explode in the public eye, the boulders would not only shatter the walls of Washington but the Great Wall itself. They needed to get the information into Congresswoman Coleman's hands; Coleman would be able to light the fuse.

As they walked toward the exit of the business center, Julia heard a cell phone ring. She turned and saw a man in a black suit stand up at the computer station behind where she and Brad had been sitting. The man caught her staring at him and immediately turned from the desk.

Julia hesitated. There was something about his demeanor that was unsettling. Their eyes connected again. Instantly, she knew.

She grabbed Brad by the arm and whispered, "Don't turn around. Walk quickly out the door. He's here."

Julia quickened her pace as she pushed open the door to the business center.

As they closed the door, Julia said, "That man…in the black suit back there. He's following us. I know it. And I think he heard everything. We've got to get out of here."

"I found them," Dirk said quietly into his cell as he quickly made his way to exit the business center.

"In the library?" asked the Predator.

"Yes. They know everything," Dirk said.

"Everything?"

"Everything! And I think they know I spotted them. Got to go."

CHAPTER 54

Brad and Julia raced out of the library and dashed to the corner of 9th and G. Brad grabbed Julia's arm and pulled her to the left. They sprinted north on 9th looking frantically for a cab but couldn't find one.

When they reached H Street, Brad turned and saw the man in the black suit come around the corner of the library. He watched as the man stopped briefly at a trash bin, pull out a paper bag, and then continue after them. Brad wasn't sure what that was about. It didn't matter—they just needed to lose him.

As they reached the Renaissance Hotel between I and K, Brad could see their pursuer gaining on them.

"C'mon. I've got an idea."

Brad grabbed Julia's hand and headed through the front door of the hotel. They immediately darted left in the large lobby and hurried through a sea of hotel guests until they saw another hotel exit leading out to K Street.

Dirk rushed into the lobby. He looked frantically in each direction. To his far left, a hundred yards ahead, he could barely make out his two runaways heading out the side hotel exit. He dashed in pursuit.

Brad and Julia hurried across K Street into Vernon Square. They passed the City Museum of D.C. Brad glanced ahead and saw the Convention Center in front of them. A large banner hung over the entrance, *Washington Auto Show*.

"That way!" Brad yelled, pointing to the front doors of the Convention Center.

As they rushed up the stairs to the front, Brad looked back and saw the man running out of the Renaissance.

Once inside the Convention Center, a large poster board resting on an easel directed Auto Show attendees up an escalator to Ballrooms A, B and C.

"Follow me!" Brad pointed to the escalator.

"Where are we going?" Julia cried, trying to keep up with him as they ran onto the escalator and up the moving steps.

Brad turned back and shouted, "We've got to get lost in the crowd for a while."

At the top of the escalator, hundreds of people were standing outside the ballrooms. Brad and Julia quickly maneuvered their way through the masses. They mixed in with a group of car fanatics walking into the giant showroom where thousands were packed in like sardines investigating the auto industry's latest crazes. It didn't take long before they disappeared among the sea of bodies.

CHAPTER 55

"Man, that was close," Brad exclaimed as they squeezed in between two large boxes. They had managed to slip unseen beneath a ten-foot platform supporting Toyota's latest *Sienna*. Tall, black curtains skirted the base of the platform. Behind the curtains were numerous large boxes of supplies being kept in the manufactured storage space. Brad and Julia were out of sight from even a Toyota employee who might wander beneath the platform in search of materials.

"How did he find us?" asked Julia, trying to catch her breath. The bustling crowd provided ample noise to drown out their conversation.

"No idea," Brad admitted, wiping the sweat from his neck.

"Could they have been following you all along?"

Brad shook his head.

"The hotel clerk," Brad realized. "I asked him for the nearest library. I bet you they figured out we were staying there and got the guy to talk."

"What do we do now?" Julia asked anxiously.

"Wait here. This is a good spot."

"But he'll keep searching for us."

Brad ran his fingers through his hair trying to think of a next step. "There's got to be more than one exit from this place. We can sneak out a side entrance with a crowd."

"What if he sees us? Or what if he catches us before our meeting with Coleman? Or what if Coleman gets further delayed? The WHC meeting is in a couple of days. We've got to get this information out."

Brad looked down. He knew she was right. Something had to be done.

Julia didn't wait for Brad to figure it out. "I say we call the Washington Post. The ICT knows a lot of what we've discovered but we need someone objective in the media who's also in the loop in case something happens to us."

"But if the story's in their hands, they'll run with it."

"We can give 'em most of it but hold back a few pearls. I could work out a deal to tell them the rest in a few days. They'll want the whole story before they go to press."

"Sure that'll work?"

"I did a deal like this with a source when I worked for the Chronicle," Julia said confidently.

"Your call."

"I know someone who might have a contact at the Post. Can I borrow your cell?" Julia stretched out her hand.

"You're gonna call now? From here?"

"Got a better time and place?"

Brad reached into his pocket and gave Julia his phone.

Within minutes, Julia had spoken with a key reporter at the Post. She shared enough of the story to catch his interest. They arranged to meet immediately at the Embassy Suites Hotel near the Convention Center to discuss further details. The reporter would get a room and then call Brad's cell to let them know the room number.

She negotiated a guarantee that the story wouldn't be run for a couple of days and that both her and Brad's confidentiality would be maintained as the sources. In return, Julia promised the reporter he'd get a story that would change his life forever.

All she and Brad had to do now was reach him alive.

CHAPTER 56

The Predator slammed down the phone. *How could they have vanished again?* he raged in disbelief. He would have removed Dirk from the job—permanently—but he couldn't risk bringing someone else into the loop. Besides, he didn't have time. Instead he picked up the phone and placed an overseas call.

"What's the status?" the Predator asked.

"Half of the group is in Beijing," Redman replied. "The others arrive tomorrow. The meeting is scheduled for 9 a.m. Thursday morning." Redman paced anxiously in front of the window of his thirty-story, high-rise hotel room with a panoramic view of Beijing.

"Let me know when everyone's there."

"And what about our pain-in-the-necks?"

"I'll have them in nooses soon."

"My life's on the line, here! Soon better mean immediately!" Redman raged.

"Don't squawk at me! All our lives are! Your flight is set for Thursday night. After the vote, you'll be like any MIA."

"What about my split?"

"You know the deal. It'll be wired as soon as we get the vote."

"I'll call you when they're all here," Redman conceded as he disconnected the call.

CHAPTER 57

*B*rad and Julia huddled among a swarm of automobile aficionados departing the 9th Street exit of the Convention Center. The crowd crossed over 9th and headed down Mass. Ave.

When the group reached 10th Street, the two of them skirted left. They bolted down the redbrick sidewalk until they reached the Embassy Suites. As far as they knew, they hadn't been seen.

Getting off the elevator at the third floor, Brad and Julia moved quickly down the hallway until they found 312 the room number they were given when the reporter had called Brad earlier.

Julia knocked.

Brad looked back to make sure they weren't followed.

"Who is it?" a man's voice called out from the other side of the door.

A surge of panic went through Julia. She didn't know what the reporter looked like. What if he had called the FBI or the police? Could they be walking into a trap? They had no choice but to take the risk.

"It's us, Frank," Julia said, and closed her eyes praying it was him.

The door cracked open slightly.

There stood a thin man in a blue, long sleeved button shirt with gray slacks. With a receding hairline and glasses, he appeared to be in his late forties.

"Julia?" asked the man.

"Yes. Frank?" Julia replied.

The man nodded his head and opened the door to let them in.

Frank Johnson was a veteran reporter for the Post. He covered the Hill exclusively and was the number one guy when a major story was about to break there. His nose was crooked from being punched a time or two after sticking it where it didn't belong. Like many reporters, he wasn't shy about going for the jugular if it meant an earth-shattering story. And from what he had heard on the phone, this one had the making of an enormous quake.

Brad and Julia entered the one bedroom suite while Frank promptly shut the door behind them. The living area contained a couch, coffee table, large cushioned chair, round desk, TV, wet bar, and refrigerator.

"Take a seat." Frank gestured toward the couch. He sat in the large chair next to it.

"Thanks for meeting us on such short notice," Julia said as she and Brad sat down. "We promise it'll be worth it."

"I pushed back a deadline on a major piece. Tell me what you've got."

Frank reached into his pocket and removed a small tape recorder and placed it on the coffee table in front of them. "Comes with the territory. I hope you don't mind," he added.

Julia looked at Brad. They both hesitated, then Brad nodded.

"Okay," Julia said, turning back to Frank.

Julia explained every detail of the story beginning with her father's taping of the massacre, the presence of the Vice President, and Redman's murder of the young Tibetan. She described Ruttlefield's resistance at her father's meeting before he was murdered, the stealing of the original tape, each of the subsequent murders, the FBI cover up, the Secret Service connection, her visit to the Dalai Lama, and their chase from the MLK library to the Convention Center.

Brad described Redman's documents admitting to Mason's murder and the violations of Chinese factories—though he didn't make reference to Sherpa's email or how he got the documents. He mentioned the connection they discovered at the library between Ruttlefield and Ingrols.

"You've got no evidence that Ruttlefield's involved," Frank said, "but it does seem highly suspicious. Do you have the tape and documents with you?"

"No," Brad said.

"Where are they?"

Brad and Julia remained silent, unsure whether to divulge the location.

"In a safe place," Brad finally responded.

Frank gave Brad a flat stare and waited to see if he would reveal more. After an awkward moment of silence, he switched his line of questioning.

"And what about the Vice President's participation?"

"As we agreed," Julia interjected, "we'll explain all that to you in the next couple of days." Julia leaned back into the couch.

"Why wait?" Frank persisted.

"We have a few more things we need to explore so that you have the full and accurate story," Julia said, being intentionally vague. She and Brad had agreed that they wouldn't disclose their upcoming meeting with Coleman. They still needed her cooperation and thought she might be uncomfortable if she knew they had given her name to the Post.

"So why bring this to me now?" Frank leaned back, folding his arms.

"We're being followed," Julia said. "And since three people have already been killed over this tape, we decided should anything happen to us in the next day or so, we wanted someone in the media to know what's going on. The International Campaign for Tibet is aware of some of the story, but we wanted someone even more objective. We're not going to the police or FBI, because we're not sure what connections Ruttlefield has. Besides, they've already been covering this up. If anything happens to us, you can go public with all this."

Julia paused and then stressed. "Again, we're trusting that you won't say anything until we give you the full story in a couple of days. Can we count on you?" Julia leaned forward.

Frank looked down. He took off his glasses and rubbed his forehead. As a reporter for the Post for five years, he had uncovered many noteworthy stories in his stint given the rocky nature of the Hill but nothing of this magnitude. If everything these two were saying was true, this one could get him into the ranks of Woodward and Bernstein.

"Well, I must say you've got my mind spinning. Of course, I want to know what else you've got. But, if it's anything you can prove, I'd say this is one helluva scandal. Okay. Not another word spoken."

"Thanks. You've got Brad's cell number. But we'll call you in the next two days."

"What about your safety? Don't you need some security?" Frank asked.

Brad chimed in. "We'll be okay. But if it's all right with you, we'd like to stay here tonight under your name. We can't go back to the Doubletree. They know we're staying there. We can pay you for the room once we can hit an ATM. We're both short of cash."

"Don't worry about it," Frank said, waving his hand. "This one's on the Post. You've been through enough."

"We appreciate that," Julia said.

They all stood up and shook hands. Frank pulled out a couple of business cards and gave each of them one. "We'll talk soon," he said as he opened the door.

"Yes," Julia affirmed.

As Frank walked out, Brad checked the hallway again to make sure no one was there. It was empty. He closed the door and hooked the latch.

Brad looked at Julia. They hadn't discussed the fact that they would be sharing a room together. They both knew the other was thinking the same thought.

CHAPTER 58

The options for food were minimal...and they were starving. Brad and Julia couldn't venture out to eat because they couldn't risk being seen. Having something delivered wasn't feasible because neither had enough cash, and a credit card could be traced by the FBI in minutes. Though they didn't want to take advantage of Frank's generosity, there wasn't much choice. They ordered room service and put it on the Post's bill—it wouldn't be a huge cost given the benefits the Post was about to gain.

After devouring their dinners at the table, they moved back to the couch. Brad glanced over at Julia. She looked tired.

"How you holding up?" Brad asked. "I can't believe all you've been through the last few weeks."

Julia took a breath and slid her feet onto the couch behind her while still facing Brad. "I wouldn't know where to start."

"Anywhere's fine by me," Brad encouraged.

Julia leaned against the cushion of the couch. "Well, with all that has happened, I feel like I'm in some cosmic washing machine. I don't know how much more I can take."

"You've handled it with a lot of grace."

Julia blushed. "I don't know about that...but I tell you, it's strange. While there's a part of me that's scared to death, I think the anxiety has actually been fueling me. I've never felt so determined in my life. I feel like a locomotive powering down the tracks doing whatever it takes to get these bastards caught while also helping the Tibetans...and...aren't you glad you asked...?" Julia smirked at Brad. "There's this intuitive sense that I can't quite put into words, but it's a feeling that we're being led. I don't mean just by whoever this Sherpa is. But...and this might sound crazy... but it's like my father's here being an angel on our shoulders. I feel like we're in some murder mystery novel and he's guiding us to find out who did it. Sounds crazy, huh?"

"Before I met you, I would have said you need some serious R&R. But I must admit, with all we've been through, it sounds possible."

Brad touched her on the shoulder in reassurance and support. He rubbed the muscle just above her collarbone to relieve some tension.

Julia felt her body relax. "That feels so good, Brad."

"Turn around. I'll get both shoulders and your neck."

Julia turned her back toward Brad. Brad scooted closer. He started massaging her shoulders and neck.

"Wow. You have no idea how good that feels," Julia said closing her eyes. As Brad continued to massage her, Julia leaned her head down in a more relaxed position.

"Pretty tight, huh?" Julia asked.

"Yeah, let's loosen some of these knots."

Brad worked her shoulders some more. After a minute, he stopped. Julia turned back around.

"Brad, listen. I want to tell you something." Julia gazed into Brad's eyes. "I don't know how to thank you for everything you've done. You've been more than incredible. I'm not used to having someone support me like this."

She stopped to think about what she wanted to say next.

"I've been a loner a lot of my life—like my father. As you know, I grew up without a mother, and no brothers or sisters. I was alone throughout most of my childhood, because my father traveled constantly for work. He'd leave me with sleep-in nannies or neighbors. There were so many nights I'd lie in the dark and cry from loneliness. I pretty much had to fend for myself ever since I can remember."

"So *that's* how you became the strong, independent type," Brad interjected.

"I guess. When I was thirteen I learned my father had lied to me about my mother."

"He told me about that when we discussed beneficiaries of his estate."

"I was so angry at him, Brad. I pulled away...and always kept it that way."

Julia looked down for a moment. Brad could see she wasn't finished and waited for her to continue.

"I know he loved me, but I always felt unsupported by him...and other men. My first real boyfriend in college cheated on me. So guys haven't exactly been my knights in shining armor."

"I can see why you'd put up a shield."

"Well, I know some people are an open book and can trust from the start. On the other hand, I don't trust until I get to the last chapter."

"And what chapter are *we* on, may I ask?" Brad questioned softly, but with curiosity.

Julia smiled but avoided the question.

"I know I'm still single because I've been too afraid to let anyone in all the way. A part of me believes they won't be there for me at some point...physically or emotionally. So that shield is pretty strong."

"Like many people," Brad added.

"Yeah. But after some soul searching in India, I saw that the walls we put up to keep others out are cages that keep us locked inside. We think we're protecting our hearts from pain, but really we're isolating ourselves and making the pain persist."

Julia stopped and leaned her head against the wall above the couch. "Sorry if that's too much to lay on you. I'm really tired."

"Not at all…and maybe it's good you're tired. You're letting down a wall or two right now."

"How about you?" Julia asked, turning the conversation around. "You mentioned you were married back in your early days. What's kept a handsome, savvy and supportive catch like you alone since then?"

"Luck," Brad said.

At first Julia couldn't tell if he was joking or not. But then Brad finally cracked a smile.

"No. I've got my share of skeletons too," Brad added, turning his eyes away.

"Such as…?" Julia prompted.

Brad hadn't expected to go into it. He wasn't sure how much to reveal. He, too, was exhausted and didn't want to say something he'd later regret. But Julia's honesty was compelling.

"Well—"

Just then the phone rang.

"Saved by the bell," he said.

It rang again.

"Should we get it?" Julia asked.

"It could be Frank."

"It could be whoever followed us."

"How would they know which room we were in?"

"True," Julia conceded.

The phone rang for the third time.

"I say we get it," Brad concluded.

"Okay. You pick it up."

Brad leaned back and grabbed the phone.

"Hello?"

"Mr. Johnson?" a voice said with a foreign accent. Brad remembered that Johnson was Frank's last name. He had to play along.

"Yes?"

"This is room service downstairs, sir. Just checking to see if everything was to your satisfaction, sir."

"It was," Brad responded curtly.

"Would you care for anything else, sir?"

"No, we're all set."

"Thank you. Have a good night, sir."

Brad hung up and turned back to Julia. "Just room service checking in."

"Do you think it really was?"

"We better hope so 'cause we've got no other choice but to stay here for now."

Julia smiled into Brad's eyes. "I want to hear more about what you were about to say before but hold the thought for a minute. I need a quick bathroom break."

After she left the room, Brad got off the couch. His body was tensing up. He started walking back and forth between the door to the room and the table. His mind was going back in time again to the dark memory he preferred to forget. *Why now,* he thought?

When Julia returned, she found Brad pacing.

"What's up?" she asked, standing in the doorway to the living area.

"It's nothing. Besides, you're tired and I'm tired. Now's not a good time to get into it."

"No, I want to know. Really, what is it?" she pressed, walking toward the coffee table.

Brad continued to pace with his head down, still hesitant to say anything. After a few more steps, he spoke while continuing to look at the carpet.

"I don't know why this is coming up now. It has nothing to do with you...it's..." Brad stopped in mid-sentence but kept pacing. He didn't know what to say.

"It's okay, Brad. Whatever is, you can tell me. Believe me, at this point, given all I've been through, I can handle it."

Julia sat back on the couch, hoping this would send a signal to Brad to do the same. But he just continued to walk back and forth between the door and the table.

"I haven't talked about this in a long time. I try not to think about it. But since I met you, it's been coming up...a lot. Not sure why." Brad stopped. He wasn't sure he wanted to go into it, but something in him decided to take the plunge.

"When I was eight, I was behind my uncle's house with my younger brother Danny. He was five. It was a cold January day, and we were outside building a snowman. A massive snowstorm had dumped a foot of snow the night before. It was that heavy, wet snow—which made it perfect for making snowmen—but hard to move. My uncle had this huge tool shed at back of the yard...the size of a four-car garage. In it were all sorts of equipment. He worked as a furniture maker and part-time mechanic. Well, I left Danny for a sec and went into the shed to get a shovel. It took a while to find one, with so much stuff in there...but I finally did. When I made it back to the snowman, Danny wasn't there. I figured he'd gone back to the house. After a few minutes of moving some snow around, I heard my name being called. I looked up and saw the shed was on fire."

Brad stopped for a moment. He looked at Julia. She tilted her head in the direction of the couch to suggest that he come sit beside her. He walked over to the couch and sat next to her.

"Well, I started running for the shed. I could tell it was Danny's voice screaming from inside. I ran as fast I could, but I fell a couple of times 'cause the snow was pretty deep. Each time I got up the fire seemed to have doubled in size."

Brad stopped again and looked down. Julia could see he was breathing a bit heavier.

"As I got there, the fire was blazing. Most of the shed was in flames. The steel door was the only part not burning."

Brad coughed to clear his throat. He was having trouble getting the words out. Closing his eyes, he took a deep breath. Julia touched his arm.

"It's okay," Julia said comfortingly.

Brad shifted positions placing his knee on the couch so he could face Julia more directly. He tilted his neck back to stretch out the tension and continued.

"Evidently, Danny had followed me into the shed. Somehow I didn't see him in there when I left with the shovel. The shed was packed with equipment everywhere. Well, Danny had found a pack of matches and was playing with them. Why my uncle would leave a pack of matches in the shed with all that wood and oil to this day I'll never know. Danny probably dropped the match when it was lit. The match struck some oil on the ground near his feet. When I got close to the door, I heard a large crash from behind it. I knew if I opened it, I might get engulfed by the flames. I screamed and yelled for help, but nobody was around. I didn't know what to do. I turned and ran back to the house as fast as I could to find my mom. My dad was on a business trip. When I ran into the house screaming, my mom came running. She immediately called 911. The blaze was too strong for us to get into the shed, and by the time the fire truck arrived, well it...it was too late."

Brad tried to rub a tear from his eyes. Julia noticed and slid closer to him. She was tearing up as well, not only from his story but also from his emotion.

"If only I had opened the door when I reached the shed, maybe I could have saved him somehow. He was my only sibling. It destroyed the family. My parents were completely torn up about it. My dad never forgave my mom for not keeping a closer eye on us. They got divorced within a year. I still feel it was all my fault...Danny dying, the divorce, the family falling apart."

"It just happened. It wasn't your fault," Julia consoled.

Though a part of Brad knew this was true, another part had never accepted it. He took a deep breath and wiped another tear from his eye.

"So how's that for a skeleton?" he joked, trying to grin through the tear.

"Everyone's got a story that would make you cry," Julia said wiping away a tear of her own.

"And make themselves cry too..." he added, sitting up a bit more upright to compose himself.

"So is that why you do all the death defying acts?"

Brad raised his eyebrows surprised by the astute question.

"You know," Julia added, "your bungee jumping, dare devil skiing, sky diving. Seems like you're just daring life to take you."

Brad grimaced. "Touché."

He ran his hands through his hair a few times.

"After that day, I swore I'd never be gutless again. I should have run into that shed to get Danny."

"Guess we both have our hearts in cages," Julia said.

"Yeah."

"Though I've got to admit something." Julia hesitated but then decided to say it. "Mine's opening up."

She looked directly into Brad's eyes. He could feel the sentiment coming through. He knew what she meant.

Brad nodded. He couldn't say the words, but his eyes let her know he felt the same.

"Guess I'm feeling like I'm nearing the end of the book," Julia said with a smile.

Brad chuckled. "I must say I kept trying not to think about you personally, because you were the daughter of my client—had to keep that professional distance, you know. And with all you've been going through, I didn't want to confuse you."

Julia reached out and touched Brad's hand. She inched a bit closer. Brad touched her face with his hand and then ran his fingers through her hair. He leaned forward, and stopped just inches from her face. Julia closed the distance, feeling their soft, warm, vulnerable lips come together.

CHAPTER 59

The red neon glowed from the alarm clock...5:57 a.m. Brad could barely make out the numbers. He peeked over and saw Julia still fast asleep. Realizing he was awake, he slipped out of bed, used the bathroom, and then quietly slipped into the living area.

He turned on his computer to check email. His eyes quickly passed over an email from a client to another email from a scrambled address. Brad clicked on the name and quickly saw that it was from Sherpa.

> *Urgent. I've got documents you must see ASAP. I'm leaving them in an envelope for you. Go to Caribou Coffee at the corner of 17th and Pennsylvania. Look under the seat cushion on the right leather chair facing the fireplace at 6:00 a.m. this morning (Tuesday). Be careful. They're searching all over D.C. for the both of you. Sherpa*

Brad was astonished. Sherpa was right here in D.C. and knew exactly what was going on! Who was this Sherpa?

Someone who worked at Ingrols? The person could easily make the trek in from Delaware.

Or perhaps it was some whistle blower within the government.

Or maybe McCarthy had some connection that needed to be anonymous.

Brad glanced at the clock again. It was now 6:01. He thought that if they hurried, they might be able to catch Sherpa at Caribou's. It would be risky to leave the hotel but the information might be crucial to their mission.

Brad went into the bedroom and woke Julia up.

"What is it?" Julia murmured huskily.

"I just got an email from Sherpa. Sherpa's leaving us documents at some coffee shop here in town. Hurry. You've got to get up and get dressed."

"What?" Julia said, still groggy.

"Sherpa's in D.C. The email said the documents would be left at 6:00. It's now 6:01...6:02," Brad added, glancing at the clock again. "C'mon, maybe we can catch Sherpa there."

Julia sprung out of bed. Within minutes, they were both dressed and out the door. As they went through the lobby, they carefully inspected the area for the man in the black suit. With the scene clear, they exited the front door. It was still dark given the early hour, but no one else was about.

Brad noticed an ATM across the street. They needed cash. While Julia asked the doorman to hail them a taxi, he ran to the machine and withdrew several hundred dollars. By the time he was done, a taxi had pulled up out front.

Getting out of the taxi at Caribou Coffee, they rushed to the entrance. Brad read a sign on the front door advertising for employees. *Work where you're appreciated. At 6 a.m. you're downright loved!* He smiled and pulled the door open. As he briskly walked in, a gentleman in a gray suit passed him and headed out the door with coffee in hand. Julia let the man exit before she entered.

"Are you Sherpa by any chance?" Julia tried.

The man stopped and looked a bit confused. "Excuse me?"

"Are you Sherpa?" Julia repeated.

"No, but I'd like to be," the man said smiling at Julia. Julia paid little attention to the comment, though she was surprised to hear it; she hadn't showered and was wearing the same wrinkled clothes from the day before.

Inside Caribou's, two people stood in line waiting to order their morning pick-me-ups. On the left of the store facing

Pennsylvania Avenue were tall tables and chairs. Further down was a small fireplace fronted by two brown leather chairs.

While Brad moved to the chairs, Julia asked whether either of the customers in line was Sherpa. Neither admitted to being their Secret Santa.

Meanwhile, Brad reached under the cushion of the right chair and felt for the envelope. No luck. He reached further. There it was—tucked to the back of the chair. He pulled out the large manila envelope and slipped it inside his jacket.

Julia ordered two double-shot mochas, and then she and Brad sat at one of the tables to view the envelope's contents. Brad almost spit out the first sip as he read the shocking information. A rush went up his spine realizing the ammunition they now had in their hands.

He passed the documents over to Julia. As she read, she also knew they had all the details needed to bring down her father's murderer, hang Ingrols out to dry, shake the foundation of the current administration, and pressure the U.S. government to forcefully confront China on Tibet.

Brad and Julia quickly agreed on their next move. Brad stuffed the documents back in the envelope, took one more sip of his mocha and then went up to the cash register.

"Excuse me. Can you tell me where's the nearest FedEx Kinkos?"

The person making the coffee turned her head and answered, "Not too far...on K near Sixteenth."

"Thanks," Brad said.

They raced out of Caribou's and made a beeline for K Street. They knew what needed to be done...and fast.

* * * * *

Inside FedEx Kinkos, using a self-service copier, Brad and Julia quickly made copies of the documents and then FedEx'd the copies to Frank Johnson at the Post. They included a cover page saying, *Do not run the story yet. More to come.*

They both agreed that they couldn't take any chances withholding the information. They were more scared than ever. The documents contained such incriminating facts that they knew the perpetrators would certainly stop at nothing to have their mouths sealed permanently.

Brad looked at his watch after they paid for the transaction. "It's too early to call Coleman's office yet. Let's head back to the Embassy Suites and wait."

"What about the tapes and the Ingrols' documents?" Julia asked.

"What about them?"

"We need to give a copy of the tape and the documents to Coleman and then get one to Frank."

Brad started to shake his head. "I don't know. Mr. Black Suit could be camped out waiting for us. That stuff should be safe in the room. We could wait 'til we meet with Coleman and then have someone under her authority get it all from the room."

"We'd have more credibility if we had the tapes and documents with us and we don't have time to waste. I'd feel much better if we had the stuff with us. Besides, whoever's chasing us probably thinks we wouldn't risk heading back to the hotel. I bet he's out combing the city for us. We could take a taxi over there, circle the hotel, and see if anyone's monitoring the area. If the coast is clear, we'll pull up front and ask the doorman to check the lobby before we get out of the taxi."

"I guess we could try that," Brad conceded.

It didn't take much to convince the cab driver to circle the hotel. Any extra ticks on the clock just moved the meter charge along. With no sign of the man in the black suit near the hotel or in the lobby, Brad asked the driver to wait out front and keep the meter running. They'd throw in an extra twenty for that, which didn't take much persuading either.

Brad and Julia quickly entered the hotel, passed the empty front desk, and got in the elevator. When they reached Brad's room, he placed the white plastic key card into the door and waited for the green light to shine indicating the door was ready to open. A red light appeared. He tried the card again thinking maybe he inserted the key the wrong way. *Dammit*...again a red light. Julia tried it. Again, no luck.

They returned to the lobby and approached the front desk, which was still vacant.

"Hello!" Brad called out while they both anxiously glanced about the lobby for anyone unusual.

A voice yelled from the office in back, "Be right there!"

A young man came out from the office dressed in a hotel uniform. "May I help you?"

"Yes. My name is Benson. I'm in room 436. My key's not working."

"Let me check." The hotel clerk looked in the computer. After a moment he looked up and said, "I'm not sure what happened. Sometimes the magnetic strip gets deactivated in people's pockets. Let me make you another key. Do you have ID?" Brad pulled out his license. The clerk glanced at it and handed it back to him. He proceeded to punch a few numbers into a machine and inserted a new key. He then handed it to Brad.

"Thank you," Brad said, as he and Julia quickly made their way to the elevator.

As soon as the doors closed, the clerk pulled out a business card from his pocket and dialed the number. "They're here," the clerk whispered when he heard the voice on the other line.

"Good," Dirk responded and hung up.

The clerk put down the phone and reached into his pants pocket. He smiled as he touched the two Ben Franklins resting there. He was even more pleased since the two bills were just half of what he was promised if he followed the instructions he had been given—to call the number on the business card if either of the young couple turned up and to delay the couple's re-entry into the room. He appreciated the reward the Secret Service agent was giving him for his cooperation to capture two wanted runaways.

CHAPTER 60

*D*irk dashed out of the Starbucks near Dupont Circle and jumped into his car. His car screeched out of his parking space, nearly slamming into an oncoming SUV.

* * * * *

Julia and Brad were relieved to see the green light appear on the hotel door this time. Opening the door cautiously, Brad flipped the light switch and peeked inside. Everything seemed to be in order.

Brad immediately grabbed the contents from the tissue box. He put the Ingrols' documents and one of the tapes into his briefcase. He gave the second tape to Julia for her to hold. She put the tape in her purse and quickly set off to her room to gather her belongings.

Once their bags were packed, they swiftly exited their rooms and headed to the lobby to checkout.

Standing at the registration desk, Julia turned to Brad in dismay. "Shoot. I left my purse in the room on the bed. I was moving too fast. It's got one of the tapes. Why don't you finish checking out and put everything in the taxi. I'll be right back."

"Okay, but hurry," Brad said, continuing to scan the area. The lobby was vacant.

As Julia bolted to the elevator, Brad took the receipt from the hotel clerk and proceeded outside.

While Brad and the doorman placed the bags in the taxi, Dirk entered the hotel through a side entrance. Dirk had checked in as a hotel guest after the chase from the MLK library. His key gave him access to the less conspicuous entrance.

Entering the empty lobby, Dirk approached the front desk where he saw his young accomplice completing some paperwork.

The hotel clerk looked up.

"I made the call and messed with their hotel keys—just like we agreed. You've got my other two hundred?" The clerk stuck out his hand.

"What room?" Dirk insisted coldly.

"426. She's up there now. He's outside with the taxi. Do I get anything extra for that? I'm going away this weekend to a party and need the extra cash," the young clerk pleaded with a smile.

Dirk reached into his pocket and pulled out his silencer. He pointed it directly at the clerk's chest and pulled the trigger, sending the clerk to the floor behind the desk.

"There. Have a blast," he added and headed for the fourth floor.

Julia entered her room and found her purse on the bed. The light brown purse had mixed in with the pattern of the bed's comforter, making it easy to miss.

As she grabbed it, she realized she'd been holding out from going to the bathroom for a while. She couldn't wait any longer. *A quick one*, she thought.

Brad looked at his watch as he sat inside the taxi waiting. He thought about calling Coleman's office but decided to hold off until Julia was in the cab so they could do it together.

Julia left the hotel room and stepped out in the hallway. As she closed the door behind her, she heard a ding from the elevator bank down the corridor. A man emerged. Immediately she realized it was *him*. Instinctively, she bolted the opposite direction with her purse in hand. The man in the black suit chased after her.

Within five strides, she turned left down another corridor. The hallway was about fifty feet long with a red exit sign above a door on the far side. She rammed open the door to the stairwell and immediately bolted down the stairs as fast as she could. After two flights, she heard the door fly open above her and the sound of feet pounding down the stairs.

Two more floors, Julia thought.

Dirk leaned over the stairwell and could see his prey a couple of flights below. He fired his gun. It barely missed her. The sound of the bullet jolted Julia and she missed a step, sending her flailing down to the second floor landing. She landed hard on her right knee and felt an excruciating pain shoot up her leg. By the time she tried to get up it was too late—a heavy body pounced on top of her, sending her face down.

Julia screamed out. "Help! Help!"

"Shut up or I'll kill you right here," Dirk warned.

She felt something metallic against her temple. Her eyes widened when she glimpsed out of the corner of her eye the black gun in his hand. Her body went limp with fear.

Using his weight to keep her face down, with the gun in one hand, he used his other to pull her arms behind her back and managed to handcuff her one-handed.

"Quite the busy bees you both have been. Well, no more buzzing around."

With her arms locked behind her back, and Dirk's body on her, Julia couldn't move. Dirk briefly put the gun down to pull out some tape out of his coat pocket. He ripped off a small piece and taped Julia's mouth. He then picked the gun back up and shoved it hard into her back. Julia winced at the pain from the force against her spine.

"Now, I'm going to keep this gun right at your back. One bad move, or any squawking, and I pull the trigger. Understand? You've pissed off quite a few people, and they've given me the green light to kill you if need be. And you already know these people haven't been shy about doing that. Now get up."

Dirk grabbed her arm and pulled her off the hard floor. He continued to stick the revolver into her back. "Start walking down."

Julia struggled with her bruised knee but limped down the steps.

Brad sat impatiently in the taxi. *What is taking so long?*

After a few minutes, he decided to go back into the lobby. He told the driver he'd be right back.

As the doorman opened the front door, Brad approached the registration desk. At first he thought the clerk was in the back office again. However, as he hurried past the desk, he halted when he saw a pool of blood coming out from behind the counter. Brad looked behind the desk and saw the young clerk lying on the ground with his chest covered in red.

"Holy shit!" Brad shouted.

The doorman came running from his post.

"Call the police!" Brad yelled as he ran toward the elevator.

The doorman ran to the registration desk, grabbed the phone and dialed.

Brad pressed the button for the elevator. He paced nervously back and forth, waiting for the doors to open. He looked to the right of the elevators and saw a short hallway with a stairwell sign above a door. Just past the stairwell was a side exit of the hotel with a glass door. Brad could barely make out through the door a flaccid body being shoved into the backseat of a tan Camry by a man in a black suit. As the man climbed into the driver seat to take off, Brad recognized the man as the one who had been chasing them and realized the body was Julia's!

"Shit!" he yelled. He knew he only had one choice.

He dashed for the taxi. It was his turn to do the chasing.

CHAPTER 61

"Follow that car. I'll give you an extra two hundred bucks!" Brad hollered as he jumped into the taxi.

As the taxi took off in pursuit of the Camry, Brad berated himself for having let Julia go up to the room by herself. He couldn't tell if she was still alive. *What if she had been killed?*

With that thought, the memory of his brother Danny hit him like a punch. The same panic arose that he felt when he had witnessed the shed burning. Unlike leaving his brother to run for help, there was no way this time he was going to abandon Julia.

Brad looked down at his watch. It was still too early but he needed help.

He pulled out his cell and dialed Coleman's office.

As anticipated, he reached the office voicemail. Brad left an alarming and detailed message explaining the situation. He ended the message by giving his cell number and clarifying that he'd give it ten minutes before calling again. If no one answered his next call, he'd contact the cops.

He hung up the phone.

Hold on Julia. I'm right behind you.

At Rhode Island and Florida, the Camry turned right. It continued straight until turning onto New York. For the next few miles, the driver kept the taxi at a distance where it wouldn't be noticed following.

The Camry passed Gallaudet University. Next, it passed Mt. Olivet Cemetery. Just before reaching the National Aboretum, it took a few left turns until turning onto Adams, a street consisting of several industrial properties. The Camry slowed down as it approached a small warehouse a couple of buildings down.

"Go past the street," Brad instructed the driver.

As they did, Brad caught a glimpse of the Camry pulling into the warehouse.

"Pull over here." Brad threw a huge stack of twenties onto the front seat and jumped out of the cab. He driver quickly took the bags out of the back.

Brad noticed an office building next to the warehouse. There were some thick bushes around the perimeter of the building. He ran over and hid himself and his bags in the bushes. He pulled out his cell phone and called Coleman's office.

"Hello. This is Bill Chelmsford," a voice answered.

Brad heard three beeps. Before Brad could get a word out, the battery on his cell died.

CHAPTER 62

When she came to, Julia was clueless about where she was. She felt queasy and dazed. It didn't take long to figure out she had been drugged—though she had no idea for how long. The chloroform had done its trick.

Julia lay on a cold floor in a musty room. The room was dimly lit. Her hands were still handcuffed and her feet tied. From the floor she could see that she was lying next to a gray metal desk and a couple of silver metallic folding chairs. An empty shelving unit was situated to the side of the desk. Her best guess was that she was in some sort of office.

Using as much strength as she could muster, she pulled herself up to a seated position. She thought she was alone in the room until a voice spoke behind her.

"You're not going anywhere," Dirk said. He had been sitting in a chair behind the desk keeping an eye on her. The tape copy was now securely in his possession.

Julia turned and tilted her head in the direction of the voice and saw her kidnapper sitting at the desk staring at her.

"Where am I?" Julia asked trying to get some bearing of the situation.

"No questions," Dirk stated adamantly.

"What do you want from me?"

"Did you hear me?" Dirk leaned toward her as he escalated his voice. "I'm going to ask the questions."

Julia felt a surge of anxiety go up her spine.

"Where did you go last night?"

"What?" Julia asked, not fully understanding the question.

"Where did you go last night after the Convention Center?" Dirk demanded.

"I don't remember. My mind is groggy from whatever you gave me," she said trying to be evasive.

Dirk stood up abruptly. He picked up the gun that had been on the desk in front of him. He walked over toward Julia.

"I don't think you realize how close you are to your grave. Tell me everything or I'll bury you right here. Don't test me. I've had enough of the two of you. Now, one more time...where did you stay last night?" Dirk pointed the gun directly at her head.

"At the Embassy Suites Hotel near the Convention Center," Julia blurted out nervously.

"Did you go there from the Convention Center?"

"Yes." She didn't give any more information than he asked for.

"What name did you register under?" Dirk persisted, having previously checked that hotel.

Julia's mind went blank for a moment. She couldn't remember Frank's last name.

"WHAT NAME WERE YOU UNDER?!!!" Dirk shouted.

Julia was frightened by his anger. "We stayed at the hotel under someone else's name. His name is Frank, but I can't think of his last name at the moment. Really!"

"And who is Frank?" Dirk insisted.

"He's a reporter for the Washington Post. It's Johnson. Frank Johnson."

The man pulled out his cell phone. He dialed 411 and got the number of the Embassy Suites Hotel. When his call rang through to the hotel, he asked for Frank Johnson's room. The hotel operator forwarded the call to the room. There was no answer, but at least he got what he needed—he knew Julia was telling the truth.

"Good," Dirk said, putting the cell down on the desk. "Now tell me how you know this guy Frank."

"I got his name from a contact I have in the business. We called the Post from the Convention Center. We arranged to meet Frank at the hotel. We asked him to get us a room under his name."

"Why?"

"Because we wanted to inform him of everything we know."

"What else!" Dirk kept digging.

"We wanted the media to know what we knew in case something happened to us," Julia stated.

"And what do you know?" Dirk had overheard some of the conversation at the library but wanted to see what else they knew.

"We know that Redman had my father killed. We know that Kennedy and Senator Green were murdered. We know about Ruttlefield's connection with Ingrols."

She stopped there. She decided she'd hold back the other scandalous information for now, as she didn't know how this man fit into the picture and how much he heard at the library.

At that moment, the cell phone rang. Dirk picked up.

"Yeah? She's in the process of telling me what she knows."

A moment later he added, "Okay. Will do," and hung up the phone.

He turned to Julia and said, "I guess you'll tell the rest of the story in a few minutes."

He went to his jacket resting on the chair. He pulled out a cloth and a small container. He dampened the cloth with some of the chloroform and held it over Julia's face. Within a few seconds, her world went black again.

CHAPTER 63

With his cell not working, Brad needed to find a phone...and fast. He left the luggage and his briefcase concealed among the bushes against the office building—it would be easier and quicker to maneuver without them.

Remembering he'd seen a storage facility across the street from where the taxi driver had dropped him off, he raced back in that direction.

As he approached the facility, he noticed the side door was open. He peered inside and called out, "Hello?" No one responded.

About to enter the building, he heard a car in the background. He turned to see a black Lincoln town car coming down the street. Leaning behind the doorpost to stay out of sight, he watched the car turn onto Adams. He knew instinctively that whoever was in the car was connected to the kidnapping and headed to the warehouse.

Brad rushed into the storage facility and found a manager on duty getting an early start to his day. After getting permission to use the phone, Brad called Coleman's office and spoke with Chelmsford. Brad explained the entirety of the situation, the location of the warehouse, and that he was now without a cell phone.

"How soon will Senator Coleman make it in?" Brad asked.

"Fifteen minutes," Chelmsford answered.

"Can you call her and let her know what's going on?"

"I'll try to do that right away. In the meantime, stay where you are. We'll get the cops and Feds over there."

Brad hung up the phone. He remembered that waiting for help for Danny didn't come in time—when the fire truck arrived, it had been too late.

Brad couldn't let that happen again. Julia was in danger. He knew he had to find a way into the warehouse. Time was of the essence...and he needed to do whatever it took to make sure Julia got more of it.

CHAPTER 64

When she awoke again, Julia was still lying on the floor. It seemed like she hadn't been out as long as the first time, but she couldn't be sure.

Dirk watched as Julia began to stir. Standing next to him were two other men who had just arrived. One was dressed in a very fine, navy blue suit with a red tie. He had thin gray hair and appeared to be in his late sixties. The other was short and stocky, had a bald head with a hawk nose, and appeared to be in his early fifties. A large gold ring shimmered on his right hand. Like Dirk, he was dressed entirely in black, wearing a long black leather jacket, a buttoned down black shirt, black slacks and black shoes. The color was an appropriate expression of his nickname—Predator.

"Good timing," Dirk said to Julia, as she looked up at the men. He picked up the gun again and pointed it straight at her head.

"Ms. Hamilton was describing how she and Benson stayed at the Embassy Suites Hotel last night under the name of Frank Johnson, a reporter from the Post who got the room for them. They met with him there and told him what they discovered. Give us the specifics of what Frank knows."

Dirk pulled Julia up to a sitting position. Julia desperately wanted to know the identities of all three men but was afraid to ask. Putting all her cards on the table seemed like a desperate...and only strategy.

"We gave him documents that we accessed from Redman's computer proving Redman had my father killed. We also gave him material proving the connection between Ruttlefield and Ingrols, as well as our supposed beloved administration. He knows we've been followed by those who killed my father, Congressman Green, and

Meredith Kennedy…and should anything happen to me or Brad, then he would know who was responsible."

The Predator took a step forward Julia.

"You goddam bitch!!!" He slapped her hard across the face. The gold ring dug into her cheek.

Julia fell onto the ground moaning. A trickle of blood came out of the corner of her mouth.

For a moment she wondered whether the truth would really set her free.

* * * * *

Brad quickly returned to the office building from the storage facility. Staying out of sight, he maneuvered through the bushes to the other side of the building in order to get a clear view of the two-story brick warehouse.

From his concealed vantage point, he determined that the front side of the warehouse contained the main entrance along with several first and second floor windows. He could only make out part of the back parking lot where both the Camry and black Lincoln were parked. Squirming his way through thicker brush to gain a better angle of the backside of the building, he stopped when he noticed a man in a gray suit standing on a short platform guarding the back entrance to the warehouse. *Dammit*, he thought. He'd have to try the front.

He made his way back through the brush until he was about thirty yards from the front of the warehouse. Though he'd attempted plenty of life defying stunts, he knew this would be one of the most perilous ones.

He closed his eyes and remembered his own advice...no thought, no fear. On the count of three, he burst out of the bushes towards the entrance of the warehouse.

Reaching the building, he ran right along the front wall so as not to be witnessed by anyone looking out a window. He quickly climbed the front steps and tried opening the door—it was locked.

Knowing he was out in the open, he immediately ran to the far corner of the warehouse. Cautiously, he peeked around the side. There was no side door, but a first floor window, about eight feet above ground, was slightly open.

Brad ran under the window, reached up and grabbed the ledge. With all his strength, he pulled himself up and tried to squeeze into the tight opening. He fit his right elbow inside to gain some leverage but the opening was too small to insert his whole body. With his left hand, he tried to push the window open. It didn't budge. He pushed harder, but as he did, he lost hold of the ledge and fell to the ground.

The noise caused the watch guard in back to turn his head in the direction of the sound. The guard—the driver of the Lincoln—pulled out his gun and walked down the steps from the platform. He headed toward the side of the warehouse.

Brad quickly stood up and tried again. This time after getting his right elbow in place, he reached inside with his left hand and found the handle. He tried turning it in order to open the window further but turned it the wrong way, causing the window to close a bit. Using all the force of his right arm, he managed to keep himself from falling a second time and turned the handle the other direction. The window slowly opened.

When the clearing was large enough, he managed to get his head and shoulders inside. Just as he landed on the floor, the watch guard came around the corner and scanned the area. There was nobody there. Seeing no trace of anything suspicious, the security guard from Ingrols dutifully returned to his post.

CHAPTER 65

Julia's head was throbbing. Her cheek was burning from the slap. The Predator pulled her up by the hair.

"When's this guy Frank going to run the story?" he demanded. Julia shrieked and the Predator let go. She toppled over in pain and tried to catch her breath.

"We...We—" Julia coughed trying to clear her throat. "We left it that he'd wait a couple of days...until I tell him to."

The Predator sat back down behind the desk. "Well, that adds another to our hit list," he said as he pulled out a cigar. He then turned to the man in the blue suit standing next to the desk. "What do you think we do now, Burton?"

Surprised, she blurted out, "You're Ruttlefield?" to the gray-haired man in the blue suit.

Ruttlefield stood there silently.

"Not bad, Ms. Hamilton," the Predator answered from behind the desk. "You should've thought about a career with the FBI...you would have made a good agent."

Julia sat up and stared at the Ambassador.

"I guess your hefty investment in Ingrols was worth taking out a few lives, including my father's, huh?" she accused—she wanted to hear him admit it.

"He gave us no choice," the Predator retorted instead. "It was unfortunate he made that tape. It would have been a wrecking ball for Ingrols, Redman, Burton, the Vice President, and...me. We thought we got lucky when Green contacted Burton. Imagine all the people in Washington who could have gotten that call. We thought we could squelch the problem if your father wasn't around to squeal. So we sent a Secret Service agent, Kennedy, to do her thing. We thought we knew her quite well...but I guess not well enough.

Our little hot secret agent was a bit hot underneath and had a secret of her own...a little resentment for not getting a bigger piece of the pie. She threatened to expose us after she did her...deed...unless we gave her a bigger slice. Needless to say, we couldn't have a walking bombshell around. So we had her...deactivated."

"What about the FBI? How were they in on the cover up? I know they were. They told Kennedy's parents that she committed suicide," Julia asked.

"Let's just say I have some pull—"

"Enough," Ruttlefield cut in, before the Predator went any further.

"So how did you and your boyfriend get all these documents?" Ruttlefield asked.

Julia decided she'd protect Sherpa's existence at this point even though she didn't know Sherpa's identity. Sherpa was obviously on the inside somehow and she didn't want Sherpa added to the list of search and destroy. Julia figured stretching the truth a bit wouldn't hurt.

"Brad's a computer whiz. He was able to sneak into Redman's office and hack his way on his computer. He found the emails Redman had sent to the Chinese Minister of Commerce."

"And Dirk said you came across my connection to Ingrols through the research at the library?" asked Ruttlefield.

"That's right."

"And what else do you know?" the Predator commanded. Though Dirk had conveyed what he overheard at the library, the Predator needed to find out if there was anything else.

Julia pondered for a moment. It was time for her to bring everything she learned out in the open. And she needed to buy some more time. She knew that once these guys felt she was done talking, she would be done...period.

* * * * *

Rays of light streamed through the small windows on the ground level of the musty warehouse. Twenty-foot tall structural racks were spread out evenly through most of the floor. The racks had recently contained pallets of Ingrols goods; they were now empty.

The Ingrols-owned warehouse had been one of their few regional distribution centers on the east coast. Having moved operations to a larger D.C. facility, Ingrols was still in search of a lessee for this space. It had been unutilized for six months, which made for a convenient and covert hideaway to hold a hostage.

Brad favored his right leg as he got up from the floor. He had fallen hard on his thigh and hip. His first few steps brought a wince of pain. He limped his way to a large forklift about ten feet away to use it for cover until he could make a plan.

In scoping the scene, all that was visible to him were the racks. He listened closely for voices or movement but couldn't detect any. He assumed that Julia must have been hauled to a room on the second floor.

Brad knew he'd be no match for what could amount to several armed men. The Feds were probably on the way by now, but he figured if he could just position himself secretly, and get a glimpse of the situation, he might be of help somehow.

Quietly, he moved rack by rack, keeping a lookout for any of the captors. On the far side of the floor was a staircase. He proceeded to the top where he peered through a small window in the door that shut off the staircase from the hallway. No one was visible on the other side.

Gently, he opened the door a crack. It creaked as he did. He held the door steady for a moment, praying that the sound hadn't been heard.

Once he realized the sound had gone undetected, he opened the door a bit more and slipped into the hallway. He slowly closed the door behind him to prevent the door from making a sound.

The second floor was structured in a long, rectangular fashion. Offices were located on both the inside and outside corridors. Brad heard voices coming from the far end of the hall directly in front of him. As he got closer, the voices were coming from what had been a large accounting office on the inside of the corridor.

Brad edged up to the door until he could get within earshot.

CHAPTER 66

Dirk took a step toward Julia and once again put the gun to her head.

"You heard the man. What else do you know?"

Julia took a breath and then looked over at Ruttlefield.

"I guess you're not the only one with a blind trust that has a steep investment in Ingrols."

Ruttlefield stood a bit more upright. Julia could tell she had captured his interest.

"It turns out," Julia continued, "that the founder of Ingrols was a man named William Pratt. When Mr. Pratt retired from Ingrols, he owned over fifty million dollars of Ingrols stock. He passed away just a couple of years ago—right before the last presidential election. Mr. Pratt was a widower and had only one daughter—Marilyn Pratt—who was the sole beneficiary of all of Mr. Pratt's Ingrols stock. And isn't it interesting that Marilyn Pratt is now Mrs. Marilyn Tenner—the wife of the Vice President of the United States, Mr. Jack Tenner. And although the stock is now invested in a blind trust, of course the Tenner family has a deeply vested interest in the financial well being of Ingrols. The Vice President and the Tenner family fortune would take an enormous hit by the publicity of the tape and these documents. And so the Vice President made a secret visit to Tibet to seal the deal."

The Predator leaped out of his chair. "He had nothing to do with the killings!"

Ruttlefield twisted around and abruptly yelled, "Let me handle this, Mack!"

Though Julia was feeling the effect of the drug, the name Mack seemed familiar. After a moment, her eyes widened as it hit her.

"Mack Tenner?" she probed.

"Well, once again, good for you Ms. Hamilton," said Mack Tenner, the Vice President's son.

Julia suddenly understood. The documents Sherpa had left at Caribou Coffee were copies of emails sent by Ruttlefield to a disguised email address. The emails described Ruttlefield's assurance that every measure was being taken to insure Ingrols success in China and that the Pratt family fortune would not be comprised. Julia and Brad assumed that the emails were sent to the Vice President. They didn't consider that it was actually his son who was mixed up in all this, protecting his and his family's interest.

"So your father has you as the point man in all this," Julia accused.

"My father is innocent in all of this," Mack defended.

"But he was there. He's on the tape!"

"We had no idea he was going to show up at that meeting. *I'm* the CEO of Ingrols. This deal was *my* baby...not his. But once a father, always a father. He wanted to make sure I or the U.S. wouldn't be damaged by the deal."

"But he shook hands with the Chinese while the massacre was taking place!"

"He tried to force an agreement *not* to do the deal. He thought he had their consent. But I wouldn't let him interfere. I pushed the deal through...we've got too much at stake."

"How am I to believe all this?"

Ruttlefield answered. "Because it's true."

"Why should I believe you, Mr. War Buddy?" Julia confronted, revealing another piece of information she learned in a note that Sherpa left at Caribou's.

Ruttlefield raised his hand to slap Julia as well but held back.

"Let me tell you something, smart ass. He saved my life in Vietnam. When I got shot after our squadron was ambushed, Vice President Tenner could have run for safety but stopped and carried me to a rescuing helicopter. I never forgot that and swore I never would. I wasn't going to let this tape ruin Ingrols and the Tenner family."

Julia looked at Tenner. "And, God forbid this deal didn't go down and the tape got out. Ingrols had bet its entire company on this deal. You'd lose a lot more than your inheritance if it blew up."

"I knew we should have taken her out," Dirk interjected.

"I've had enough of this," Tenner added. "She won't be any more trouble." He got out of the chair and grabbed Dirk's gun from his hand. "It's time to get rid of this bitch like we did the rest of them. She knows way too much."

Tenner walked around Ruttlefield closer to Julia. He pointed the gun at her. Julia heard the gun shot, but she was startled: the sound came from *outside* the warehouse. Several shots rattled off. Tenner spun toward Dirk, tossing the gun to him.

"Go check it out," Tenner commanded.

Dirk raced to the door. He opened it and scanned the hallway in both directions. The corridor was empty.

CHAPTER 67

Dirk darted across the hall from the office into another room that contained a window overlooking the back lot.

He snuck up to the corner of the window and looked outside. A few Crown Victoria plain-wrappers with flashing lights were spread throughout the lot. Several Feds were securing the scene—some in firing position. At the base of the steps to the warehouse's back entrance, the Ingrols security guard lay outstretched in a pool of his own blood.

Suddenly Dirk was blind-sided by a body that lunged from behind. The force from the collision sent both bodies plunging to the floor.

Brad landed hard on top of Dirk and immediately grabbed Dirk's right wrist to shake the gun loose. Dirk's left elbow came out from underneath and drove a blow to Brad's gut.

Brad buckled and Dirk shoved Brad off his back. As he did, Brad jerked hard again on Dirk's wrist and the gun flew out of Dirk's hand, sending it ten feet away from where they were entangled.

Dirk slid along the floor toward the gun but Brad grabbed Dirk's leg and stopped him. Brad landed a punch into Dirk's head smashing it hard against the floor.

With Dirk dazed, Brad quickly climbed to his feet to get the gun. Dirk stuck out his leg, tripping Brad.

Brad reached for the gun but couldn't quite touch it. He tried to inch his way to the gun when Dirk rolled onto his knees and leaped at Brad. But just before Dirk landed on him, Brad reached the gun, instantly turned and pulled the trigger. Dirk fell directly on top of him—blood pouring out from the dead man's head.

CHAPTER 68

With gun in hand, Brad stood once again outside the accounting office listening intently for Julia's voice. He needed to know she was still alive and well. Earlier he had overheard the conversation involving Ruttlefield, Tenner, Dirk and Julia. Having just killed Dirk, it was now two against one.

Brad leaned in towards the door. Complete silence emanated from the room—and throughout the second floor as well. The door was partly open so he inched closer and peeked through the crack.

The room was empty. He could see the desk and chairs where the group had been but no was one there.

He slowly opened the door ready to shoot but the entire room was vacant.

Where are they? Could they have taken off during the fight? Are they hiding in another room or did they take Julia down to the first floor?

Brad noticed another door across the room. For a moment he debated whether to check it out or to go downstairs and find the Feds. On the one hand, he didn't want to push his luck. He was fortunate to have survived his fight with Dirk. However, he knew he'd be a sitting duck. The Feds didn't know who he was. They might mistake him for one of the captors. He figured he might as well explore where the other door led—Julia was still in danger.

He crossed the room and placed his left hand on the knob and held the gun in his right. Pointing the gun, he took a deep breath trying to calm his trembling hands.

On the count of three. One. Two. Three. He shoved opened the door.

"Freeze right there! FBI! Drop the gun!" a voice shouted from behind him.

Brad immediately raised his hands as he stood looking into an empty storage closet.

"Drop the gun, I said!" bellowed the agent.

Brad dropped it. Behind him, in the doorway, was one of the Feds with a .45 caliber pointed straight to the middle of his back.

"Don't shoot!" Brad called out, keeping his hands raised. "I'm Brad Benson—the one who called Senator Coleman's office. My...girlfriend, Julia, is being held hostage in this building!"

"Keep your hands up and slowly turn around!" commanded the agent.

Brad slowly turned. Blood stains covered his shirt from his fight with Dirk.

"Move against the wall away from the gun!" the agent demanded. Brad complied.

"Now put your hands on the wall; keep them above your head."

The agent made his way over to where the gun had fallen while continuing to point his gun at Brad. He reached down, picked up the gun and shoved it in his pocket. He proceeded to pat down Brad. After determining Brad was clean, the agent let him put his hands down and checked his ID.

"What are you doing here?" demanded the agent. The guy had short black hair and a goatee.

"Like I said, I came into the warehouse to find Julia. She's being held hostage."

"What's this blood from?"

"I killed one of the guys who kidnapped her. He's dead across the hall. Two other men were holding Julia hostage in this

Red Tape

room. One is Burton Ruttlefield, the United States Trade Representative and the other is Mack Tenner, the Vice President's son!"

"What?"

"Yes. They were just in this room a few minutes ago. I was in the hall listening to the conversation when I heard gunfire outside. I went into the office across the hall to hide when one of the captors came in. I knew if I didn't jump him first, he'd see me and kill me. So I knocked him down and got his gun loose. We fought until I shot him in self-defense. I just came back to this room, but the rest of them are gone."

"I've been checking the entire floor and you're the first one I've seen. We've got agents swarming this place and there's been no word of anyone else."

Brad turned to look at the desk and chairs. "But I'm telling you, they were right over—" Brad stopped as he pointed at the desk. What he saw was clear evidence that Julia had been there. "That's Julia's Tibetan bracelet!" Brad said.

Brad reached down and picked up the twined bracelet she had been wearing.

"She was wearing this for good luck."

The agent stood over Brad's shoulder as Brad ran his fingers over the bracelet, wondering where she could be. It had only been a few minutes.

The agent scanned the room. He found a vent but it was clearly too small for anyone to fit through. The agent then walked behind the desk and scanned the bookshelf. He stopped when one book seemed peculiar.

"Hold on. I've got something."

He immediately pressed a button on his collar and spoke into a two-way radio. It was then Brad noticed the agent was wearing a headset with an earpiece.

"Hack? Mav here. I need cover. I'm on the second floor. Large office in the center."

Within sixty seconds, Hacksaw appeared in the room. He went over to where Brad and Maverick were standing.

Maverick pointed at the bookshelf as he spoke to Hacksaw.

"I think they're behind this case. Be ready."

Maverick asked Brad to get down behind a desk on the other side of the room.

He then pulled on what seemed to be a book in the shelf. Instead of it being a book, it was a fake hardened casing. As Maverick pulled on it, an entire section of the bookshelf opened like a door. Maverick swung the door open and immediately yelled, "Freeze! FBI!"

Behind the door was an eight-by-ten-foot ventilated vault. The secret vault had been used for cash storage and essential records of Ingrols operations. Inside the vault Ruttlefield and Tenner were standing with their hands up. Julia was lying on the ground in front of them.

"Don't move! Keep your hands up!" Maverick yelled.

Maverick and Hacksaw immediately entered the vault and frisked both men. Neither was armed. Ruttlefield and Tenner were immediately handcuffed. Hacksaw leaned down to feel Julia's pulse—she was still alive.

Hacksaw called for Brad. Brad ran into the vault and over to Julia. He leaned down and picked her head up into his arms.

Julia then opened her eyes and saw Brad holding her.

Thank God, she thought. *The nightmare is over.*

CHAPTER 69

As they came out of the warehouse, Maverick escorted Ruttlefield and Tenner to his car, which was parked on the far left side of the back lot. They were to be hauled off and booked.

Following closely behind, Brad and Julia were led by Hacksaw to his vehicle, which was parked just to the right of Maverick's. They needed to be taken down to the Hoover Building for debriefing.

Also in the parking lot were several FBI agents gathered around the Camry and Lincoln. One of them was arranging for the vehicles to be impounded.

Julia had regained consciousness in the vault and was in a dazed state from all the chloroform still permeating throughout her body. She was rubbing her wrists and held onto Brad for support.

When they reached Hacksaw's car, Julia turned and watched as Maverick nudged Ruttlefield and Tenner into the backseat of his car. Despite her dazed state, Julia noticed a lengthy scar on Maverick's neck as he tucked Tenner's head under the frame of the back door. She knew she had seen the scar recently but couldn't remember where or when.

As Maverick closed the back door, sealing in Ruttlefield and Tenner, Julia took a closer look at the FBI agent. She knew she knew him. Just as Maverick opened the door to the driver seat, it dawned on her—it was agent John Carlton from Denver! Maverick was just his code name.

Julia immediately screamed. "Wait! That's agent Carlton! He's in on all of this!" Julia was sure it was Carlton. Carlton had grown a goatee but she was certain it was the same agent who had covered up her father's case, as well as Green's and Meredith Kennedy's!

Brad turned. "That's the guy that was following me in Denver!"

Carlton immediately jumped inside the driver side, slammed the door shut and started the car. Ruttlefield and Tenner were ready to escape with Carlton as their driver. Their plan had almost worked to perfection.

Carlton's car screeched in reverse and passed the other agents in the lot who were momentarily stunned. He swerved his car past the other agents, shoved the gear into drive and burned rubber as he sped towards the driveway leading out of the warehouse back lot.

At first, Hacksaw was also taken by surprise by Carlton's sudden evacuation. However, he had been briefed on the way to the warehouse about the cover up. He immediately realized that Carlton was the co-conspirator.

Hacksaw pulled out his gun and fired. The bullet blew out the windshield of Carlton's car. The car swerved and turned toward the corner of the warehouse. As it did, Hacksaw fired again but missed.

Carlton's car whipped around the corner but immediately slammed into another agent's car entering the back lot. The crash immobilized both cars.

The other agents immediately swarmed Carlton's car with their weapons ready to fire. Carlton came out with his hands up and was quickly handcuffed. Ruttlefield and Tenner were removed from the car.

As they watched the scene unfold, Brad held Julia tighter. This time, their nightmare was truly over.

EPILOGUE

For the first time in a while, Julia wasn't looking over her shoulder or contemplating her next move. She was completely relaxed in Brad's arms as they sat on his couch at his Denver townhouse watching TV. After spending two long days with authorities in D.C. recounting the details of what happened during the previous weeks, they had returned to Denver for some down time.

It was now 10:00 a.m. and CNN was about to present a comprehensive story of what had been named the Sino-Ingrols Scandal. Wolf Blitzer came on the air to report from the Situation Room.

"Good morning. For those of you who have been following the last few days, I want to give you the most recent update of the unprecedented Sino-Ingrols Scandal.

Frank Johnson, from the Washington Post, broke the story this past week of an unprecedented conspiracy of murders organized by Mack Tenner, the Vice President's Son, Burton Ruttlefield, the United States Trade Representative, Kurt Redman—the Chief Operations Officer of China Operations for Ingrols Corporation, FBI Agent John Carlton, and Liung Xilai, China's Minister of Commerce. First, to take you back..."

Wolf Blitzer described in detail the series of events that took place starting with the Tibetan Massacre in Lhasa up through Julia's rescue at the warehouse. He then continued with various consequences of the scandal.

"As a result of this story, Ingrols stock has plummeted from $79 per share to $16 in just two days, one of the greatest two day drops in history. Ambassador Ruttlefield, Mack Tenner, Kurt Redman, and John Carlton have each been indicted on several accounts of fraud and murder. Vice President Tenner, who secretly showed up at the massacre, did so to try to impede the deal. Though innocent of any charges, clearly his family name will be ruined as a result of this scandal. Also, a historic meeting between President Whitmeyer, Chinese President Jintao, and His Holiness The Dalai Lama will take place in two weeks at Camp David to outline the steps for creating an autonomous Tibetan region within China. This meeting comes on the heels of overwhelming international pressure put on China to acknowledge and change their human rights violations. The United Nations Security Council voted 14-1 last Tuesday mandating that China meet with The Dalai Lama to discuss creating an autonomous Tibet. Congresswoman Marjorie Coleman organized an emergency meeting with the Senate; they voted to revoke China's MFN status unless China's policy toward Tibet changes. Serendipitously, the World Trade Organization's Ministerial Conference took place a few days ago in Geneva. A consensus was reached among its 150 members that China's membership be halted unless the policy changes. China's trade policies, factories, and human rights practices will also be intensely investigated. Saudi Arabia even threatened to severely sanction China's oil supply unless China changes its stance on Tibet. China is the second largest importer of oil from Saudia Arabia. In light of all that has transpired, President Jintao has finally agreed to meet with the Dalai Lama. And on one final note, in another significant move, UNESCO, The United Nations Educational, Scientific, and Cultural Organization released a statement yesterday assuring that under no condition will the Jokhang Temple in Lhasa be destroyed. It will forever remain as an international heritage site and be preserved as a sacred honoring of the Tibetan community. Well, that's it for now. More to come tonight on Larry King, as he will be interviewing the Dalai Lama. This is Wolf Blitzer from the Situation Room."

Brad picked up the remote and clicked off the T.V. "Your father would be incredibly proud of you," he said as he leaned forward to grab his coffee cup.

"Thanks."

Julia touched the bracelet that was back around her wrist and for a moment felt her dad's presence.

"And all this wouldn't have happened if it wasn't for Sherpa," Julia added.

"That's for sure," Brad said. "Can't blame her for wanting to remain anonymous... though she really deserves public credit."

"It's hard keeping her identity a secret, but we can't betray her. We owe her everything."

"We need more of her in Washington."

"Yeah, she's got a lot of integrity. What a contrast to Ruttlefield, huh? I wonder how she was able to be his assistant all that time?"

"Well, at least Jessica doesn't have to worry about that anymore," Brad said putting down the coffee. And it's amazing you picked out Carlton. Don't know how I missed that one," Brad said.

"You never got a real close look at him. And how were you to know that he got a text message saying that they were in the vault?"

"Yeah."

Julia closed her eyes. She leaned back into the couch. "It would be so wonderful to see the faces of the Tibetans when His Holiness returns to Lhasa. They've prayed and survived for so many years anticipating that day."

Brad pulled her closer in his arms and kissed her on the forehead. He then looked at his watch.

"We better get going or we'll be late."

Julia opened her eyes and looked out the living room window at the snow flurries.

"Think I'll be warm enough with a sweater and raincoat?"

"I think so. Besides you'll have the warmth of eighty thousand screaming drunks to keep you warm."

"Sounds like a blast," Julia smiled. "Who would have guessed? I've gone from my father's funeral, to a Buddhist retreat in India, to being kidnapped at gunpoint in D.C., and now to a Broncos playoff game. Go figure."

"And what about me?" Brad leaned over and gave her a warm slow kiss on the lips.

Julia melted into the kiss. As they both pulled away, she looked in Brad's eyes with a slight grin. "If there really is a *you*."

"Oh, no...here we go again, Ms. Buddha."

HOW YOU CAN HELP TIBET

1. Keep informed about the plight of Tibet through the International Campaign for Tibet (ICT): www.savetibet.org.
2. Donate to Tibetan organizations such as the ICT. *(100% of proceeds from buying Red Tape go directly to the ICT. Please note that the author is not affiliated with the ICT.)*
3. Write your congressman/congresswoman to take stronger action about Tibet.
   https://writerep.house.gov/writerep/welcome.shtml
4. When buying products "Made in China," consider alternatives.
5. Ask yourself two questions:
   "What can I do today to live my deepest truth and values?"
   "What can I do today to bring more inner peace?"

To contact the author visit: www.redtapethenovel.com

Made in the USA
Charleston, SC
13 July 2011